I0603787

Airfield Aptitude

America's Fabulous Fifties, Book 2

By Cindy M. Amos

ISBN-13: 978-1-0880-1377-9

Dedicated to
The valiant men and women who dared to
design, build, and fly airplanes,
endeavoring to keep innovation aloft
and balanced between two wings
Ad Astra per Aspera
"To the Stars through Difficulties"

ACKNOWLEDGEMENTS
The author would like to acknowledge the following
for their support and encouragement of this book:
Kansas Aviation Museum, Wichita, Kansas
Jeffrey L. Rodengen, *The Legend of Cessna*
Jay M. Amos, NDE Technical Review
iStock for vintage black & white photograph
Pamela Bower for final proofreading
Cynthia Hickey of Winged Publications
& The Inspiration of the Holy Spirit

*If I took flight on the wings of the morning and
flew as far inland from the sea as possible,
even there your hand would hold me, and
your divine guidance establish my purpose.
Psalm 139:9-10*

In Memorial to

Dwane D. and Velma L. Wallace

For their ongoing scholarship endowment for outstanding

Aeronautical Engineering students at Wichita State University

Including Parker M. Amos, Recipient (2013-2017)

With highest appreciation

Chapter 1

Weston Durand pressed his hips onto the hangar's balcony rail as the shop floor sprang to life down below. Postwar progress came through a combination of American muscle and clever ingenuity, and he'd arrived last month to supply both. The first fuselage-piercing rivet sounded with a metallic bang, and the pulse of the airfield began for another productive day.

A row of aircraft hulls stretched to the hangar's back wall, all L-19 Bird Dogs heading for the latest U.S. Navy order. Hired to guarantee these planes met the company's highest standards, he'd make sure that quality had been designed at every level, not merely inspected for the final product. Quality control had assumed the lead as a top paradigm for the industrial world. Fortunately, he'd completed his specialized engineering degree right in time to ride the wave straight to prosperous Wichita, Kansas.

Sounds of footsteps descending caught his attention as safety manager Duncan Reed made his way to post another entry on an oversized blackboard near the employee check-in station. There, the detail-oriented manager noted a sequential success for safety. Reed used a rag to wipe off the last digit and marked a seven in its place to make the board read three hundred forty-seven days of consecutive safety in the workplace. No one could argue that 1953 was adding up to be a safe year. Metal tapping soon gave way to a flourish of riveting, lending the morning a raucous pace.

He started toward the steps when the first shout echoed through the hangar doors, left open to welcome the balmy April day. Drowned out by the shop noise, the worker's message failed to register. Weston started down the steps, ever looking out on the tarmac to assess the situation. A man in coveralls appeared in the doorway, crossing his arms over his head.

Reed side-stepped to him in rigid posture for only a second, and then turned toward the hangar interior. "Mayday! Clear the shop floor—brake failure on the taxiway." A tall man, Reed motioned toward the back of the hangar with foreboding gestures, routing the evacuation away from the front entrance. Tools clanked on the floor as laborers cooperated in haste.

Close to the intercom, Weston rushed back up onto the balcony and pressed the microphone to amplify the announcement. "All employees to the back of the hangar. Mayday called on the taxiway. Clear the front hangar now." A harsh metallic click sounded as he hung up the receiver.

He ran down the first flight of steps onto a landing midway down and spotted the aircraft in trouble. Still wearing its dull primer coat, a state-of-the-art turbocharged light airplane floundered on the tarmac, circling in broad arcs. One wheel of its landing gear, dragging from a locked brake, had begun to emit black smoke.

Watching to estimate the diameter of each advance, Weston calculated that impact would occur within the next two sweeping circles. The twirling turboprop would make fodder out of the hangar's tin doors, and metal would rain like hailstones across the shop floor. A sick feeling made his stomach lurch, as partially-constructed airplanes and hailstones didn't mix. Projecting he'd have to inspect every fuselage damaged, he'd have his work cut out for him over a month of Sundays.

Reed motioned him down the steps as he escorted a portly older woman on his arm. She carried a length of leather seat coverings in her hands as if trying to baby the material through the calamity. As he descended, it struck him that more than cow skin needed to be sheltered from flying metal shards. One last glance across the shop floor made him stumble down the last few steps. The window of a fuselage centered right in front of the door now framed the torso of a lone worker, seemingly unaware of the crisis at hand. The figure turned, and he made out the face of a young woman wearing headphones to cancel out the shop floor noise.

A growl rose in his throat. He had a split second to decide whether to retreat or not. He locked gazes with Duncan Reed, and his distress soared to a higher level.

The portly woman straightened her Rosie-the-Riveter headband. "Where's the kid? Wasn't she right behind me?" Her jaw gaped with disbelief.

"Someone's working in the front plane. I'll go get her." Weston began to run, dodging tools as he ducked between two plane hulls.

"That's Myla Templeton of Interiors," the woman called after him.

"Stay low," Reed shouted.

The air turned electric as the circling plane approached the hangar, its propeller cutting the tension into a thousand ribbons of sanity. Weston hoisted up the roll-away steps and lunged into the fuselage, grabbing the worker around the waist.

"Mayday on the taxiway." He pulled her out with only a gasp of resistance and down they came together. His muscles straining, he shoved her toward the rear of the hangar when the deafening impact sounded right behind him. Men's voices exchanged commands out on the tarmac as the first metal fragments hurled past him to the right. "This way," he shouted, veering left. He caught her by the waist as the propeller struck the tin door a second time and minced its panel into a fresh wave of shrapnel.

Agile but petite, her short gait would prove to be the death of them both. Weston felt the impact of metal tear across his right calf, a sharp blow. Desperate, he eyed a wheeled creeper used for underbelly work and headed them both right toward it. In a lunge, he hurled her onto the board first, covering her from the rear. Like clockwork, a third propeller strike released another round of shrapnel as the plane's nose foundered hard against the hangar door. Unavoidable, he splayed across her body, using his momentum to shove the creeper well under the closest fuselage, seeking refuge between the landing gear.

The rise of her breathing mingled with his for several drawn-out seconds. The shop floor shrank into a miniature world that contained only the two of them. He struggled with where to put his hands and finally settled on extending them in push-up position to alleviate some weight off his rescue victim. Her cropped black hair pressed against his chin, not entirely unpleasant as a floral scent wrapped around him.

She turned to him and locked onto his gaze. "Father God, shelter us under your protective wing," she whispered.

"Lord, yes—and minimize the aftermath." He tried to fake a smile to make light of the situation, but her eyes held all the honesty of the universe. Trapped in their sincerity, he felt her chest rise and fall as his calf sent a stinging reminder up his right leg to take stock of his situation. "Are you hurt?"

"I don't think so." Her lips lingered in a pout as she knit her brow. "It's kind of difficult to feel anything right now."

He lowered his head onto her shoulder about the same time the test flight technicians shouted that restraining chocks had been thrown in place. His arms began to shake from fatigue, so he lowered his frame to alleviate the strain, shifting his hip beside hers on the creeper. "I think we're safe now. Let's give it a few extra seconds, just in case."

She nodded, her crystal blue eyes now rimmed with unshed tears. "Thank you for coming back for me. I never heard the mayday warning."

"I didn't spot you until almost too late. I'm Weston Durand, by the way, the new quality control supervisor."

"Myla Templeton, Interiors. It looks like you might have your work cut out for you for the rest of the day." With that, the first tear broke the dam and a stream readily followed.

A cramped reaction worked through his sternum straight into his midsection. He'd never been this close to a crying woman before. Instead of sensing weakness in her tears, he somehow detected strength. "You're a brave woman, Myla. I have a great deal of respect for that."

Footsteps raced up to their location. A man stooped beneath the landing gear to lend a hand. Duncan Reed soon tugged at his shoulder. "Let's get them up to first aid."

Mindless of duty, Weston inched off the creeper, his focus targeted on the petite woman. At physical separation, an elastic tension stretched between them as Reed forced him back. A red stain on her coveralls off her hip leaked into his peripheral vision.

Reed motioned to a couple of men. "She's been hit. Help me

get her upstairs."

"I'll take her." Weston regained his feet, whereupon his right leg immediately went gimp.

"You'll not be taking anybody, Rin Tin Tin." The portly woman locked her arms across her heaving chest and darted a forced wink in the direction of his leg.

Myla clamped her hand against her hip and rolled off the creeper with a moan. Two men took her by the arms and hoisted her onto a roll-away tool chest to facilitate the trip over to the infirmary. He stepped toward the tool chest and grimaced, his calf hitching with the step.

"Get up on here, too, and let's get you both seen by the nurse. No wasting time, Durand." In charge of safety, Duncan Reed commanded control, denying any derision along the way.

Weston lowered across the chest stomach-down, avoiding Myla as he draped his lame frame onto the makeshift gurney to comply with orders. When he exhaled, it sounded like a pitiful retreat for a hero. His sole consolation came with a hand's tender landfall on his shoulder blade. The cart lurched forward, its casters complaining against the concrete floor. The hand made a small circle of commiseration, circumnavigating his back. Squeezing his eyes shut, he hoped to high heaven the hand belonged to the woman with mesmerizing sapphire eyes.

~

The familiar front stoop of her home loomed before her as Myla made her way up the walk. Her boss had been a chatterbox all afternoon, but now seemed to lack for any final words. She took the well-padded arm offered and limped along, trying to shorten her gait. Every time she brought her left foot forward, the stitched-up skin over her hipbone screamed bloody murder.

A sheepish look flitted across Alice Granger's face before her steely countenance took up residence once again. "Let me tell your mother what happened. It's the least I can do, seeing how I put you out there in harm's way and all."

"Miss Granger, you must not feel that way. I chose to work out on the shop floor knowing it held hazards. Today I found one. That's the most peacetime action I'm liable to see this side of the Pacific Ocean." She gave a bit of a chuckle, hoping to prod the older woman toward forgiveness.

"We're half a continent away from the Pacific Ocean, young lady. If we can get these Bird Dogs out to the Navy boys, they'll do the rest. I still haven't heard what the new exterior color will be, have you?"

"My father used to say the Navy only sees one color, ship-deck gray." Myla paused before taking the bottom step. When she lifted her left leg, her waistband pinched against the newly acquired row of stitches. "Ouch, all right then. Steps are no longer my friend."

"Which means I'll have to keep you out of those fuselages for the time being. No matter, you're slated to cover that crackpot quality control meeting for me next week. You take the cutting jobs and hole up in the Interiors lab. I'll conduct the installations, fair and square."

"But what about your arthritic knees, Miss Granger? I'm making matters worse for you in a roundabout way."

"Don't worry your pretty little head about me, Miss Templeton. We've got to get you on the mend first, and then we can redistribute the wealth of work between us. Those Bird Dogs have to roll out by summer's end, come what may."

"Yes, ma'am. They will, and you can count on me to be right back on the job. A two-inch cut won't keep me down."

"That's the spirit. I knew you had pluck that first day I hired you. Mighty fine seamstress with upholstery, too. Now, let me do this next part, so we don't shock your mother half to death."

"Okay." Myla pulled the front door open and led the way into the foyer. "Mother? Miss Granger is here with me. She'd like a word with you." She soon felt a tinge of guilt when her mother appeared, her brow arched in worry. "Mother, this is my supervisor, Alice Granger."

"Good evening, Mrs. Templeton."

"Please call me Effie. Won't you come in?"

"Only for a few minutes. I've got to get on home to my dogs, you know." Alice worked her way around the recliner and perched on the edge of the sofa, looking uncomfortable.

Myla took a seat. Her mother came close by and leaned on the chair's thread-bare arm. She made a mental note to make slipcovers from coordinating fabric to better hide the wear.

"We had a situation at work today, what they call an on-the-job accident." Miss Granger drew a breath and continued her account.

"A test flight went wonky on landing when the throttle stuck and the brakes failed on one wheel. The aircraft circled its way down the tarmac all the way to Hangar C where we've got those Bird Dog fuselages lined up thick as thieves. Myla worked in the front fuselage right in harm's way when the airplane crashed into the hangar door."

"Oh, goodness me. Are you all right?" Her mother held a helpless look that blanched her cheeks pale. "You know how I feel about you working out there."

"A gentleman saved me right before the plane hit the hangar door, Mr. Durand, our new quality control supervisor." Myla clammed up, deciding not to share much more than that. Some of the particulars were personal impressions, not to be repeated.

"The safety manager sent him to retrieve Myla once I noticed she hadn't evacuated with us. They followed protocol, I'll give 'em that." Miss Granger rocked back on the sofa to allow herself a deep breath. "Just about ruined the safety manager's record though, as three hundred and forty-six days without an injury on the job is nothing to shake a stick at. Guess he'll have to start all over tomorrow."

"You're hurt then, Myla?" Her mother's voice dripped with concern.

"I took a metal shard on my left hip. The nurse in the infirmary stitched me up and now it's healing. It could have been so much worse. I truly thank God for sheltering me from what might have been."

"And you may consider sending a note of thanks to our Mr. Durand. He ran a lot faster than I would have, that's for sure." Alice stood with a groan and motioned to the door. "I'd better hit the trail."

Effie followed the bulky supervisor to the front door. "Thank you so much for getting Myla home to me. I'll surely write that note to Mr. Durand and send it with her on Monday."

"Yes, Miss Granger. Count on me for Monday. That quality control meeting is first thing, so I'll report in to Interiors right afterwards." Myla shifted in the chair to make eye contact and instantly regretted the motion.

"Do take good notes in the meeting for me. You know how I hate being left out." The department head pulled the door open and stepped past the threshold, turning to give her a mischievous wink.

Her mother shoved the door closed and hung on the doorknob as if weakened. "Myla, you know how I feel about you working in such a rough place. Since something awful has happened, I wish you'd reconsider."

"For now, I have to focus on getting well. Can you start the bath water for me, Mother? A soak in a hot tub would do wonders right now."

"Of course. I want to see the stitches when you get out. At least your immunizations are current. We wouldn't want you to come down with lockjaw, would we?"

"No, Mother. We don't want any complications." She stood and limped toward the hall. She'd be plenty lock-jawed about what she discerned when peering into Weston Durand's depthless brown eyes. Even with an airplane propeller chewing away at the hangar, she hadn't been daft enough to miss the high-grade specimen of a man pressing her into the underbelly of safety. No, she'd take that tactile impression to the tub and steam over it awhile.

"Thank God it wasn't any worse, Myla Renee." Her mother popped out of the bathroom wringing a clean washcloth in her hands.

"I have already…and plan to again at bedtime. Mr. Durand also got wounded, Mother. So we need to pray for his recovery as well. He took a gash across his right calf, which earned him eight stitches to my four."

"It sounds like he sheltered you. Praise God someone was there when you needed protection." She handed over the wash cloth and feigned a smile. It came and went without wholehearted support.

"Yes, with some quick thinking, he shoved me onto a mechanic's creeper and jumped aboard, launching us under a fuselage for protection by its landing gear."

"Oh my stars. I trust you don't consider that an average day's work."

Myla entered the bathroom and jacked off her work shoes to feel the coolness of the tile floor beneath her feet. "No, Mother. Any day that stands out from the others is considerably better than average." She heard the gasp as she pulled the door closed, not meaning to leave her mother off-balance by her honest remark. Rising steam began to cloud the mirror as she regarded her reflection. Tucking an errant strand of wavy hair behind her ear, she imagined her rescuing knight running to claim her while the dragon began chomping at the metal drawbridge. The dramatic analogy pleasured her so much, she replayed it several times as she undressed and dipped into the healing waters.

~

Weston hobbled to the back door of the Pontiac Catalina and opened it to retrieve his new friend, a single crutch. The nurse at the infirmary had insisted he keep his weight off the injury, allowing it to heal. He tucked the padded collar under his armpit and headed for the apartment entrance. For once, he didn't regret the shoddy two-step entrance off the bungalow's back porch. Two steps seemed like child's play in comparison to the sixteen he'd have to navigate Monday morning to access his office. He gritted his teeth and made the ascent without using his right heel, which kept his stitched calf muscle from flexing.

He entered the mudroom where his landlord did the laundry on an antiquated ringer-washer. Nothing looked state-of-the-art about this place, but it was only temporary lodging. He'd pick up searching for a permanent residence after he could get around without the crutch. With the Catalina nearly paid for, he could assume a mortgage without much financial difficulty and improve his quality of life. Not meaning to, he banged the crutch against his weightlifting bench which announced his entry.

In no time, his landlord had shuffled to the doorway. "Say, what's happened to you, Weston? Did the Red Baron shoot at your airplanes?" The old-timer chuckled into his fist and waited for an answer.

"Brake failure on a turbo-prop prototype, Mr. Godfrey. It ran afoul and chewed up a hangar door with its propeller. I had the honor of saving a young woman in danger and received a cut on the leg for my heroic efforts. The worst news came after an inspection revealed the throttle stuck and the brake line failed, so it likely wasn't happenstance."

"Aha! Intentional trouble is the worst kind. At least you have the weekend to be on the mend. My sister just brought over a plate of her famous chicken-fried steak. How about I throw it in the oven and knock on your door when it's warmed up? I can't let you scrounge around back there on one leg to scrape up a meal. What do you say?" Mr. Godfrey's salt-and-pepper brows arched up, crinkling his forehead.

"Throw in a can of creamed corn and you've got yourself a dinner partner, Mr. G." He pulled the apartment door open while his landlord slapped his hands together and disappeared into the kitchen. Weston dragged his crutch tip over the threshold and hobbled into the main living area. He pitched the crutch onto the tan vinyl couch and plopped into the Windsor chair at the dinette table nearby. A bold-typed headline stared back at him from yesterday's paper, hailing the prototype turbocharged airplane as the next star in the nation's air fleet. He ridded the paper from sight with a hasty shove and dropped his head on his forearm to clear the shrapnel-filled day from his system. Somewhere between ache and aggravation, wavy black hair that smelled of meadow flowers began to soften the recollection. He lost himself in the redemptive sensation until he couldn't remember anything else.

Chapter 2

Weston shifted on the padded stool as more participants filed into the meeting room. Unlike other Mondays, this day would not begin with the lead-balloon dread of repetition in the workplace. For once, they could cut the fetters that bound them to routine and be free to dream a bit. Not just grateful to be a part of it, he had the privilege to launch the initiative that would help Cessna take wing to greater heights. Two more men sauntered in, quelling their conversation at the door. He nodded, recognizing the older man with broad shoulders from the shop floor. With the committee's circle mostly filled, he turned and printed "poka-yoke" on the blackboard.

"Thank you, gentlemen, for meeting with me today." Weston wiped the excess chalk from his fingertips and squared around on the stool. A flurry of activity at the door caught his attention, so he held his next comment until the late-arriver could join them. To his immediate pleasure, he saw Myla Templeton sweep into the room in a trim brown dress. After she'd taken the closest empty seat, he cleared his throat. "I already have to amend my welcome. Thank you, lady and gentlemen, for attending.

"You now hold a place in what is called a Quality Circle. For the next hour while we meet, I'll ask you to clear your minds of what departmental tasks await you, to help me dream of something broader for the company's future. Through our brainstorming together, it is my hope that we will keep Cessna on the cutting edge of competitiveness through a paradigm of continuous improvement in every facet of our operations. Here, I want to solicit your ideas for specific improvements—and we won't just give it lip-service either. I intend to see that every idea holding merit moves forward toward implementation.

"But first, before I get too far into faulty product detection and quality management, let's go around the circle to identify ourselves and tell what department we represent. "Ladies first, Miss Templeton, if you please. And let me add that it's good to have you back at work today."

Myla shifted in her seat and crossed her ankles. "Thank you, Mr. Durand. I'm grateful to be here, I assure you. My name is Myla Templeton. I've worked for Interiors as an upholstery seamstress for almost two years." She nodded to the man on her left and looked back at him with pink-flushed cheeks.

"Ted Halyard, sheet metal." The middle-aged man clamped his mustache tight against his bottom lip, content to have minimally obliged.

The next man gestured with open palms and revealed an impressive set of calluses. "I'm Ernie Pike from tools and fixtures. I'm glad to be here—if it means improvements."

"I share that sentiment, too. I'm Skip Sellers from production and assembly." He rolled his broad shoulders forward as he dropped his elbows onto the chair arms. "I want to add that the two of you gave us quite a scare last week on the shop floor, when the turbocharged prototype decided to pay Hangar C an unwelcome visit." He nodded across the circle to Myla, making her cheeks flush pink again.

"Thank you for your concern, Mr. Sellers. I thought I recognized you from the assembly floor." Weston made eye contact with Myla and couldn't fight back a slight smile. "Guess a weekend comes in handy for recuperation now and then."

"Yes, remarkably so." Myla nodded to Sellers and soon busied her hands with opening a bound notebook she'd brought along.

"I'll be the last one in the huddle then." A thin man stuck a thumb into his chest, striking his name badge. "I'm Rich Yost, paint shop."

"Aha, Mr. Yost. Perhaps you could enlighten us as to what color those Navy-ordered L-19s will be when they roll out of your shop." Weston gave a good-natured laugh as several members perked up, ready to hear a secret.

"More than one color, mind you. But that's all I'm at liberty to say." Yost zipped his lips closed and tucked the imaginary key inside his breast pocket.

"All right. I'll consider that a lead-in for our introductory teaser today." Weston turned toward the blackboard and gestured to the phrase he'd written earlier. "Let's shift our thoughts back to quality management for the duration of our time together. I have to thank our Japanese counterparts for this term, 'poka-yoke.' Anyone want to guess what it means?"

"How about 'guard your back' for a guess?" Halyard, the sheet metal worker, gave a boisterous laugh laced with condescension.

"Well, I think since we're helping them rebuild post-war, we have trust on our side this time," Weston replied. "Anyone else want to give 'poka-yoke' a shot?"

"How about polka-dot? I've been asked to paint worse." Yost chuckled and threw an elbow toward his neighbor.

Sellers studied the phrase on the board. "I'm going to guess something like 'if it's broke, then fix it.' Seems like common sense, but we don't always abide by it."

"Good point. I want all our efforts to make common sense— and I think your guess is close to the actual translation. 'Poka-yoke' means 'avoid error,' which is what we'll be all about in our continuous improvement effort." Weston paused to take a breath and saw that Myla employed her time by taking vigorous notes. A pleasure birthed at the unprompted sight, and his aspirations for the group took wing. "All tethers aside now, we're heading for the unchartered territory of vast improvement. Give me a sign if you're with me."

"Aye," Skip Sellers replied.

"Here, here," Ted Halyard added.

"I'm in—but it wouldn't hurt to throw a doughnut at me now and again," Ernie Pike said. The comment solicited a round of chuckles.

Rich Yost flashed a thumbs-up sign, his nail rimmed with last week's paint work.

Weston glanced over at Myla and tried not to focus on her slim ankles. When she dropped the pen and applauded, his spirit took wing. "All right then. Let's look at our individual departments. You call out some of the current problem areas, and I'll write them up here on the board. For every problem, there's a solution—if we're innovative enough to recognize and develop it." He picked up the chalk and held one finger in the air for their first suggestion. Quiet filled the room.

Myla looked up from her notebook with an open expression. "What about the problematic mindset of settling for status quo? It's not a tangible part or product, but it does pose a barrier to innovation for the future of our company."

Weston squelched the urge to hoist his frame off the stool and wrap her in a giant hug. Instead, he hid his pleasure by turning to write "status quo" on the board. "The primary cause of sickness in American industry is the failure of management to manage for the improvement of quality. While I'll not own that quote, it could be construed as a veritable definition of status quo. Thank you, Miss Templeton, for bringing it to the forefront of our discussion, so we know to avoid such a mindset as we enter into the domain of the innovative. Now, does anyone else have a problem, perhaps something more concrete?"

"I think we have a ventilation problem in the paint room." Rich Yost leaned forward and gave a shake of his head. "Put that on your list, because I sure would like to see it improved."

Weston scratched the chalk across the blackboard. The group's ready engagement bolstered his effort. It represented a good start.

"I can't get the right parts on the shop floor when I need them," Skip Sellers added.

Weston pointed three fingers at the foreman and wrote his problem on the board. By the time he'd finished taking input, he had fourteen entries ranging from short-circuits in production to shoddy vendor products. He turned and faced the group that arched around the circle from knee to knee. "Improvement starts right here and right now. Let's brainstorm some solutions, shooting from the hip. Focus on inadequate air circulation in the paint shop and give me your first idea." He glanced around the circle's perimeter until Skip Sellers lifted his hand with a suggestion. He clicked his fingers at him and solution-oriented innovation began to swirl around the room. To his budding delight, Myla continued writing everything down. The group had a self-appointed secretary, one he could work closely with and not mind it for one belabored second. What a delightful happenstance.

~

Myla reread the note from her boss: *Bring ten layouts to the shop floor this afternoon.* Unfortunately, the Quality Circle meeting had gone on for so long, she'd lost a good chunk of the morning. She'd have to work through lunch to get the material cut and divided into sets, or face getting a reprimand from Miss Granger. That woman could be so unyielding at times, especially when it came to efficiency. In her case, haste didn't make waste, it made status quo. A worry dug into her confidence that her sketch-up of a new décor scheme would fall flat, given such an old-school welcoming committee. Maybe the Quality Circle would provide more fertile soil.

Myla gave it further thought as she stretched the leather roll out to cut a seat cover from it. She affixed the pattern, reflecting back on the morning's meeting. Hadn't Weston Durand's face simply beamed each time a new idea had been tossed out? What if she planned a pitch for her western-style interior at their meeting next month? He'd certainly asked them to bring back further development to fuel the innovation discussion.

The more she thought about it, the more certain she became. She could put the mock-up together at home and give the Quality Circle members first dibs at critiquing it for aesthetics and marketability. With the scissors aligned, she made the first decisive snip around the pattern. "Changes are coming, Madam Leather. You're not the only fabric in town."

~

The wheel hub that had saved his skin last Friday sure looked the worse for wear, especially for an aircraft that hadn't even rolled off the shop floor. Weston laid flat on his back, examining the scratches left by flying metal scraps. The flex strut seemed sound despite the cosmetic damage, but he would measure and document the superficial flaws for now. He grabbed the caliper from his shirt pocket, took the reading, and committed it to memory.

When he rolled the creeper out from under the plane, something wedged it into an abrupt halt. Forgetting about the instrument, he put his hand out instinctively to thwart the threat. What a shock to find a woman's trim ankle as the interloper. The caliper dangled in his fingers, mere inches from making contact.

"I wouldn't ruin that pair of nylons if I were you, Mr. Durand." Myla's warning filtered through the shop noise. When she knelt nearby, her dress hem swished the edge of the creeper as if protecting its territory.

Catching the tease in her comment, he gave her a boyish grin and sat up beside the wheel mount. "I agree, there's been quite enough damage around here already."

"Is this beyond salvaging?"

"What? This wheel hub? No, I don't believe so. Most of these scratches are shallow nicks. We'll give it the standard proof test before this plane test flies, just to be sure."

"Better it than me, as I'm on light duty this week. Say, you ran a pretty inspiring meeting this morning. If I'm an accurate judge, your devotion to quality control became infectious around the circle."

"Glad to hear your impression. By the way, thank you for taking notes during our session, which brings me to ask a favor."

She squinted the slightest bit. "I'm sure you wouldn't ask for any extra time, since I don't have any. Short of getting a summer intern, I don't know how we'll get these Bird Dogs outfitted for the Navy order. My fingers are sore from all the constant cutting and stitching as it is."

Weston stood and stretched, prompting a jab of pain from his calf. He winced and knew she'd seen it. "I've got sore stitching of my own, Miss Templeton. What I really wanted to ask is for you to keep doing what you've started—taking notes in our meetings. I'll have clerical staff type them up as formal records at the close of each meeting, then forward your notebook through office mail back to you. Would you please consider it?"

"Only if you might consider my proposition in return." She rose and raised one eyebrow so high, it appeared to touch the hangar rafters.

"It seems I'm suddenly open to negotiation. With the exception of another maelstrom of raining metal scraps, what might you have in mind?" He opened his stance and pocketed the caliper. Remembering to personify the quest for innovation, he intensified his gaze.

"I have a proposal I'd like to pitch at our next month's meeting—for a new product on the Interiors line. It features a state-of-the-art textile better suited to more arid climates. Its durability ratings are high. I'm planning to give it a western twist with saddle stitching and maybe even a dab of hand-worked tooling along the console. All I need is the guarantee of ten minutes at your meeting, Mr. Durand. Do you think you can spare it?"

Somewhere amid the rise and fall of her eloquent delivery, he'd been transported into a higher realm, one of mindless appreciation. Yes, he'd heard the product description and had been impressed with her vision-casting, but the lull of the words leaving her well-curved lips caused a precipitous daydream for which he had no resistance. He raised his hand to his chin and stroked it to collect his composure. "That's amazing—the whole concept I mean. Why don't you plan to lead off then? I'd much rather launch a new Interior line right off the get-go than rig a circulation fan for the paint shop. This concept is most exciting. Really, you've lent me hope anew."

"Well, thank you, Mr. Durand. Let me express my regret for your continued discomfort from the wound you sustained during my rescue. I trust you'll be done with your crutch friend by the end of the week."

"Friend would be pushing the relationship, Miss Templeton." At this point, he wouldn't give the crutch a sideways glance, as he held something much more lovely in focus. "Could you drop that notebook to me in the office mail? I promise to have it back to you by week's end, even if I have to deliver it myself."

"Of course I will, since it sounds like the notebook will fall into capable hands. As for my part, I'll start that prototype mock-up on my own time this weekend. I already have a sample swatch of the fabric."

"Then you have a jump on the status quo, to borrow your term and serve it right back to you. I'm glad you're part of the Quality Circle, Miss Templeton. Who knows? We just might turn a few heads by what we come up with to improve things around here." He shifted ever so slightly in her direction to better demonstrate his sincerity.

A booming voice rolled over the fuselage. "Myla? I need those skins over here pronto."

She stiffened at the beckon and pushed the cart bearing a stack of seat covers forward. As she rounded the nosecone, she glanced back at him. "Status quo," she whispered in slow motion, her lips exaggerating the words.

Weston chuckled, but wiped his mirth away with his hand, hoping not to lose his professional edge out on the shop floor. He withdrew the caliper and gave her a farewell salute with it. The scene played out with his discerning eye on the back seams of her nylons, a quantification that didn't require employment of the caliper—not in the least.

~

"Just a spattering of mayhem, that's what I'm after." He walked around the table and pulled the Frigidaire open. All he could find was watered-down orange juice. *How pathetic.*

"You'll need to lay off a couple of weeks—or they'll start suspecting something." She opened the wrapper and spooned out the crushed remains of a moon pie. Once she got the contents into her mouth, she gave him a long look while she chewed.

"I'm not due back over there until the end of the month. My route takes me to Hutchinson next. I have a couple of dolls on the furniture line I'm selling to. They admire my company."

"The Snap-lite Rebel, that's my brother. He has a dame in every port, just like James Dean. And it never hurts his end-of-the-month sales quota."

"No ma'am, it doesn't. Having women in the workplace has bolstered my commissions like jet fuel. I won't be complaining any time soon." He took the juice and drank it right out of the jug.

She took the remaining hunk of damaged treat and plopped it into her mouth.

"If you would lay off those sweets, you could manipulate your own subtle negotiations."

"If I gotta pick a flaw that's taking me to the mat, this is what I pick." She held up the cellophane smeared with the moon pie's chocolate coating and began to lick it clean.

He slammed the refrigerator shut and looked at her in disgust. "Story of my life—a doo-whop spirit with lousy back-up singers." He headed to his room, unsatisfied with the damage.

~

Congratulations for the prominent part you have played in the early development of aviation. Your work has been a splendid contribution to this great industry, and Kansas can be proud of your memorable pioneering in this field.

President Dwight D. Eisenhower to Founder Clyde Cessna, February 23, 1953

Weston allowed his gaze to linger on the engraved plaque while the chatter of the secretarial pool swept around him. He drew in a long breath, thinking how his work continued that pursuit of excellence for which Cessna had become internationally renowned. For his part, he would hold high the mark and extend others the same opportunity.

A tapping on his bicep added to the mayhem of the clerical suite. "Here's your notebook back, sir. I've tucked the notes inside the back cover." A middle-aged woman with a silver streak highlighting her hair gestured with Myla Templeton's notebook.

He took the notebook and gave the typing work a cursory review. "Thank you very much for getting to the meeting notes so readily. I'll plan to do this the first of every month, immediately following our QC meetings."

"That's fine. End of the month is usually when we're busiest, so you've selected a good time to need clerical support." She started to retreat and then stopped herself. "I wanted to mention the personal correspondence tucked inside, in case it had slipped your detection, Mr. Durand." With that, she gave a faint smile and turned toward the typing console.

With a flurry of thought-provoking questions darting around his brain, he made it into the far hall before opening the notebook. There inside the front cover was a linen envelope with his name handwritten on it in a pinched flowing font. Determined not to make a public show of it, he slammed the notebook closed and made a beeline for Hangar C. When he stepped outside, April seemed to have put on a new bonnet. The day unfurled as fair as spring allowed. He took his time crossing the corner of the tarmac, glad to be shed of the cumbersome crutch at last.

He stepped through the open hangar doors and entered the clickity-clack zone of constant riveting noise, grateful for the sound of progress. As he headed for the stairway, he tossed a wave to Skip Sellers. A uniformed service vendor retreated from the snack room, her arms balancing a cadre of empty boxes. He feigned a nod her way and headed up to his office. In route, he opened the front cover, removed the personal correspondence, and placed the notebook in the mail basket, having already affixed the routing slip back to Interiors. With a turn of a knob, he entered into the sanctuary of his small office and closed the door behind him.

The envelope beckoned like a daily-double bonus from his palm. He stood facing the file cabinet and tore at its flap, eager to read the message. He slid the card out and pressed open its center fold.

Dear Mr. Durand,

Upon learning that you were present to quell every mother's nightmare of harm coming to their child by some unexpected circumstance, I want you to know that you hold my sincere appreciation for taking care of Myla under such a calamitous situation as the recent accident. We would like to extend an invitation to dinner at our house, 32 Magnum Street, on the evening of April 29th to properly thank you. I look forward to meeting you then. Effie Templeton

Anticipation birthed in his chest. No question. He would most certainly attend.

Chapter 3

Myla fussed with the chintz chair covers that she had added to the mahogany dining set in an effort to lighten the antique furnishings while adding a touch of spring. Their dinner guest would be arriving any minute. She quelled an ice cold trickle that slid through her chest and decided to check in with the cook one last time. Worried about presentation, she grabbed the Fiesta Dinnerware platter and headed for the kitchen. The aroma of roast beef made her stomach growl.

"This gravy isn't thickening like I want it to," Effie said, hunched over the black skillet. "Bring me the flour canister, will you?"

She picked up the second largest canister, but held it ransomed against her midsection. "Okay, Mother, about Mr. Durand. Can we agree that we don't have to tell him all the family stories on this first visit?"

"Oh, is this a first of many visits? That's putting the cart in front of the horse, isn't it? I really need my Gold Medal, hon." She motioned for the flour with a flap of her wrist.

"He's…interesting. Duncan Reed, our safety manager, said he recruited him from Iowa State where Weston had finished up his post-doctorate work in quality control. That gives him more aptitude than most of the men out on the shop floor." She carried the canister to the range and sat it between the burners, where a pan full of her mother's garden peas simmered.

"I'm certain the company will benefit then. Can you take the lid off for me?" She stopped stirring with a fork and looked up from the pan. "I promise to restrain my storytelling, if that's what you're getting at."

Myla tugged at the gasket safeguarding the flour until the lid popped off in her hands. "Thank you, Mother. I don't want to rush into a personal conversation with a work associate, that's all." She dipped the scoop into the fine powder and put the handle toward her mother.

A door chime sounded from the front room as the flour found the pan. "You answer the door, Myla. I simply must get this gravy to thicken. Please keep him entertained in the living room until I can join you."

All her preparation seemed to melt like wax as she stepped to the front door. When she opened it, a well-groomed version of Weston Durand stood on the stoop. Having chosen to wear her most form-fitting dress, Myla suddenly grew self-conscious. "Mr. Durand. How nice of you to come for dinner."

"I wasn't about to decline an invitation like this. Between the cafeteria at work and re-heated leftovers with my landlord, I think my taste buds are in rebellion." He laughed and followed with a sincere look. "Please say you'll call me Weston tonight. While we're away from the aircraft industry, I'd hoped we could be, well, just regular folks."

"Yes, if you'd like. Please come in before mother accuses me of keeping you on the stoop like some pushy vacuum salesman." She smiled and gestured into the living room.

He stepped into the foyer. His gaze made a quick appraisal of her, halting where the tucks of her dress bodice conformed to the rounds of her hips. "Your injury—I trust it's healing without complication."

"Yes, thank you for asking. I'm looking forward to having those itchy stitches taken out soon." She winced and led him into the living room, conscious of having to turn her back toward him. She'd no more than alighted on the edge of an overstuffed club chair than her mother appeared in the room.

"And what she won't tell you is that all those appalling bruises have finally faded, too. Good evening, Mr. Durand. I'm Effie Templeton, Myla's mother."

Still standing, Weston shook off his surprised expression to greet her, extending his hand to take hers. "Mrs. Templeton, it's so nice to meet you after your thoughtful note. The dinner is a special gesture, one not underappreciated by a starving bachelor such as myself. Your home is quite lovely, by the way."

"Thank you, Mr. Durand. That's mostly Myla's touch, I'm proud to report. She has a way with fabrics and décor. Always has, from the time she was a young girl."

"Mother, Mr. Durand has asked that we call him Weston tonight. If it helps him feel more welcomed as a hero and less like a quality control advocate, I think we should oblige. After all, my slipcovers may not hold up as quality work, should he decide to remain an inspector."

He laughed, giving the front bay window his immediate attention. "I don't think that would be a possibility, really. But I'd answer to Weston, ma'am, if you'd be willing to use it."

"Very well then, I need to swing back into the kitchen and turn off the oven. Myla, you carry the conversation until I return. We'll head into the dining room in a bit. Make yourself comfortable on the sofa, Weston." With a dusting of her hands, she turned and disappeared from the doorway.

"Always in a pinch and a dash—that's my dear mother." She tilted her head with the jest, hoping to make him more at ease.

He lowered onto the sofa cushion in one deliberate slow movement, his gaze ever upon her. "I never imagined there would be bruising. I trust there wasn't much discomfort from them. I am apologetic to have caused them in the first place."

Her ruse of trying to be the hospitable-yet-impervious hostess began to crumble under his genuine concern. She shifted in the chair, causing the seam selvage from a tuck to draw tight across her injury. She pinched at the rayon fabric and tried to remedy the rub, but only managed to give his gaze a new target. With honesty being the only way out, she blinked to focus her attempt. "Anything I feel, any scratch to recover from, or any bruise to shed is the grander part of being alive enough to retell the story of a wayward airplane. My Father used to tell me to search for the silver lining, and one might say your being here tonight could suffice as such."

He pointed toward the mantle. "Is that your father?"

She knew the picture without having to look around. "Yes. He was an officer in the Navy. Mother moved back here to Wichita after being widowed by the Pearl Harbor attack."

At that, Weston got to his feet and approached the fireplace for a closer look. He stood contemplating the framed photo for some time. "I'm more than sorry for your loss. And forgive me for using a Japanese term to start our QC session. I'd not given any prior thought to wartime losses, a shortcoming on my part."

She stood, partly to alleviate the tug at her scar, but also to extend him a gesture of understanding. "Poka-yoke, how ironic a term, especially when 'avoid error' manages to become one—a mistake, I mean." She stepped closer to him and regarded the stern figure in the photograph, hardly the man she remembered as her father. "Bruises fade and we get well."

"So all is forgiven? The shove I gave you and my indiscretion at touting the Japanese?" His expression softened while he reached for her.

Myla looked up into his penitent brown eyes and sensed it again, that feeling of glimpsing deeper into his soul. The mental reminder that she didn't trust men came too late. Though she'd intended the friendship to remain guarded and superficial, such a candid encounter worked against her initial efforts. Now, she had to do what she always did when she felt her resolve slipping away—she prayed. Her next thought came under divine inspiration. "I believe the Lord set the example of forgiving seven times seventy."

His face enlivened with immediate relief, which soon birthed a warm smile.

"Looks like you have at least five more errant slips to go."

"Oh no. Don't forget the multiplying factor of seventy. Jesus had to add that to loosen up those disciples beyond the limit of the law, don't you think?"

She laughed and the once-weighty conversation turned the corner to much lighter content. "That will teach me to measure twice and cut once, won't it? Math is such a bother."

He gave her a look that spoke of a mystery. "Or a key, if one can harness it to unlock the yet-to-be-known."

"That's an intriguing perspective. I'll try to stay more open in the future."

Effie pushed through a crack in the kitchen door. "Dinner's ready, you two. Myla, show our guest to the dining room, and then come help me bring the roast in, will you?"

"Please say 'yes' to halt this infernal rumbling in my stomach." Weston's cheek crinkled into a smirk as he nodded in reaction to the announcement.

"Yes, Mother. Weston had just finished a most elaborate apology…almost a lesson, you might say. I'll be right there."

Squelching a smile, he extended his elbow to escort her to dinner.

She placed her hand in the crook of his elbow. The cottony touch of his oxford cloth shirt brought unexpected comfort. "So we're both nearly well then?" She stepped toward the dining room, and he soon followed close beside.

"Absolutely. With these stitches out the first of next week, all that will remain is a spot made tender." He touched a button on the shirt front and flexed his muscles beneath.

When his hand formed a fist, Myla felt the taut ripple of strength rise up his arm, a masculine mix of tender resolve and restrained power. Her knees grew weak right at the table's edge, where she let him go and held onto trusted mahogany. Needing a diversion to more neutral territory, she thought of the meal. "I hope you like green vegetables. Mother is serving the last of her home-canned garden peas."

"I can hardly wait." He shifted to the chair opposite hers and played with the slipcover tie. "It seems that your creativity knows no bounds."

"Oh, I'm positive there's a limit," she replied. The kitchen never seemed so far away, but she somehow managed to find it.

~

With the end of the month at his doorstep, Weston had pushed his inspection schedule into overdrive. At least the assembly floor in Hangar C had been brought back to fully functional, though a pile of damaged parts now rested in his newly appointed lab space. He examined the rough-edged piece of corrugated tin that had lacerated the pilot seat Myla had been installing at the time of the accident. Routine for his follow-up, he placed it on a scale and read the gauge to the ounce. Once he recorded the information, he pushed back from the workbench with a thought to keep the relic for sentimental reasons. Who knows, perhaps Myla would be interested to see what might have been. He tucked it onto the file cabinet and turned to leave.

A glance at the hallway clock reminded him of his final task for the morning. He exited the lab and headed for the far end of the hangar in search of Skip Sellers. In a team-building effort, he had pledged to accompany him to a local vendor to pass along their paradigm of quality control one stroke removed from the Cessna facility. He'd use this encounter as a prime example of supplier partnering in their next QC meeting. With a little up-front attention, they could turn a once troublesome spot into a trustworthy component supplier. After having passed a dozen Bird Dogs in various stages of prep, he walked smack dab into a confrontation off a cockpit entry. There, in the middle of the heated exchange, stood Myla, her arms laden with custom-cut upholstery pieces.

Alice Granger seemed swollen to the size of a dirigible, her face a deep crimson. "Scram, that's what I say. This aircraft is next in line for Interiors. It's where we're headed and where we're going. Tell that to your cockamamie supervisor."

Weston diverted toward the disagreement. "Could I be of some help here? It seems there's plenty of work for all without having to huddle up in one place at the same time." As he squared his feet to demonstrate he wasn't going anywhere, he heard Myla gasp to his left.

A stocky man filled the cockpit doorway. "The Interiors department knows we have to get the wiring done first. Sorry we're running behind on this line, but I'm nearly done here."

Weston focused on the crusty veteran upholsterer and gave her his undivided attention. "There now, Miss Granger. First things must remain first on the assembly line. I'm sure there is another candidate ready and waiting for your avid attention nearby."

The electronics worker pointed off the tail section. "I finished that plane first thing this morning. She's all yours, gals." With that, he nodded and disappeared inside the cockpit.

Miss Granger harrumphed, so deep a resignation it must have originated at her boot soles. "All right already. We'll move up one beast. Come on, Myla."

He quickly thrust his arm out separating the two women. "Miss Templeton, might I have a brief word with you? I have some follow-up data from your accident scene."

Myla's jaw dropped as she stood speechless, her eyes widening at his reference.

Miss Granger reached for her load. "Give me those covers. I'm not above getting started without any assistance." She took the seat covers with a grunt and headed around the tail of the wingless fuselage. In short order, she turned back with a pruned expression. "Remember Myla. Ask him."

Weston waited for the large woman to fade into the background while Myla's gaze scanned the floor. Maybe he should say something to make her a little less uncomfortable. "I'm sure life can get a bit tenuous when you find yourself being dragged around in the wake of a battleship for most of the day. Maybe quality control should leak over into employee relations and bring everyone up to a more courteous professional level."

She looked up with a spark rekindled in her eyes. "Sign Interiors up when you get that program running, Mr. Durand. I could stand a little less high drama around here."

"Speaking of high drama, I took a measurement of the metal scrap found in the fuselage you were prepping the morning of the accident. Given its mass and estimating its velocity, I can assure you, it would have been a lethal blow had you remained inside."

Myla squeezed her eyes closed. "For the love of God, what a fate that would have been."

Why the sight of her standing so pure and tranquil amid such a ruckus of shop noise affected him, he'd never understand. Its fragility gripped his heart, so he lingered admiring her for a peaceable instant. With his throat tightened, he whispered what came to mind next. "In retrospect, you claimed the protection of God—and he lent it. Those are the telltale moments our faith is forged into something more real."

Her eyes fluttered open and her lips curled into a private smile. "Yes, it was a faith moment, I assure you. Things like that happen for a higher reason, though from an outside perspective it all seems accidental."

He tucked his hands into his pockets. "Now that I've run into you, let me ask how that western mock-up is developing. Our next QC meeting is coming up on the seventh."

"I'm getting there, but I could use better tools for the finish work. Guess I'll justify those once the design gets approval."

"That's the spirit—the spirit that ushers in change. Just know that I'm pulling for you. It will be ladies first on the agenda, so get that dog-and-pony show prepped and ready."

"Say, would you be interested in seeing the damage to that seat cover where your hunk of metal landed? I had to strip it off and start all over again."

His hand flew to his chin in thoughtful reaction. "Aha. Is that the question the battleship had to remind you concerning? Not to say that the cut cover wouldn't be tantalizing to an inquiring mind, but I may have been hoping for something along a more personal line." He squinted to let her know he had her under his immediate scrutiny.

She flung her palms open as if to divest herself of the whole matter. "Blast the time-clock that turns April into May. It's the Open House this weekend. Some higher-up had the predilection to make the invitation for participating Sadie Hawkins style. I think they're trying to boost attendance to showcase our work to more of the general public."

Somewhat acquainted with the coming event, he tilted his head incredulous to know more. "Sadie Hawkins?"

"The single women must invite the men, not vice versa. It has something to do with the moon, or leap year, or something hilariously harmless." She rolled her eyes at the sentiment.

"So, Miss Granger is not-so-subtly reminding you to ask—that is, if you want to go?"

She struggled to swallow before looking up at him. "Would *you* be interested in attending Open House, by any chance?"

"By every chance, in fact, as I'd heard rumors that they would be giving plane rides in our 140s—which may be my only opportunity to experience the comfort of the spring steel landing gear first-hand."

"As my guest, I mean." She knit her fingers together at her waist and waited.

The personal aspect of the invitation had shot right past him at first mention, but now that she posed the offer in no uncertain terms, the vacuous hangar space seemed to shrink around the two of them. "It would give me great pleasure to be your guest for the day—if you'll fly with me. It's my only condition, as we'd have to agree to face the day together in all aspects."

"That's a deal. I need to go now. Miss Granger remains

gracious only for so long."

He stepped back as if to free her to leave. "Let me pick you up Saturday at nine-thirty. I heard the gates open at ten o'clock."

She waggled her finger at his presumptive plan while her gaze trailed down the tail section. "Sadie Hawkins though. Don't forget."

"Which renders me your driver, and yet, your humble guest." He bowed ever so slightly to seal the deal. He now had a date for Saturday, wonder of wonders. Her wavy hair flounced as she ran to catch up with her workload, a reminder that her hair smelled of flowery meadows. The sensation made him long for the closed-in cockpit experience all the more.

Someone hailed him from the snack room door, and he looked up to find Skip Sellers waving him inside. The promise of another thought-provoking rendezvous filled the final few minutes of morning, however, his last one would be hard to beat.

~

Inverted, Myla stapled the seat cover with one hand while pulling it taut with the other. For the umpteenth time, she replayed the amicable conversation with Weston Durand which helped the mundane afternoon pass. When his conditional came to mind, she took a labored inhalation. She had pledged to ride in an airplane, no simple feat since even hopping on a merry-go-round gave her motion sickness. She'd quell the unstable beast, though, if it meant spending a day accompanied by such an intriguing man.

Her head began to swim with possibilities of how the day might go, giving her the sensation of a fish moving upstream to follow a mindless sudden urge. Wasn't she the girl who didn't trust men within an arm's reach and didn't ride in anything with tight quarters moving faster than a mule? She had two days to resolve this before everything went up, up, and away.

The fabric resisted conforming to the rounded edge of the seat, so she reworked tiny folds in the leather getting it to comply. *Why, oh why, do you have to be an airplane?* She squeezed the stapler to end the difficulty, and then added two more anchoring shots for good measure.

The sound of someone striking the metal gantry drifted from down below. "Are you done in there, Myla? I'm ready to move up the line."

She sat up and shimmied to her feet. "Just finished, Miss Granger. I'll be right down."

"Say, did you get your Sadie Hawkins question asked awhile ago?"

"I did—and he said yes. So we're all set to attend Open House."

"Good. Now, I've got to screw up my courage and take a dose of my own medicine."

"Choose wisely, Miss Granger, or it will make for a long day come Saturday."

"Good golly, Miss Molly. Men—a girl can't live with 'em and can't live without 'em."

Myla backed down the ladder, unwilling to touch that last remark with a ten-foot pole.

A stranger approached her wearing an exaggerated smile, his black leather jacket accentuating his sharp chin. "Hey, you ladies appear to be the crew I'm looking for. Interiors, right? The sewing gals said I might track you down out here. I'm the Snap-lite Tool rep."

Her boss made a disgusted noise in her throat. "I don't have time for this. You take the pitch, Myla, and make it quick."

She faced the man who seemed to favor the luck of the draw. "Okay. I'll be over there right behind you, Miss Granger. Now, what can I do for you today?"

He lowered his gaze briefly to the tool set he carried along, and then gave her a look filled with mischief. "I'll keep this straight to business, though it won't be all that easy."

"Save my time and yours, please."

"I *am* trying to save your time—by getting you the right tool for the job. Snap-lite has a new set of leatherworking tools out that I thought might be of interest to your department."

"Let's have a quick look at what you've got."

He set the tool kit down and extracted a small case. When he popped the top open, half a dozen or so leather punches jiggled inside.

She held her hand out for the set. "I'd like a closer look, if I may." Not wanting to seem eager, she took the case with deliberate slowness, while her mind raced with options on how she could use these for her western prototype. "Tell me. How much does this set run?"

"Right now, it's seven-fifty. But, that comes with a bonus punch a quarter-size larger than the end one there. I don't have that bonus on me, but I'll order it and bring it to you the next time I'm servicing this facility." He flashed a wolf grin that attested to his willingness to return.

Myla flattened her lips and regarded him in a direct stare that meant business only. "I need these three decorative punches, so I'll go ahead take the whole set. I can't wait to run this through purchasing. Let me pay out of my own pocket today. I do expect that bonus piece, but there's no rush on it. Just leave it up in the department office for me. Here's a ten, if you can make change." She dug the bill out of her coverall pocket and flapped it at him.

"Yes ma'am, Myla. Say, that's one of the quickest sales I've ever done. My rebel charm must be working overtime." He snatched the bill and worked his hand into his far pocket.

"That's Miss Templeton to you. Plus, I highly question the charm part."

His face contorted at the jab. "Ouch. Guess I set myself up for that one. Here's your change." He held out two ones and clamped the coins under his thumb. When she turned her palm up to receive it, he caressed the underside of her hand as he slipped it into her grasp. "I'm Hague Amherst, your personal tool salesman, satisfaction guaranteed. Until next time, Miss Templeton. I look forward to it immensely." He gave her a little wink and bent to retrieve his traveling sales kit from the shop floor.

A large form shifted into the aisle close by. "Myla, are you ready yet?"

"Coming, Miss Granger. I'm all done here." She iced a look at the tool salesman to make sure he knew she wasn't interested in his wink, his wolf smile, or anything that went with them. The weight of his hungry stare made her want to run down the aisle. *Thank goodness for the battleship, a handy weapon in hostile waters.* She tucked the tool set away and didn't look back.

Chapter 4

The turnout for Open House had been nothing short of phenomenal. Weston could not have been enjoying it more. Reveling in the static display area on the tarmac, he'd lost Myla momentarily, but soon found her studying the intake of one of the Continental-Teledyne engines on the XT-37. A svelte turbojet, Weston shared the company's pride, given this first-built aircraft was destined to take the world by storm.

Myla nodded him over, her brow knit. "Hey, help me out here. I don't get how having this jet engine lends itself to flight."

He straddled his feet front-and-center on the intake, giving the turbofan blades a quick once-over. Maybe he could toy with her inquisitive mind and command her attention all the while. "Do you remember Newton's Third Law of Motion?" He leaned in toward her as several others had come alongside the turbojet.

"Uh, help me recall those particulars will you, Weston?" She shaded her eyes with her hand as if to focus on the answer.

Trying not to water down his physics lesson just because his student looked impishly darling standing there with rapt attention, he decided to up the effect by downing his volume. "For every action, there is an equal and opposite reaction."

"Like touching a hot iron and retracting your fingers—or something akin to that?" She tipped her head toward him and wet her bottom lip.

He lost a bit of his focus when the overhead sun seemed to accentuate her faint smile. "The air gets sucked in here by the fan." He wiggled his fingers ever closer until they touched the fan blades. When several more people crowded around the engine,

Myla stepped closer to him.

"Then what, after you have an influx of air to start off?"

"After the fan, a compressor compresses the air and then it mixes with fuel." He balled his hands up like lathering soap. "Then the mixture is ignited."

A young boy stepped between them, pinching his balsa wood glider in his stubby fingers. "And then BOOM, right mister?"

"Very good, young man. Yes, the compressed air-gas mixture ignites, expands with a tremendous force, and then gets expelled from the rear of the engine to generate thrust."

Myla locked her arms across her chest. "The equal and opposite reaction?"

Weston hooked his smile into his cheek. "Right again. When the air is exhausted from the rear, it propels the aircraft forward. Thus, we have generated jet-propelled flight."

Members of the attentive crowd began a smattering of applause at the conclusion of his explanation. Myla pursed her lips. Dimples appeared in her cheeks.

He offered his elbow for a gentlemanly escape, and they stepped away from the static turbojet for their next pursuit. He paused in front of the Model 308 prototype that had been demonstrated to the U.S. Army a month prior and unceremoniously declined. He pointed out the small blackboard propped against the identification plaque as he read the inscription, *Rejected by our military. Next step?* Some nearsighted attendee had torn off a corner of paper and written *scrap it*, tucking it into the message board's frame.

Myla exhaled with a sigh. "All that original work down the drain. That doesn't really encourage me to whip out that western prototype in all my non-existent free time."

"Ah, now, Miss Templeton. If at first you don't succeed, try, try again. Otherwise, Cessna's next greatest contribution to aviation won't even get off the ground." He leaned into her with a weighty shoulder nudge.

She capitulated with a chuckle. "Your point's well taken. Where to next?"

"Should we dare go flying next, or are you hungry for lunch? It's barely eleven-thirty."

She turned and gave the waiting line a fleeting inspection.

"Flying first would suit me better, if you are ready to go up."

"I'll race you over there. Ready, set, go." He hooked her elbow and lit into a mad dash to beat out other interested parties headed in the same direction.

Myla laughed and kept up with his pace. When he tried to nose-dive into the first line, she pulled him deeper onto the taxiway and planted in a shorter queue.

A woman leaned out of line ahead of them. "Well, look who decided to finally get their feet off the ground."

Myla gave her a brief wave. "Hello, Miss Granger. Good to see you made it."

When the supervisor nodded, Weston wondered who in the world would have come out as *her* Sadie Hawkins date. Skip Sellers soon poked his head out and gave him a snappy salute. His jaw must have hung open for several seconds before he received a jab in the ribs.

Myla hoisted one brow, her eyes full of laughter. "I think you might be having one of those equal and opposite reactions things, Mister Newton."

"That's Sir Isaac Newton, the incomparable." He rubbed the back of his neck, wishing he'd worn a hat. "Glory be, what I know about interpersonal relationships could fit in a pillbox."

"I'll take a Dramamine if you're dispensing cure-alls, Doctor Regret." She stepped up when the line shifted and pulled him along by the elbow.

"You're not bringing up motion sickness at this late point in time, are you?" He turned her shoulders so she squared up to his on-the-spot inspection. A sheepish expression gave him the truthful answer she probably wouldn't admit out loud.

The line moved up, and she side-stepped forward. "We'll see how it goes."

"If that's truly the case, we don't have to go up."

"No, nonsense. You want to test out the 140, so we'll go. That's all there is to it." She held up one finger, pointing toward the sky.

He gave her a corrective look over his brow when an eager participant gave a little shout of hallelujah up front. He looked around the line to see the guide taking Alice Granger by the elbow to escort her around the awaiting aircraft. Skip Sellers followed right in her wake. "Today, the Navy is joining allegiances as the battleship goes airborne."

She jabbed at him with her elbow, but failed to make contact. "Let's allow her some fun today, shall we? I think you're jealous, that's all. They look like they're having a good time."

"Jealous is the one thing I'm not. Sunburned yes, and getting hungry, maybe. But I'm not jealous by any stretch of the imagination." He closed the gap in front of him as the airplane taxied off with Alice riding shotgun in front. That reminded him that he needed to claim his seat.

"Would you mind if I sat up front with the pilot? The view is much more sweeping up there—unless you want to experience that open-to-the-sky feeling behind the windshield."

"Absolutely not. Be my guest. I'll take the back seat where I can double up, if my stomach starts to flip." She crossed her arms over her abdomen as a preventative measure.

"Thank you, Miss Templeton. Just for the record, Miss Battleship and Mr. Push-broom Mustache aren't the only ones having fun today. Your company has been most delightful."

She shifted forward in line, but her fleeting smile somehow forgot to advance with her. "Hope you can say the same after we land."

He patted her shoulder with his left hand. Subtly, he checked for his handkerchief with his right, just in case. He liked to be prompt in saving someone's dignity, especially his own.

~

Finally standing in front of their line, Myla allowed the sunshine to play across her cheeks. She practiced slow breathing in an effort to allay her mounting fears. Standing on the ground seemed well and good, but add a twitchy pitch, or a wing-stretched yaw, and the whole thing might cavort across her grain from the inside out.

The guide hastened toward the front, holding up three fingers. Weston replied by flashing two fingers back. He waved them toward the aircraft where a propeller made it difficult to hear any further instructions. Weston lent her a hand up into the rear seat.

Myla took a quick assessment of the neat interior work as she tumbled onto the seat. Outside the door, she could barely make out that another passenger had been paired with their flight. She scurried to the far seat when Weston lunged toward the back joining her. He looked like a boy as he donned the headset, giddy for the adventure. He soon handed her a set and helped her center them over her ears, clearing a wayward wisp of hair that only seemed to add to his pleasure. When he snapped his seatbelt into place, she searched for hers and did the same.

A female's voice came in loud and clear over the headphones. "You guys all ready?"

"Absolutely," Weston replied.

"The back seat's ready," Myla added.

The man up front gestured with a vigorous thumbs-up and when he turned around to give them a smile, it was the slick tool salesman, Hague Amherst. He gave a foxy wink before he straightened around toward the front.

Myla felt the bottom of her stomach fall out, but blamed it on the pilot who could have eased the throttle a bit more gently to start the flight. In seconds, the call to the tower for clearance to take off gave her all the more reason to collect her composure. *Get on with it.*

Weston reached over and gave her hand a squeeze. His face remained animated as he watched the landscape whiz by out her window. "This is going to be so amazing."

"You're right," she replied. When the headset amplified her voice back to her, she sounded like a complete stranger.

"Let's take this baby off the ground," Hague said, his hands hovering level over the horizon. Almost at his command, the wheels gave a bounce and the craft lofted airborne.

It only took Myla five seconds to abhor the sensation head to toe. The plane nosed up to gain elevation, making her stomach flatten out proportionally. She closed her eyes to deal with the sensation and felt Weston's hand press against her forearm. Somehow, his touch seemed to help, and the queasiness leveled off. When the plane banked, she opened her eyes to take a look at the town of Wichita. The perspective captivated her, a bird's-eye view of her industrious city. One wing tip lowered and the entire downtown area emerged.

"There—look at the Arkansas River," Weston said.

"And the Little Ark branching to the north," Hague added.

"See the blue-topped building just off the wing-tip?" the pilot asked. "That's where Clyde Cessna built his first plane."

"Hats off to your cunning, Mr. Cessna…and thanks for my incredible job," Weston said, his chest swelling with excitement.

"Yeah, thanks for nothing," Hague added.

"And over here is my old neighborhood," the pilot said. "We lived just south of Quaker College. Those were the good old days."

Myla caught the nostalgia in her tone and began searching for something familiar down below. "I think I spot my old school, South High."

"That's right," the pilot replied. "And look how much the town has grown. Why, soon we'll be as far south as Haysville. Let's circle around and head west. I'll show you Lake Afton before we head back."

"Now, that's a deal," Hague said. His affirmation soon came with his trademark wink.

The pilot seemed to enjoy the flirtation and gave his knee a cordial pat before gripping the throttle again. "I'll put the lake off the right wing. Say, Sugar, you might have to unbuckle and lean across Mr. Handsome back there if you want to catch a glimpse."

Weston beckoned her over to his side of the cockpit.

Apprehensive, Myla depressed her buckle and the strap went limp. When the plane tucked into a tight coil, she climbed toward Weston and got a glimpse of pure blue waters.

He tapped the glass and eased her onto his lap, not resisting the trespass.

She alighted and followed his point with her gaze, her nose only inches off the glass. For a moment, the world seemed suspended on a thread from which they hung like a Christmas ornament. When his arms tightened around her waist, she leaned into his chest and received the full hug, glad for the mountaintop elation that came with the flight. Once the plane leveled off on the far bank of the lake, she felt obligated to revisit her side of the compartment. She squirmed back into place as a man's throaty acknowledgment came across the headphones.

"I'll never forget that sensation," Hague said. A satisfied hum followed.

Myla looked up between the two front seats in time to see Hague turn back toward her and blow her a partly-cloaked kiss. The foxy wink repeated as the plane descended with an atmospheric bump. Inseparable, the two actions knocked the bottom out of her stomach, and she lost her composure.

"Sorry about the air pocket," the pilot said, "but the rest should be smooth sailing."

Myla tried to look nonchalant as she folded her arms across her midsection.

"I'm interested in giving that flex strut a test drive when we land," Weston explained. "My job is to look for flaws and defects, so general process comes with the territory."

"Aye-aye, captain," the pilot cooed. "I'll be sure to give you a worthy demonstration. Stay buckled up, everybody."

"This is going to be cool," Hague added. He shifted in his seat and braced his hands up on the instrument panel.

Myla pressed back in her seat, regulating her breath to keep it even. In a thought for self-preservation, she stripped the headset off and tossed it to Weston. She squeezed her eyes closed and planned to keep them like that until the doors opened to let her out onto terra firma. In seconds, Weston's hands eased around her right arm and held her, his thumbs stroking her skin just below her sleeve.

"Comfort, comfort ye my people," Weston whispered. He brushed her hair back and laid his cheek on hers, warm and full of life. Seconds ticked by and then the lurch of striking land occurred. The aircraft seemed to buoy up like landing on a wave of water. "That's all there is to it," he whispered. "You're safe and sound."

She opened her eyes as the plane decelerated, a grassy meadow opening beyond. She dared to glimpse into his eyes while another sensation wrecked her stomach, a different depthless type of feeling. When the plane stopped moving, the door tore open and there stood the guide, the same as before. Only she had changed. In that short lapse, she'd sat in a man's lap and let him hug her, taken an air-kiss from yet another man, and viewed the earth as only the angels do.

Weston slid out and clasped the guide's hand, shaking it vigorously.

Myla moved to the airplane's door, concentrating on her own dilemma. Though she tried to angle away, she spied Hague giving the lady pilot a kiss on the cheek for her efforts. That last straw cracked her tolerance, and her head began to swim. Weston guided her to the ground and her breath hefted out of her lungs. In mayday mode, she looked up at him in a panic. "Give me a few minutes to redeem my composure." With that she tore away, running until the heavy door to the women's restroom gave way to her shove. She entered the safe haven a land wreck, her pure intentions bundled into a tight knot at the bottom of her stomach.

"Unforgettable, huh?" a brunette said, tightening her ponytail at the mirror.

"Positively," she replied, angling toward a stall. She caught her reflection in the mirror and thought she looked more green than pale. *Great.* Weston would want to stop for lunch next. "You have prepared a table for me in front of mine enemies, dear Lord. Now, I'm asking you to help me want to eat." Regrettably, the wild blue yonder had pressed her straight into an airlock between two men. *So much for my arms-length away strategy.* She would have to stay awhile, as her ground level composure proved nowhere to be found.

~

The beautiful woman he'd wanted to kiss at least twice during their flight now sat across the table from him, her delicate fingers wrapped around a hot dog loaded with catsup only. Weston threw another crunchy tater tot in his mouth while he searched for fair neutral territory for their conversation. Unlike his typical inspections, the signs of weak spots came and went with this particular model, making her ever the more interesting in his estimation. A sip of fizzy cola helped wash his hesitations away, and he cleared his throat. "Are you mutinous on mustard, or what?"

She shifted on the bench and looked over at him. "Mixing it with honey is the only way I like it. My grandmother used to make it from scratch like that. Good homemade mustard can ruin you to this bitter bottled stuff." With that, the end disappeared off her hot dog.

He noticed her color looked better. "I think you're regaining your zest, now that you've had something to eat. Sorry if I asked too much of you with the flight—but I thought it was incredible, especially that view of Lake Afton. You'll always be tucked into that particular memory, a most unforgettable facet, if I do say so."

She chased her mouthful with a sip of yellow-tinged soda.

"Looking back with my feet firmly on the ground, I'm glad I went along. Flying has a weightless release to it, that's for sure."

"What was the point of your discomfort, if you don't mind me asking? Was it the confined space—or the spurious company?" Another tater tot found its way into his mouth.

Her expression traveled through a realm of indecision before she could reply. "Maybe if we could have eased into some of the transitions better, my stomach wouldn't have flipped at the sudden motion. I took that better than I imagined, given the mix of characters involved."

"So, that points a guilty finger at the questionable company." He slapped his palm against the sewn insignia on his knit shirt. "What a direct blow to my ego, Miss Templeton."

She leaned across the table toward him, placing the hot dog on her paper plate. "Not you, Weston, for pity's sake. I meant the greaser in the front seat. That guy rubs me the wrong way."

Honest relief washed over him. He stabbed two tater tots with his fork. "There's a real art to ignoring the inopportune. Not that I was thrilled a stranger took my seat up front, but it did put me in back beside you to lend a hand with your…vulnerable condition. Your Father might have considered that a silver lining, though he may have frowned upon my opportunistic hug over the lake. I apologize if that seemed untoward in the moment, Myla." He downed the potato nuggets before he said anything further that might get him into deeper hot water.

She smiled and wiped her lips with a napkin. "No apology needed. I took it as part of the overwhelming sensation of floating above the crystal blue waters. If Hague Amherst had been in back, rest assured I would have opted to miss the lake entirely."

"Perish the thought. I take it you two had met before?"

"Only briefly on Friday. He represents Snap-lite Tools and brought a new set of leather punches out on the floor for me to preview. I needed the decorative punches for my western prototype, so I purchased the set, all the while trying to quell his inappropriate flirtatious behavior."

Something about her rendering matched up with his observations in the cockpit. A needle of concern poked his chest. For today, he'd dismiss it as unfortunate happenstance. He wouldn't want Myla spending time with anybody like that guy, though. "Cads like him are a dime a dozen. It's best to avoid that type when possible."

"What do you suppose he meant by the 'thanks for nothing' comment to Clyde Cessna?" Myla reconnected with the hot dog and gave it a whopper of a bite.

Weston knew a sour grapes attitude when he saw it. Regret often carried such a mocking tone. "Let's guess that he's a tool salesman for a reason. The plant has hired hundreds of capable men since the war ended." He forked down the last tater tots which had become lukewarm.

She took a sip of her soda and shook her head. "You mean capable men and women. So, you think he may not have measured up to the mark?" Taking notice of a dab of catsup on her fingertip, she popped it between her lips to clean it off.

Distracted by her lip movement, he tired of the subject matter. "Look, Myla. I don't believe this individual is worth one more second of consideration on such a promising day, so I refuse to share you with him a moment longer. Can I tantalize you with an offer to see the paint shop? You can view Rich Yost's predicament firsthand and maybe catch a glimpse of a partly painted L-19 in the process. What do you say?"

She leaned back over the table, her lips tightening around a smile that brought the dimples up again like magic. "You sure know how to tempt a girl, Mr. Durand. Company secrets are fair contraband."

"I'm using your bent toward finishing touches as a fulcrum to have my way with you," he replied. With an impish grin, he stood and took her empty plate with his.

She grabbed her unfinished soda bottle and rose to her feet. "Well, whatever the strategy you've employed, it seems to be working." She raised the bottle toward him, and her smile eased into something more intriguing.

He worked one hand free and found his soda, lifting the bottle to click against hers. "Here's to the afternoon—dressed in a fetching paint scheme and all that comes with it."

"Here, here. Say, thank you for escorting me today. I'm having a great time. However, though my head may be in the clouds hatching out lofty ideas with you, Weston, my feet intend to remain firmly planted on the ground for the duration." She smiled after delivering her tongue-and-cheek message that confined their afternoon to ground level.

He stepped toward a barrel and dumped their trash inside. "Perhaps it may be construed as manipulative of me to rig having you get high on paint fumes, so that your feet might stray from their obligation." He jutted the crook of his elbow in her direction.

She tried to hide her smile inside the mouth of the soda bottle, but took his elbow with her free hand. Her dimples reappeared free of charge.

He had her companionship for the remainder of the afternoon. A monopoly of possession, he planned to treat it like a generous bonus. He pulled her closer and eased his pace, thinking the paint shop might be less than scintillating as a destination. Maybe he could do better.

~

Myla watched the sunset peek from behind the western bank of Lake Afton, where her escort had driven them as an afterthought. The sky had already donned a crown of vermilion red, a brilliant hue difficult to maintain for long.

Weston stooped and skipped a stone across the lake surface. It rippled the waters and streaked uneven patterns across the sunset's reflection.

Her emotions battled with a similar mix. *Arms-length away* fought against a newfound *hold me close*, leaving her not knowing what to expect from the magnetic quality control manager. His wit and wisdom had made the day special, but how would he mark the close of it? A vermilion sunset would be hard to beat.

Weston came up the bank and stood beside her. "Are you ready to go?"

She glimpsed his focused attention and then regarded the far bank. "Lend me a minute more to watch the colors change on the horizon."

"Absolutely. There's no hurry on my part."

"Oh, look there. A great blue heron is coming home to roost." She pointed above the lake as the large wading bird swooped past them on steady wing strokes, heading for an island on the northern lip of the lake.

"One last flight to seal the day." Weston's tone seemed airy, as though he was dreaming out loud. "I dare say May first has ever been more beautiful."

She turned toward him and found him looking right at her. His comment landed like draped chiffon, pleasurably elegant yet light. "I agree."

He dropped his chin to his chest. "Thank you, Father God, for all things inexpressibly lovely. What craftsmanship your hands have wrought. It humbles us through and through."

She closed her eyes to join him in his petition. "Yes, Father, we accept the blessings of this day, and thank you for each one of them, in Jesus' name, amen." She glanced back at the evening sky, and the sunset's brilliance had suffused into a dusky peach aura.

"As if God would have his own amen to the day." He touched his fingertips to the small of her back.

"I believe you're right about that. I'm ready to go now." She managed a light smile while he guided her to the Pontiac's passenger side and opened the door. She slid across the supple upholstery and fingered the piping along a seam, waiting for him to settle behind the steering wheel.

He grabbed the mechanism two-fisted as if anchoring his fortitude to something substantial. "Promise me we can do this again—or I'll not be able to force myself to leave."

She blushed at his struggle, not dissimilar to her own inner tug-of-war. "Yes, I promise." The vow ebbed like the sunset, giving a horizon of glow all its own. The lake darkened as they drove beside it, caching its surface-strewn crystals for another day.

Chapter 5

Only a king deserved the exquisite woven leather fabricated into her new design—a sky king. Myla checked the corner of the tarp to be sure it cleared the cart wheels. Every spare moment of her last ten days had birthed this prototype, one that she could scarcely wait to show-and-tell at Weston Durand's QC meeting this morning. She pushed the cart toward the industrial elevator at the far end of the hall, her speech running through her head.

Impossible to separate, her personal feelings infiltrated her professional expertise as she thought about her place on the circle to the left of Weston. To maintain focus, she'd direct her attention to the other men of the group while she explained the particulars of her new interior design. Weston would stay in the periphery of all that, so she could avoid the sensations he prompted. Ignoring would be too strong a word, but she could redirect her focus for the sake of the project. When her notebook slid off the tarp, she caught it before it hit the floor.

The elevator pinged and opened as she arrived, which she took as a sign her timing would be favored today. She pushed the cart across the threshold gap and hit the first-floor button. A whir of noise announced the floor drop, and her stomach took the movement with its regular flip. Good thing she'd gone light on breakfast. She wanted to be lithe in her presentation so tea-and-toast would have to do. Her knees bent when the elevator halted. Its doors opened and the first floor beckoned her out. Three doors down, her new seat cover would meet its destiny.

When Myla approached the meeting room, she found Weston

standing inside. She angled the cart and waited, while Skip Sellers hastened to move a few chairs and allow her entrance into the circle's interior.

Weston moved toward her. "Good morning, Miss Templeton. So good to see you're ready for the first item on our agenda."

"Thank you, Mr. Durand. I wouldn't have missed this opportunity for anything." She pushed the cart past Skip, nodding her greeting to him. His mustache twitched in response.

Weston peeked out into the hall before coming toward the circle. "Looks like we're waiting for Mr. Pike, and then we'll get started."

Myla took her seat and opened the notebook, writing in the date and names of attending members. The handwork came like therapy, as her mental state swirled with details of fabric durability and cost analysis figures. A shadow passed over the page, and she looked up to find Weston looking down at her, amusement enhancing his facial features.

"We probably don't deserve your efficiency, Miss Templeton—but I sure appreciate it." He smiled and pulled a folded paper out of his pocket marked with hand-written entries. "My scrawled agenda suffers compared to your adeptness."

She looked up at him remembering a technical matter she'd meant to address. "Oh, Mr. Durand. I thought to ask—could someone take the meeting notes while I'm presenting? It would be impossible for me to do both."

He held out his hand, gesturing for the notebook. "What at relief. You're lending me purpose in my own meeting. I'd be glad to footnote the specifics, although you might consider putting your pitch on paper sometime in the near future."

"Please don't assign me the next thing to be flustered over, Mr. Durand. I'm treading water already this morning." Uncomfortable, she shifted in her seat.

Skip Sellers leaned forward, his fingers combing his sideburns. "You'll be flying at a higher altitude than the rest of us by virtue of what's already under that tarp. All we ask is a glimpse at what you're up to. That'll elevate the rest of us, for sure. Then maybe we can ask some intelligent questions and look half-professional."

She looked up and Weston's eyes were shining. She knew it could be attributed to his QC dynamic, as they were seated in a circle here for a reason. Skip's support demonstrated the wisdom of it, and Weston's appreciation became contagious. "Thank you, Skip. You can have the first shot at the Q & A then."

Weston slapped a hand against the notebook. "Aha, Mr. Pike is here—that makes the whole gang. Let's take our seats so we can begin this Quality Circle meeting. I trust you've all had a good month, especially with the Open House festivities." He glanced around the circle, his gaze alighting on Myla upon mention of the special event.

Skip cleared his throat. "Talk about innovative thinking. Why, making that Open House based on a Sadie Hawkins invitation made it downright memorable in my estimation."

"Well said, Mr. Sellers," Weston replied. "This goes to show us what one slight twist on something familiar can lend to the feature. If we can grasp the power of continuous improvement with such a twist here and add a tweak there, imagine what tomorrow could be like."

Rich Yost coughed into his fist. "Yeah, such as being able to breathe like a real human."

Weston sat back on his stool. "Yes, we're all anxious to get back to our paint shop brainstorming, Mr. Yost, but first Miss Templeton has been promised the lead-off position on our agenda. Without further ado, let's have Myla Templeton of Interiors make her presentation." He gestured toward the cart and opened the notebook.

Myla stood to accomplish her first task—removal of the tarp. Not intending to still have the pen in her hand, she turned to place it in her seat, only to see Weston pat his shirt pocket and come up empty. In two steps she delivered the pen to him, which he accepted with a sheepish grin. When she turned back toward the cart, Skip waited to lend her a hand. She nodded and took the front corners while he operated on the back. Together they hoisted the cover for the grand impact she'd intended. When Skip took possession of the cover, she held out her hand to showcase the two-tone seat with dual lines of contrasting stitching. For the briefest moment, she felt like a game show hostess.

"Oh, wow," Rich Yost said.

"Now that's a cut above," Ted Halyard added.

"Thank you, gentlemen. What you are looking at is an

upgraded interior option I'm calling 'Western Durango.' As you may know, Cessna incorporates leather into its cockpit schemes because the material lasts five times longer than other upholstery fabrics. My question is, why settle for durable but plain? I'd like to introduce to you the newest product from the tannery process, used in my inset panels here…and here." She pointed out the deeper hue of tobacco-brown leather that lacked the smooth surface of the leather surrounding the edges. "This is called woven leather— every bit as durable as the leather we've traditionally used, but look at the aesthetic character it adds."

Skip smoothed his mustache. "That's definitely a good-looking fabric."

Myla took a breath as she nodded in agreement. "Here, I have teamed the woven leather in what's called 'Shoemaker Tan' with a darker lot of matte finish leather we've kept stockpiled for just this purpose, an alternate model. The western nuance is picked up with the double saddle stitching using a lighter hue of bonded nylon thread, plus a premier feature that will be new for us—hand-tooled leather trim."

"Oh, my. Now, you're really talking upgrade," Ernie Pike said. "Tools and fixtures are my specialty. When anyone says 'hand-tooled' to me, I start to see dollar signs in the margin."

Myla held up a finger to arrest his objection, knowing the proof would be in the product. She stooped and removed the mock-up of the prototype she had developed. "Here's the matching throttle cover, encircled with hand-embossed crescents and cross-hatched down the leather seam. The woven leather has been repeated for the cap inset to tie the seat craft to the trim." She circled the cap with a fingertip.

"Here, Skip, you start this piece around. For something like the 140, we can also add padded leather to the edge of the instrument panel, like so." She bent to retrieve a longer strip of smooth matte leather that bore a single row of crescent embossments, all perfectly aligned. When she held it up, someone behind her began to applaud, so she turned to face him.

Weston clamped the notebook closed between his knees while he clapped one last time. "I have to say, this project has the wow factor going for it. Great job, Miss Templeton. You are gifted at what you do. Can you provide some specifics for the group on cost analysis, product availability, and so on? Inquiring minds—like Mr. Pike here—might want to know as much as possible about such nitty-gritty details."

"By all means, Mr. Durand. Industrial standards have their place, even though the final product need not be mug-shot ugly." She smiled to prove her point, fishing out her specification list from her pocket. For the next five minutes, she regaled them with durability statistics, weight projections, cost comparisons, and time estimates for completing the installation, start to finish. True to her earlier promise, she bestowed the first question to Skip Sellers.

"I guess everybody's heard we're remodeling the 195 this summer, right? Those double-sized wing flaps and the propeller spinner are still getting the bugs worked out in design mode, but we'll be in production on them before the month passes. What if we added an interior upgrade with the remodel to catch the buyer's eye? It seems only natural to add a tweak. Good golly, that woven leather is some striking stuff, if you ask me."

Weston held out his hand toward her. "That remodel will become Cessna's 195A, Miss Templeton. What if A stood for 'artful' and contained your groundbreaking concept?"

"Well, the western styling has been conceptualized as an option, not meant for full production," she replied. The copious amount of time that might consume began to swarm her analytical thinking.

Ernie Pike snapped his fingers as if to sweep in to her rescue. "What about this compromise? We use the woven leather inset panels on the 195A like we would regular matte leather, cost-for-cost a comparable trade-off as upgrades go. The labor-intensive western part—the contrast stitching and the hand-tooled stamping—can be reserved for the custom finish job called the 'Western Durango.' If buyers want the stylish add-on, they have to pay for it."

Rich Yost slapped his hands together. "For the 'Western Durango' the paint shop could add an emblem on the nosecone. You know, we can make it resemble a cattle brand to lend it that rich rancher look. How about a stamp of the letters WD with a circle around it?"

The idea exploded across the design board in Myla's mind. She held up one finger. "No, only partly around it, Rich. You know what an open circle stands for, don't you?"

Weston growled like a hungry bear as he slid off the stool. "Now we're on fire with this thing. Yes, an open circle is the letter C for Cessna. That way we get the company identified in the new logo as well. Who in this circle can draw up something like that?"

"Let me take a stab at it," Rich Yost offered. "I draw the designs for all the stencil work for the paint shop. I think I can handle this western logo."

Skip Sellers stood, the tarp folded across his arm. "I can't tell you what a hand-in-glove fit this seems like to me. You know that brag line for the 195 is 'a cabin as roomy as a car's interior.' So now we have a chance to make it look more like an upgraded stagecoach. If you ask me, the timing couldn't be better. Bravo, Miss Templeton—and thank you for all this hard work up front."

Weston tucked the notebook under his arm. "Yes, thank you Myla. Skip hit it right on the bulls-eye. Upgrades in aesthetics must accompany advancements in technology, as the client cannot always see the mechanical improvement, like Ted Halyard's sheet metal upgrade. But they can feel the comfort of butter-soft seat covers and enjoy the eye-appeal of that woven leather product. I have one last comment, one I've been saving for last."

Myla's head shot up. Dread began to pulse through her veins at the thought that anything he might say could halt the prototype right where it sat. In the seconds that elapsed, she could scarcely breathe. Skip came and stood with her, offering her the far corners of the tarp. Was it a protective covering, or a death shroud for a doomed project?

Weston began to walk around the inner loop of the circle. He rubbed his hands together and chanced a glimpse in her direction with an expression impossible to read. "I admit to being in-the-know somewhat in advance, thanks to some specifics Myla shared with me earlier. Based on those comments, I paid a visit to our marketing department and discovered that a successful rancher from Montana will be visiting Wichita at the end of this week to order his new custom airplane. What would it take for us to offer him the 'Western Durango' fresh off the conceptual design board?"

"Well, sakes alive—here it is right on a cart," Skip replied. "We can deliver this down to marketing and let their window dressers fancy it up for public display."

Ernie Pike harrumphed. "You'd need to get those durability ratings written into some type of sales pitch—or give marketing the specifics and let them write it. Whatever you do, Myla, don't leave it for them to make it up, or their pitch won't have a single fact in it."

She felt a nudge to step back into the fray. "I get your point, Ernie. They tend to be all gloss and no guts down there. I'll give them the specifics on the materials, including colors and textures, plus provide a cost breakdown for pricing the upgrade. Can I get that to you, Weston?"

He placed the notebook in her seat and extended both hands toward her, palms up as if ready to receive it at a moment's notice. "With this and any other product or idea generated in this QC setting, I am more than happy to serve as the connecting middle man. Now, about that nosecone logo, could we have that in a couple of days to become part of the ad package?"

Rich Yost stepped up to the prototype to run his hand over the woven panels. "Consider it a done deal. I'll even walk it back over to you, so we don't have to wait a day for company mail to deliver it. I've got a feeling about this—a good one."

Weston turned and extended his hand, which the painter readily accepted. "Thanks for the extra effort, Rich. Drop it off at my new lab, Room 155 downstairs in Hangar C. Something tells me you might be right about your hunch. Miss Templeton may have an unmitigated hit on her hands. Let's extend our appreciation to her before moving on with our agenda this morning." He began to applaud and was soon joined by the others.

Unprepared for their accolades, Myla hid behind the pretense of covering the prototype, while Skip stuck the extra trim pieces back in place. When her gaze connected with Weston's admiring stare, the buzz rocketed up into a full-scale tingle. She bowed ever so slightly and headed for her seat while Skip wheeled the cart through the circle's opening. She picked up the notebook and slid onto the chair where she first noticed the tremble in her legs.

Weston dragged a chair into the opening in the circle as Skip retook his seat. "It's time to move into our brainstorming session for problem-solving. I'll bring up each case presented last meeting, and we'll offer suggestions for improvements. At the end of this discussion each month, we'll add new case studies to keep our process moving forward. Hence, the continuous improvement aspect of our quality control paradigm will be allowed for—and common sense will lead to defect prevention. Up first—availability of parts on the shop floor. I believe Skip can enlighten us on this issue as a result of the eye-opening vendor visit we paid last week." He laughed and sat in the new chair, right beside Myla on the circle.

On impulse, she needed to record the topic before the resolution could be posed. When she tapped her pants pocket for the pen, she came up empty. A shoulder nudge followed as Skip began to hem and haw setting up his story. She looked over at Weston who had a silly grin on his face. That's when she found her pen, happily resting in the breast pocket of his shirt.

Seconds passed without his extracting it for her. It soon became crystal clear he wanted her to retrieve it. As she lowered two fingers into the pocket, he flexed his pectoral muscles on the sly, sending her a private signal. *What a suggestive sneak.* She printed the words "availability of parts" and tried to redirect her attention to Skip, but her technical mindset had been sloshed with an emotional overcoat too muscle-clad to ignore.

Spanned between them, the pull of attraction had nowhere to go until Weston shifted in his seat to cross an ankle over one knee. That move left his shoulder permanently pressed against hers, a solid contact of the flammable kind. His finger soon tapped the notebook.

She inhaled and forced the pen to the page, recording a shortened rendition of the manpower issue of the vendor. In two short lines, she had the account caught up. When her eyes skimmed the notes Weston had taken for her part of the agenda, she had a bit of trouble reading his handwriting. The two final words he'd underlined sure snagged her attention though. There the block-printed words *AMAZING PRESENTATION* filled the closing line in synopsis of his assessment. Surely, it must have been amazing…if only she could remember one word of it.

~

Weston studied the furrows on his lunch partner's brow and could feel the stress load across the table. The cafeteria grew noisier by the minute as more laborers broke for their daily bread.

Even the air seemed heavy. When a genius carried a burden, he paid extra attention. He slid the salt shaker over when the man fingered the slice of boiled egg garnishing his salad.

Duncan Reed looked up at him and nodded. "Thanks for the flavor additive. This meal is about as bland as they come. Lorna Rae has been spoiling me at home. I fully realize that every day at lunch." He shook a dusting of salt on the egg.

"A good job sometimes comes with other attributes that aren't as sterling." He paused and animated his point with a slight smile while checking under his bun for any trace of condiments. "I hope you don't mind my observation, but you appear a bit weighed down by some matter today. Isn't Friday supposed to present itself more carefree than that?"

Duncan ate a bite of the egg, chewing as he held up a finger to beg a moment's reprieve. He winced and picked up the pepper shaker, dousing the remainder of the egg. "My morning meeting opened up a whole new can of worms for me—all attached to the XT-37's state-of-the-art jet engines. We might as well get this on the table, as it affects both quality control and safety."

Weston paused his sandwich half-way to his mouth. He had meddled, and now he stood a chance of being mired in the muddy situation, too. He jabbed the corned beef into his mouth to block the protest his gut wanted to express.

Duncan leaned across the table to counter the surrounding noise. "Have you experienced the intake force on those Continental-Teledyne engines? The turbofan has to pull an enormous amount of air into the engine casing for the entire process to generate enough thrust. Now, imagine our hangars and the clutter we typically leave littering the shop floor. Turn on a turbofan and watch what gets sucked into the intake. The ramifications are enough to keep me awake at night, I assure you."

Weston popped a potato chip in half with his index finger. "From a safety perspective, are you worried about people in harm's way? What about permanent hearing damage? That jet engine has to be noisier than propeller chop." He took a chip fragment and ate it.

Duncan leaned back from the table and wiped across his face with a napkin. He threw the crumpled paper over the remainder of his salad and took a wandering glance around the cafeteria.

"There's a boogeyman out there that accompanies the jet engine technology. His name is FOD—which stands for foreign object damage. I don't even want to tell you how much one of those jet engines costs Cessna, because it's staggering. That intake power is an invitation to disaster, and now part of my job is to see that calamity doesn't happen."

"Not to seem naïve, but wouldn't the turbofan chop up most of what's sucked in? I'm thinking about loose pages of a schematic that's been left around on a tabletop."

Duncan shook his head. "You need to up your trouble scale. This thing doesn't suck in paper dolls, Weston. Uptake of metal objects is not outside the realm of possibility. Imagine the fan ingesting a tool left somewhere forward of the fuselage. What havoc would a metal object wreak inside the combustion chamber?" His eyebrows rose into his hairline.

The skin crept up the back of Weston's neck while his appetite sauntered out the back door. He'd touched that exquisite turbofan intake at the Open House. He now realized he'd caressed a sleeping dragon—one with a huge lung capacity to draw a breath. Logic shifted into high gear as his thoughts skittered into known solutions, though this would be an intrinsically different beast by design. "Well, the first thing that comes to mind is that prevention will be paramount."

"Welcome to my world. Evidently, the jet engine arrived with a caution section in the operator's manual so extensive that it would choke Churchill's bulldog. I have to retrain employees not to be lax in their tool placement, a task that ranks high on my to-do list. Hangar A becomes a whole different ballgame, the stakes are higher, and therefore the enforcement must be more stringent." He made a growling sound as his gaze shifted to the rear windows.

A test flight landed off the end of the runway. Weston observed as the flex struts worked according to specification, a thing of beauty. The more technical the advancements in aviation became, the more stringent the manufacturing process would need to become. They were battling against the chronic potential for human error, a fact that made him uncomfortable. How this affected him still sat in a distant haze. "Duncan, you mentioned that somehow I would get sucked into this vortex of FOD concern. I always thought prevention fell under your jurisdiction—not that I wouldn't do anything in my power to support your work."

The safety manager placed a hand around his chin and seemed to be trying to force his midday stubble back into his pores. He closed his eyes and when he opened them, the man's eyelids seemed to be made of lead. "I will assume sole responsibility for the education of the work force. I remember from our previous conversation with regard to mistake-proofing, that sometimes a guard on a saw is the apt prevention for making too deep a cut. Likewise, we'll keep the engine intake covered at all times except while the aircraft's in use."

"Glad to have been a service to you on that. I've found that logic always defeats happenstance, though it takes the collective sway of mindset for all involved." He relaxed a little and took another bite out of the corned beef sandwich. The sauerkraut soon sullied his taste buds.

Duncan wove his fingers together and rested his hands on the table. "I'm not quite done with Quality Control ramifications yet. There are other matters of incidental intakes while flying, such as bird strikes and other ancillary ingestions that may have a lasting effect on the engine's performance. The problem lies in knowing whether the object has compromised the mechanism—or not."

The inference poured cold water into his veins. "You cannot really expect me to be able to inspect that jet engine, can you? Why, I'd practically have to tear it apart. That's totally unlike my airframe inspections."

"Tear it apart? Not quite. Continental-Teledyne suggests a thing called nondestructive evaluation. It's a hot research and development topic, evidently. Researchers are looking for ways to peer inside without compromising the engine and without tearing down the base components. You know, I can't help but compare it to the doctor at Lorna Rae's eighth-month check-up. Even from the outside, he could palpitate, weigh, and measure to make sure our infant is coming along at a normal development rate. Perhaps the fan blades would be much the same. I don't know, this is way out of my expertise, sort of like becoming a father." He sighed and leaned back in his chair, glancing at the far window again.

The test plane came in for another landing. This one seemed even more controlled as the landing gear barely flexed at all. Weston took a bite from the edge of the sandwich, an attempt to avoid the kraut-tainted middle. Unfortunately, the inspection challenge that had been thrown onto the table had stolen all the saliva from his mouth. The corned beef became his lunchtime FOD. He forced a sip of water down past the lump and worked harder to clear it. As he swallowed, it occurred to him that FOD danger wasn't a baby at all. It was a bomb—and should be handled as such. They really had their work cut out for them. "Duncan, count me in. Can we tour Hangar A together? In this case, two heads are definitely better than one."

"Let's go, I'm available right now," he replied, his relief evident.

From the cafeteria, they walked out onto the tarmac toward Hangar A. Weston eyed the XT-37 as it sat half out of its nest like a precocious chick impatient to fledge. "What happened with your follow-up on the brake problem on the prototype 308? Was it a faulty mechanism?"

"Not hardly," Duncan replied. He shoved his sunglasses over the bridge of his nose as his facial features pulled gaunt. "And don't forget the happenstance of a stuck throttle. Since that represents a highly questionable simultaneous occurrence, I suspect premeditated tampering. Mum's the word as I investigate who may have had access to the hangar."

Weston gestured ahead at the swarm of workforce seething in and out of the facility. "Who doesn't have access? You have your work cut out for you."

"Which is why I need an understudy." The seasoned safety manager crooked an arm around his shoulders to bring his shared responsibility point home.

Weston bristled as a chill shot down his spine. He'd much rather prevent FOD and guard against the rock-paper-tools threat of ingestion damage. At least it wasn't premeditated.

~

Myla tucked her hair behind her ear while she flattened the seat cover across her lap. One of the seamstresses had a lax moment and forgot to cut her thread tails off, so she sat on top of the gantry steps to do it for her. A hot day, she shoved the headphones off and endured the tat-a-tat of the rivet installation nearby. If only the Kansas wind would blow, she could get some alleviation from this stagnant heat.

A figure moved down below and headed for the gantry. Instead of walking by, the man stopped and looked up. It was Weston Durand. "Hey, can I steal you away from your task?"

She bit off the last thread tail and cleared it from her lips. Struck by a coy impulse, maybe she should deny his request. She climbed down a couple of steps to test him. "I suppose this is important, right? After all, these seat covers don't attach themselves."

Weston shuffled his feet and appeared guilt-ridden for the intrusion. "Well, important in the long run. I'll keep it brief, I promise."

"On second thought, I should be grateful for a break. This work has its constraints, and all of them aren't time related. Is there something I can help you with? You seem a bit at odds."

"Yes, at odds with a turbojet engine, a technological prima donna. I need your advice on a cover for the intake fans. Duncan Reed and I are working to safeguard the engine from harm."

She took a seat on a step about eye-level with the quality manager. "What is he trying to achieve by covering it? That purpose might make a difference in the fabric we choose."

"He mentioned the prospect of a bird building a nest inside. It is spring, after all. I could tell you some of the more horrid potentials for harm, but one of us should get some rest this weekend." Weston pressed his brow into a sharp divot to accentuate his meaning.

She laughed and evened up the toes of her shoes with the edge of the step. "I'll suggest some cotton fabric we use between the leather and the padding. It has a fairly open weave so it won't cause moisture build-up inside the engine, but it will keep the birds out, as well as other accidental inclusions like gum wads, candy wrappers, and diabolical soda bottle caps."

"Now you're onto the dreaded human error aspect of our dilemma. That's most insightful of you. Well then, I need two of those cotton covers for the XT-37 prototype, the sooner the better. How might I go about ordering those? I have the dimensions of the intake right here." He pulled a scrap of paper from his pocket to verify his claim.

She propped her chin in her palm. From this vantage point, they were eye-to-eye. She relished the level perspective. "I guess that depends on when you want your covers. If you're aiming for next week, then you process the request through Alice Granger."

He grabbed the hand rail and moved the gantry ever so closer to where he stood. "And what if I wanted to expedite that request? Would there be a means, besides saying pretty please?" His head tilted as if to better scrutinize her.

Myla's heart began to pound as his word choice hit home. The *pretty* had been meant for her and she knew it. Somehow, her stiff-arm defense mechanism hadn't popped into service like it normally did. Maybe that was because a twenty-three-year-old woman needed to pay attention when the smartest man at the plant sprinkled a tiny bit of attention in her direction. Plus, it was springtime. "Then you need to keep talking to me, Mr. Durand. I may somehow find the time for such an endeavor before I leave today."

A bean-pole of a youth came up behind Weston. "Are you Mr. Durand, by any chance? I have a note here from Marketing."

He turned to face the messenger. "Yes, I am Weston Durand." He flashed the ID card clipped to his shirt pocket to confirm the claim.

The young man handed over the communication, gave her a nod, and disappeared around the nosecone.

"Oh, I had better read this aloud then." He glanced up at her, his tone much lighter. "'I clinched the deal for the new 140 over lunch. The Montana rancher ordered your Western Durango upgrade. Yahoo! It looks like we're in the cowboy business. Nice work. Al Parsons.'"

She pressed her hands over her mouth to hold in some of the celebration which restrained everything but the tears. Maybe she'd let a few of those take wing, as they came from sheer joy. She blinked and set them free without shame.

He reached through the gantry rail for her, his smile a mile wide. "We have to celebrate. I mean it. Let me take you out to dinner."

She grasped his hand and took the squeeze, more like holding hands than shaking them. "I...I don't know. There's so much to do in setting up production, which means working late today. Plus, I have to fit in these jet engine covers."

"That part is my fault—but I'm in no mood to accept a decline of my offer. How about next Friday? The dust should settle by then. Is it a date?"

She tried to pull her hand away, but he'd have none of it, so she sat there locked in circumstance, a delicious predicament. Happiness fluttered in her chest. She swiped a tear from her cheek with the back of her free hand and capitulated. "Okay, next Friday it's a date."

He held up one finger as if ticking off a list. "Dinner comes first, to toast the new interior line. Entertainment might be next, perhaps a movie."

"Well, I have wanted to see Burt Lancaster's new movie 'From Here to Eternity' soon."

He gave her hand another squeeze and released it, only to point a finger in her face. "Our plans, Myla. I'll look at the cinema listings to see where it's playing. Now, about those covers." He motioned in a circle, expanding the distance between his hands to adjust the estimation.

"Oh bother. Let me have those written dimensions. I never work off estimates. It's such a huge waste of time." When his eyes widened, she sugar-coated the terse comment with a nice smile. She wiggled her fingers at him and soon got what she wanted. Hand gestures painted the vagaries of a temporary mirage. She could count on paper.

Chapter 6

Myla looked over the top step of the gantry and spotted the handle of a leather punch she'd left in the cockpit. The whirlwind week had left her only half a brain, and she somehow couldn't settle into her routine this morning. After all, Friday marked her freedom from work, which today came capped with a date. She shimmied back up the steps and made a boarding house reach to retrieve the forgotten tool.

Extra time reading her Bible had not yielded the peace she needed to cover the bold step of actually going out on a date. Yet, when she thought of Weston Durand, it seemed the most natural thing to want to spend time together. A reward in a sense, hadn't he been the epitome of encouragement for her brainstorming project? She dropped the tool into her kit and started down the gantry. Wet palms caused her to lose her grip, and she took the last three steps with unintended haste.

A woman made a throaty noise beside the portable stairway. "Glad to see someone's got some sprite in their step this morning."

"Hey, Susie." Myla gave the young laborer a shallow smile before assessing the cart she'd escorted to the shop floor. "Thanks for bringing these covers down from the sewing room. You've saved me some time, which I sorely need today. By the way, that wasn't being spritely. It would be more accurate to say clumsy."

"You're fit as a fiddle, ma'am. Now, Miss Granger is another matter. I don't know how she keeps up her pace, quite honestly."

She leaned closer to share a wisp of collusion with the seamstress. "I think her bones are made of iron. She's a tough one, Grade A tough."

"Oh yeah, your shipment of woven leather came in. I had to open the packaging to inspect it. My word, Miss Templeton, that leather is gorgeous. I can hardly wait to get my hands on it in the sewing room." She rubbed her fingertips together as though warming up for the tactile treat.

"That makes you and me both, Susie, but that will be next week's thrill. I'd better get moving on down the line, or Miss Grade A will call me out, I'm afraid." Myla dried her palms on her coveralls and reached for the seat covers.

The young woman shifted between her and the cart. Her eyes darted down the shop floor and then back to her. "Someone came looking for you up in the office, Miss Templeton. Said he's with Snap Right Tools and has something for you. I told him you were working down here this morning. I hope that was the right thing to do."

"That's Snap-lite Tools, Susie. Yes, he owes me a bonus punch for a set I bought two weeks ago. I wish to high heaven he'd just given you the thing and been done with it. Don't worry about it. I'll keep a watch out for him."

"Better you than me," the girl mumbled. She grabbed the cart handle.

"Thanks for helping me get my guard up in advance. Now, let me have these top sets and take the rest down to Miss Granger, would you?" Myla ran her hands under half the pile and flung them over the gantry steps. "Eureka—a cart and a ladder all in one. Thank the Good Lord for tools on wheels."

"You're a hoot, Miss Templeton. Enjoy your work." Susie circled the cart around and rolled it past the next fuselage.

Myla stooped to release the wheel locks and surveyed her clearance past the tail section. "How can work be enjoyable when I've got two men on my mind?" Her palms began to sweat again as she guided the stairwell to its next destination.

~

Weston looked up as the lab door opened to find Skip Sellers coming in for a visit. He put down his test panel and met the man half way. They shook hands, and he motioned to a makeshift desk he'd arranged along the far wall. "What brings you down my way this morning, Mr. Sellers? Don't tell me another problem has developed in production and assembly."

The man groaned in response and wiped a hand across his chin. "We sure have our flair-ups, Mr. Durand. Yes sir-rie, Bob. We do that."

"Look, the lab door is closed. Call me Weston, will you? I

think we've been on enough capers together to go by first names."

He straightened in his seat. "I appreciate that, Weston. No, today it's not my problem I've come in about. Duncan Reed met with me about improvements to the orderliness of the shop floor, so I came to follow up with you at his request. I'm guessing this is more about safety than quality control. Am I right?"

"Let's say it's more about prevention than reparation. The neaten-up effort is Priority One in Hangar A, but it stands to reason the rest of the facility should follow suit. Of course, the jet engines of the XT-37 lead the way for such change, but there will be other models in the future requiring the same standard of protocol on the assembly floor."

"Guess we've been slobs long enough. Not that I treasure the aspect of playing housemother to my crew at the end of the workday."

Weston propped his elbows on the desk and leaned forward. "Every laborer must be responsible for his own equipment. That's mistake-proofing at its best."

"I wrote that at the top of my list after our last QC meeting. That monthly gathering is helping me more than you'll ever know." The comment accompanied a sparkle in his eyes.

"Glad to hear that. What else do you have on your list?"

"No faulty product left in the workshop is next. It's staggering what we leave laying around underfoot. To take the surplus items off the floor, I've put an order in for new shelving along the hangar's back wall."

"Strange, isn't it? One day you look up and see that the way you've been operating will no longer suffice. It's like ushering in a new era. Quality control forces you to move forward by its competitive design. That's what I find so stimulating."

"Well, thanks for getting more of us on board with you, Weston. It's been a breath of fresh air for me. I can tell you, work isn't the only place I'm ushering in a new era."

Weston straightened up and angled his head like a sleuth. "Would there be another horizon under improvement, Skip? You do seem to have a bit of pep in your step lately."

The man's straight-cut mustache took a dip to one side. "I'm taking Alice Granger out to my uncle's farm in Goddard to shoot skeet on Saturday. The loser has to cook dinner afterward, and it won't be me."

"Okay. You blindsided me with that one, I confess." He laughed and Skip joined him. The camaraderie of the moment led him to his own revelation. "I have a celebratory date myself tonight, testing much the same waters, I suppose. Miss Templeton has agreed to let the likes of me escort her to dinner in commemoration of her success with the new Interiors line."

"Myla sure is something else. One second she seems like a petite cowering cat, but then you go empowering her through the WC group and look what she comes up with. I think that goes to show you that we underestimate folks as a rule. What a change to lend them wings, so they can soar, now and again."

"I'll match you one set of wings and up the ante by throwing in a temperamental jet engine." Weston followed his challenge with a curt laugh.

"To date Alice Granger, I'm already linked up with a temperamental turbo-prop, Weston. Believe me, I've cleared my personal shop floor and tried to get myself back in line for that. Seven years as a widower has left considerable room for refurbishment."

"Looks like both of our prototype relationships are set for take-off at the same time. I've called in to the control tower on mine. How about you?" Weston pressed his hands together in prayer mode.

Skip stood and shoved his hands in his pockets. For a second he looked like an impish teenager. "Been on my knees a good deal about dating again, and it seems the right thing to do."

"Good for you. That's clearance to take off, if I've ever heard it. For your benefit, let's hope Miss Granger is of the same persuasion." Weston stood with his guest and motioned to the door. Both of them had more productive things to accomplish before the day grew too old.

"Oh, I meant to tell you. The Hutchinson plant is having a big furniture clearance sale Saturday a week from tomorrow. They're refitted for hydraulic components now, and that surplus Army furniture is nothing but in the way. Maybe your Interiors friend would be interested."

"That might give me something to aim for down the road. I'll certainly ask her. As for aim, I hope yours is solid tomorrow for the trap shoot. Keep Alice entertained, will you?"

The man chuckled and grabbed the doorknob. "And you be sure to convert your quality control into gentlemanly charm tonight, Weston. Enjoy the celebration." With that, he ducked out of the lab door to a clattering of background noise.

Weston crossed the lab floor to resume the test work on the panel. He picked up a pencil and studied his last marks. The phrase *gentlemanly charm* resurfaced to interfere with the mathematical formula he needed to recall. Couldn't it suffice to simply be himself? Myla had seen his character at work. He was a numbers man, a crack and defect guy. From out of nowhere, the realization struck him that such astute inspection might not suffice at a personal level. He cringed, at a loss as to what to do about it. Before he knew it, the pencil snapped in half.

~

Myla fingered the piping into place along the arched seam of the seat back. The surplus leather trim gathered on her knee as she brought the last step to its finale. Her stomach growled, so she didn't have to look at her watch to know lunchtime had arrived. She'd finish this task and take a break.

A figure darkened the cockpit door. "So this is what you do. You're like a darling little pixie up here." The tool seller leaned in, insistent on gaining her attention.

Myla cut the tail to length and pulled the trim end beneath the seat. Secured by her thumb, she grabbed the stapler and made the placement permanent. "Hello, Mr. Amherst. I hear you've got my bonus punch for me today. Please feel free to leave it right there on the top step if you want. I'm kind of busy here."

"I'm ashamed to say I don't have it with me. Guess my hands were too full of those filtration masks for the paint department."

She ran the corner of a rag over a line of glue that had oozed out from under the piping. "So will it be another two weeks before I get it? We're going into production on a new prototype. I'm going to need it before then." She stopped packing up long enough to shoot him a none-too-encouraging look, her best attempt to keep it all business.

He flinched. "No, not at all. I have your punch. It's still out in my car. I'm super pressed for time, though. Any chance you could walk out with me to get it? I'm due at the Hutch plant by one-thirty. That's a Friday for you." He grimaced and appeared a touch vulnerable.

Myla weighed her options. She had her lunch break ahead, which lent her the time off the shop floor. Maybe the best thing to do would be the simple thing—follow him out to the parking lot and be done with it. She could tell Miss Granger what she planned to do, in case anyone saw her leaving.

"Hey, I really gotta head out. Will that work for you? I'm not scheduled back through here until mid-June as my boss put Hesston on my route now." He started back down the gantry with one eyebrow hooked up for her answer.

She wiped the glue from her fingers before picking up her tool kit. "All right. Let's go. Since when did a bonus get to be a burden?" She turned back to him and climbed down.

"Oh, it's never a burden when I get to walk with a pretty gal," he replied.

Myla put the tool kit on the bottom step where she would retrieve it after lunch. When she stood, a vein pulsed in her temple. This tool guy was a headache in the making. She couldn't get to the parking lot fast enough. Headed for the hangar door, she locked her stiff-arm fortitude in place with a deep breath as he caught up beside her.

"So tell me about this new production line you mentioned." He gave her an alluring look to coax her response.

Myla looked across the tarmac and saw a ground crew bringing out the XT-37 aircraft, her covers in place across the two jet engines. The sight lent her a touch of satisfaction and put her in a better mood. She shaded her eyes with one hand and turned to the tool salesman. "The prototype is for the 195A. We plan to upgrade the upholstery to complement the elegant instrument panel for the model. The bonus punch is for the woven leather we'll add to the seat panels, a gorgeous look for the upholstery, but thicker to handle for installation."

"Well, it takes gorgeous to know gorgeous, that's for sure." He winked before sliding his sunglasses into place.

So the wolf had returned. She'd have to thwart that familiar bent for the remainder of the walk. "Let me take you through some of the specs." Her QC speech came to mind and she launched into it without a pause. Before she knew it, they had arrived at the controlled access. She went through first and then hesitated, not knowing where to go.

He touched her elbow with a warm hand. "To the left here. I have to park in visitors parking, which can be a pain on busy days. Fortunately, I found a spot today. Right there, the blue Ford." He led her toward the back door.

Myla tried not to judge the man based on his vehicle, but it had traveled a few thousand miles past its peak. A copious layer of dust dulled the paint job. Distracted, she hadn't noticed he had opened the door.

After he removed his sunglasses, he buried half his frame into the car to search for the bonus tool in a messy floorboard. "I know it's in here somewhere."

Myla shielded her eyes to make out more details. "Try to remember where you put it. That always helps me." Her suggestion had no more left her lips when a huge tool box careened off the back seat and dumped its contents on top of the salesman.

"Whoa. Can you lend me a hand?" He dropped to his knees to deal with the avalanche.

"Oh, sure. Let me get this wrench set first." She stepped closer and soon had two fists full of brand spanking new silver tools. Once she'd put them back in the tool box and scooted it further back, she leaned in further to retrieve another load.

He turned his shoulders toward her, a huge smile on his face. "At least I found the bonus punch." He pushed up on one arm, and tools clanked all around him.

Myla exhaled through a wayward wisp of hair. Not a breath of air moved through the sedan as May grew momentarily unbearable. She dipped back into the floorboard to clear away one last load.

The tool rep pushed out of the carnage and in one sleek move had her back pinned against the tool box. "Hope you like the punch," he said in a husky voice. His lips clamped across hers in a surprise personal attack.

It took only a split second for shock to ramp up to rage. Myla let it cut loose. She elbowed him away and laid a slap on his cheek that landed with a loud whack. With her other hand, she clawed the bonus punch out of his grasp, more than ever determined to have it. To escape, she kneed the seat and the tool box dumped its contents into the floorboard again. Relieved for the diversion, she stood up on quaking legs and pulled her hair back behind her ears. Unable to hold back, she set her ire free. "Don't ever touch me again—or you'll be sorry."

Headed back through the controlled access, Myla pocketed the punch and fumed. She pushed through the turnstile as the memory of the slippery lip assault replayed in her mind. Instead of the fond first embrace she'd always imagined, it struck her as a wretched breach of personal space. *Dear Lord, please cleanse me of all iniquity.* The urge to gargle hit her in a wave of nausea. She pressed an arm against her stomach and headed for the restroom. The whole thing had been a set-up, planned and masterminded by a sleazy tool rep. *What is this world coming to?*

~

Weston sat across the table from Myla, a vision of elegance with her hair swept up by decorative combs that matched her silky peach dress. He'd pinched himself twice already as it all seemed like a dream. Tonight for some reason, she'd been almost reticent to engage in polite conversation with him, but he'd managed to warm her up by sharing some of Mr. Godfrey's early aviation stories with her. Not that he wanted to talk about aircraft all night.

She wiped her lips with the linen napkin and caught him staring at her under the chandelier's prismatic lighting. "What? Do I have something on my face?"

Shame bubbled up inside his buttoned collar. He fumbled for a response. "No. It's the lighting." He'd been assessing her beauty for an obvious duration. Somehow, Skip's guidance came back to him to nudge him out of quality control mode. "Please excuse the gentleman hiding inside me. He doesn't get out nearly enough."

She gave a soft laugh and placed her napkin on the table. In seconds, the waiter came and took her plate. "Please let your gentleman know that he's deserving of a night out now and then." Her fingers played with the stem of her water glass.

The celebratory aspect of their evening popped into mind. "We should toast your success with the new Interiors line—a true stroke of creative genius." He raised his glass and gave her an engaging look.

"This once I'll let you, since I know benchmarking is important to you." She raised her glass and looked at him through her lashes.

"Here's to the success of Western Durango, the brainchild of a talented woman who accomplishes our paradigm of continuous improvement every day by merely showing up for work. To you, Myla. Cheers." He clicked his glass with hers, unable to look away.

Her gaze softened. The waiter came and went again. She pressed her lips together, a glimmer of soft lavender. When she blinked, her lips relaxed into a smile. "I wonder what your inner gentleman might like to add."

"You look resplendent tonight, Myla," he replied without hesitation. "A beauty amid the plain. I'm out of my league here, in every sense."

She brushed at the tablecloth and then lifted her gaze to meet his. "Not at all. I admire your ingenuity. How attractive to inspire your fellow man for the better. Part visionary and part implementer, what's not to esteem?"

He could scarcely find a proper response as her question hung in the air just beneath the chandelier. No one had ever used *attractive* in a compliment to him before. It had a rich feel to it, like velvet. "I never thought aptitude would be considered meritorious."

"Yes. It is."

Though her tone and head nod were plenty persuasive, when her shoe jostled against his in intentional caress under the table, he started to become a believer. He folded his left arm in front of him and caught a glimpse of his watch. "Oh, my stars. Look at the time. We'll have to get the Catalina wings to make the movie in time. Waiter, check please."

"I'll get him to come," Myla replied. She stood and brushed a hand over the peach silkiness of her dress as though she had spilled. True to form, the attendant rushed to her side.

The trip over to the movie locale sequenced through a spattering of small talk. Weston tried to hide their destination for as long as he could, but when he turned onto the lane beside a mammoth outdoor screen, the big secret tumbled into sight.

"The drive-in theater?" Myla turned to him as she crossed her arms over the bare skin revealed by her dipping neckline. A look akin to fear filled her eyes.

"It was the only place running 'From Here to Eternity' this

weekend. Scouts honor. It's plenty warm this evening, don't worry. If you take a chill, I promise to run the heater." He rolled down the window to pay at the entrance booth. In minutes they sat front-and-center on the big screen, a metal speaker clamped to his window for sound. He weighed his options and chose silence, not used to the uneven ground of assessing a woman's mood.

Soon, a familiar stooge-faced trio appeared on the screen in a tumble of vaudeville antics. Once she giggled, he took a deep breath and settled in for the duration. At the end of the skit he copied the lead man's two-fingered eye-poke and she played along, getting the preventative guard up against the bridge of her nose just in time. They both laughed as the feature film filled the screen.

He glanced sideways at her. "Let me know if you want something." He picked at a speck on the windshield and it was stuck on the outside, of all the luck.

"I'm fine, really…and quite happy."

The movie unfolded its plot in beautiful Technicolor. Toward the end, he heard a sob or two but he allowed her the decency of a private reaction to the melodrama. He had not been unmoved himself, and when the hero had the heroine pinned in the surging surf, romance seemed to splash the Pontiac's windshield. He reached over and took her hand in his.

With her eyes rimmed with the next set of tears, she gave him a quick smile.

Soon the final credits rolled. He hesitated to move and break the spell.

Myla released his hand. "Weston, get the speaker out, so you can roll up the window."

"Oh, right. Goodness, when did the rain start?" He fumbled with the metal contraption, until he had worked the clip free and hung it up on the stand off his right front fender. He sat back and gave a good-natured laugh about being so unaware.

"Here, let me dry off your arm." She unfolded a napkin and dabbed at his forearm.

A natural lead-in, he leaned past her and planted his palm on the passenger door. Now, he had a close-up view of those gorgeous blue eyes. Even in the dim light, they held a bit of heaven.

She finished the dry-off and crumpled the napkin. "There, you're not too wet, after all." She locked gazes with him, and all the giddiness seemed to drain from her face in an instant. She shrank back on the seat.

"Thank you for agreeing to come tonight. I've had the most wonderful time and hope you have, also." He paused, mesmerized by her eyes.

Her chest rose and fell. "Yes, it's been extraordinary. I can't say when I've enjoyed myself so much."

He touched a tendril of her hair that had escaped the fancy comb. It felt like silk, a tensile fiber that drew him ever closer.

Her eyes misted and her breath became shallow.

To taste that lavender tint on her lips became his sole thought as he searched her face for any sign of resistance. With none obvious, he leaned in to plant a kiss.

Two flattened palms struck his chest. At the same moment, a set of tears rolled down her cheeks. "I can't," she whispered. "I truly wish I could, but I can't."

He pulled back, but kept his arm across her seat. "Maybe the gentleman inside me would like to know why, since you wish you could. Nothing's stopping you."

She closed her eyes, but it didn't stop the tears. "Nothing—but my own honor."

Such a beautiful sight despite the meltdown, he chanced to stroke her cheek with his thumb. She turned into the caress and laid her cheek on his palm, a delicate surrender that stole his next breath. He had to get at the root of this matter, or else carry the guilt. "What then?"

Her eyes opened, and she straightened in the seat. "A man kissed me earlier today…an unwanted trespass." She sobbed, but worked to control it. "I'm very strict with myself, to honor my body as a temple of the Lord, like it says in the Scriptures." Her eyes welled up with tears as strength played out against tenderness.

Anger rose up inside his chest, a white-hot anger like he'd never experienced. Whoever the bloke was, he'd like to hold him down for an old-fashioned thrashing. His arms soon shook from the unbridled reaction.

"So, if I kiss two different men in the same day, what does that make me?" She looked up at him, her honor damaged—but its keeper resolute.

The lavender well out of reach, he blurted out a response

before filtering it. "Once kissed…and once missed." He retracted back to his side of the car, wrecked of any further romantic notions. The screen up ahead went dark, and the parking lot lights flickered a warning. He keyed the Pontiac and threw it into drive, though the last thing in the world he wanted to do was to take her home in tears from their celebratory evening. Shrapnel of a different sort flew through the night's air. He didn't have one iota of an idea how to have prevented it, much less how to repair it from here. Such lack of chivalry was hardly to be admired. When Myla gave a soft sob, the hurt sank deeper.

Chapter 7

Myla retreated to the employee snack room and shoved the door closed with her foot to hold back the infernal riveting noise. What a headache she carried along today—the ruination of a great spring day—though Tuesdays never gave her much to appreciate. She took the chair furthest away from the hectic shop floor, crossed her arms on the table and sank her forehead onto them. How long the bang-bang world of aviation lasted without her, she couldn't say, but a clatter from the food shelves nearby soon brought her back into the work day.

A heavy-set young woman adjusted the placement of her merchandise trays. "Say, sorry about that. I didn't mean to startle you. Good nap you had going there."

She smiled and smoothed her hair back into place. "Repair work from this weekend, I suppose."

"A rough one, huh?" She brought the top tray full of square crackers up to the display and began to restock the supply.

"Caught in the middle of something, that's all. It puts me in a fragile mood, one not well served by the constant noise on the shop floor today."

"Sounds like man trouble." She winked as she straightened up the packages.

"Double man trouble. You'd think a twenty-three year old professional woman would have this department figured out. Then, it all comes cascading down on you in a day."

"And wop-bam-boom, you have a killer headache. I feel for you, I do." Her smile revealed a set of misaligned front teeth.

"Don't remind me."

"Uh-oh. Damaged merchandise. Here, try these—on the house."

A package of slightly crushed graham crackers slid across the tabletop. She put her hand out in time to keep them off the floor. "Hey thanks. Misery loves company. I'm Myla, by the way." She peeled back the plastic wrap and attempted to nibble her problem away.

The woman slung the next tray up on the counter. "Bette here. I'm always here—it's on my route. One of my better stops, though. The change never comes out short, and the folks are nice to me. You could say, I'm window-shopping a couple of the guys out on the floor, too."

Her mouth too full of goodness, Myla could only moan in response.

"Naw, really. I slip certain ones an extra pack of crackers now and again, just to keep 'em interested. That way when they see Big Bette coming, there're plenty glad about it."

Myla cleared her mouth, but the cracker only seemed to travel half-way down. "You're too nice," she managed.

"Thanks, Myla, but nothing comes for free." Bette gave an exaggerated wink and stuffed a handful of moon pies into a canister.

"Now you tell me. I'm sitting here nursing this headache all because of a little bonus." She stood and pocketed the remainder of the snack. Break time had come to an end.

Bette tried to straighten her trays to allow clearance for the door to open. "You know what they say, better late than never."

"Right, now I'm seasoned and forewarned. I do appreciate the snack. It helped like you said. Hope you have a good rest of the day." She pulled the door open and winced at the volume of shop noise.

"Hey, you too, Myla. Remember, don't go 'round hungry."

Myla gave her a chuckle for working in the product's tagline. She patted her pocket where the crackers rode to indicate she sure wouldn't. With her headache diminished, she thought to go check the office mail before she took on another installation. The dim light of the hangar suited her more than the sunlight, so she took the interior route and soon arrived upstairs at the cutting room door. She spotted the Western Durango line in process. "Hey, Susie. How are you getting along with the woven leather?"

She looked up from the cutting table, her typically plain face animated in the task. "Like a dream, ma'am. Like a pure dream." She stroked a palm across it like petting a Siamese cat.

"You wouldn't be interested in learning how to install, would you? There's been some talk of us taking on a summer intern, but we could pull you out of seamstress duty and put the new gal in the sewing room—if you're interested, that is."

"Yes ma'am, Miss Templeton. I'd sure appreciate trying something new. It can get monotonous around here."

"Okay then, I'll put in a good word for you with Miss Granger and see if we sink or swim. I'd guess that it might happen around the first of June. Personnel Department is working on the request, but I think our QC group lent some unsolicited support to make sure it gets approved."

"Oh, that reminds me. Your QC notebook came back in the mail today. You might want to check inside." She gave a tiny smile and leaned back over the table to resume her precision cutting task.

Myla's stomach tightened at the mere thought that something might be tucked inside. More than anything, she needed to avoid Weston Durand at work, until she could come to some sort of peace as to how she felt about him. She walked into the department office and saw the notebook in her in-basket. After a deep exhale, she retrieved it and sat at her work station.

With no time to spare, she opened the cover and there taped to the inside rode an envelope. Dread with a sliver of curiosity ramped up her pulse rate. She tore the flap open and read the message printed inside.

"Dear Miss Templeton,

Please tell me you won't leave me foundering in my furniture selection at the Hutchinson plant sales event on Saturday coming. Be assured, I would enjoy both your opinion and your company for the day, as I'll need the furnishings when I move into my new house.

The gentleman in me also wants to promise you lunch. I believe a place in the old-fashioned community of Yoder serves a home-cooked meal family style and has pies galore. Let's get an early start. Plan on a nine o'clock pick-up.

Thank you for keeping your word that you'd accompany me, even though my late trespass came ill-timed. Will be on my best behavior with God ever watching us.

Your true admirer, Weston Durand

Myla closed the card. Was there any wiggle room to get out of this commitment? She'd promised him over dinner she would go. The outing still held some intrigue, if only she could relax and enjoy being in the company of such a nice man. A nice, handsome man. A nice, handsome man who mentioned that he enjoyed her company. She stood up with extra force as though she fought some invisible tether. A mental alarm sounded. She needed to get back on the shop floor, or Miss Granger would have her head. Should that headache return, she just might let the boss put her out of her misery.

~

Weston pulled up to the curb with a glimpse in the rearview mirror to check on the trailer. Before he could even turn off the ignition, Myla appeared down the front walkway. She wore a blouse that resembled her curtains, a whirl of color that offset her dark hair. Mrs. Templeton appeared on the front porch with a wave. He jumped out of the car to return the gesture and guided Myla off the curb to the passenger side.

"Goodness, a trailer comes attached to the day. You are serious about needing furniture."

He opened the door with a smile. "How a man can go from nothing to everything in a day beats me, but I hope we're about to pull it off." He gave her room to maneuver and shut the door behind her. With a feigned interest in the chrome grill, he passed back over to the driver's side and got in. Patti Page sang out the popular question, "How Much is the Doggie in the Window?" Right now, based on how he felt, his answer would be several hundred bucks.

"Are you a dog man, Weston—or a cat fancier?" She looked at him as though the answer mattered.

He shifted the car into gear, gave a look in his side view mirror, and eased away from the curb. "Guess you might say that I'm a neatness-and-order fancier, so I don't lean toward either type of pet. That's boring old me." He gave a disconcerting laugh at the realization he'd just put himself down all the while intending to gain her favor. He'd have to do better.

"Hmm. Looks like I'll have to work on you then. I like cats because they are prone to snuggle and show affection." She tucked her purse onto the seat beside her and settled in for the hour's ride to Hutchinson.

He eased up to the stop light at the access to her neighborhood. He'd need to change the subject before they came home with two rooms of furnishings and a feline. "Tell me, what do you think about the College Hill area?"

"Some houses possess a quaint charm in that neighborhood, especially along the river's edge near Sims Park. When the architecture of the home manages to play with the eye and hide its interior function, that's when you have a winner, Weston."

"How do you know so much about design? Have you studied?" The light turned green and he headed north.

"Only informally. With one parent, there were insufficient funds for college. But, I've picked up numerous books from the public library downtown to study fundamentals of interior design, employment of offsetting colors, and the like. I also try to keep up with the latest trends shown in magazines."

"Aha. Now we have parallel interests, as I try to stay abreast of the latest in quality control by reading my trade periodicals. Not too many swags of color in them, mind you, but they keep me ever interested in the subject."

"I'm guessing that yours have more math." She glanced over at him and laughed.

"Miss Templeton, I assure you. Numbers can be your friend." He scowled at her in jest and drifted into the turn lane for the highway west to Hutchinson.

"I admire numbers when they add up. One plus one equals two. That kind of thing." She smoothed one hand up and down her thigh, skimming her baby blue clam diggers. Her sleeves fluttered in the wind and gave her the appearance of an angel.

He pointed one finger at her across the seat and then jutted a thumb into his ribs. "One…plus one… does in fact equal two. Today's equation favors our outing, doesn't it?"

"Yes, at the outset anyway. I'll let you know how I feel, once I see my sales total on the furniture I select." She patted her purse to connect it to the math.

"Everything can be negotiated, Myla. Let me handle your dickering, if you don't have the stomach for it." He raised one brow as though launching a challenge.

"Not everything, Weston. Take things like cats and other terms of affection. One cannot barter one's way into those purchases-of-the-heart." She turned half toward him and propped her loafer on the center hump of the floorboard that housed the drive train.

Something about how the conversation had shifted toward the sentimental made him think things between them had advanced beyond the need to mend. God and time had somehow taken care of that difficult aspect. He brought the Catalina up to highway speed as the city limits gave way to boundless wheat fields, green with the promise of high yield. "Our Father, who art in heaven, we ask you to give us this day our daily bread. We wouldn't want a day to go by without your provision."

"Yes, Lord. We thank you in advance for what this day brings, with its new treasures and time spent getting to know each another. Should you want to throw a cat in, I promise to cherish it as one of your more adorable creatures, amen." She looked up at him, her hands still tucked under her chin from their impromptu prayer.

He could scarcely suppress his smile. "You had to ask for a cat? Goodness. What happened to the beauty of one plus one?" He repeated his pointing gesture to give her plenty of time to think about having tipped the private equation out of balance.

"I simply added a teeny-weeny number after the decimal point. Say it's two point zero, zero, one. That gives a girl hope she'll get to cuddle a cat, doesn't it?" She leaned back on her door and locked him in her gaze.

He harrumphed, a trace of his smile still dimpling his cheek. He wouldn't answer her right away, not with her fixed on him that way. The voice of Perry Como came over the radio and began to croon "Don't Let the Stars Get in Your Eyes." Not to speak in double negatives, but he sure hoped they would. Cat or no cat, he had a crackerjack date with him and intended to live it up for the day. If the box held a toy prize at the bottom, he'd take that, too.

"A cat," he repeated under his breath with a shake of his head. He checked the traffic ahead and let his gaze wander back to the passenger side with a casual slowness. Myla held her impish gaze on him, but a blush now stained her cheeks. Better yet, he had made it back into her good graces, and they still had forty-five more minutes in the car.

~

The deep, rich walnut veneers on the Army surplus furniture made Myla's creativity hit overdrive. She'd only traveled a quarter of the sales floor, but already had her eye on several pieces. That would force her into some decision-making before too long, but for now, the joy of discovery propelled her along for more. A green-eyed cat hopped onto the credenza she'd been admiring and before she could reach out and stroke its arched back, Weston shooed it off.

"That's at least half a dozen cats I've seen." He shoved his hands in his pockets in obvious disdain. "And to think, you asked God for them. Tisk, tisk. What a wasted prayer."

"Not at all, though I do agree this place is swarming." She giggled and swatted at his arm. "I've heard there's a cat lady who keeps them all fed. They probably find a mouse or two around the warehouse as payback."

"Remind me to check the drawers in my two filing cabinet night stands before I load them. I don't need any vermin freeloaders hitching a ride back to Wichita."

"Okay. Let's move ahead. Remind me what else you're looking for. Was it dining room furniture?"

"Yes. I do admire this walnut finish. That should look grand in a formal dining room, don't you think?"

"I do, but since this is Army surplus, you may not find anything so refined as Duncan Phyfe. That would better lend it to being masculine, and match your other furnishings."

"Solid built is welcome because it will last. They might have a conference room table or something similar. And I prefer oval to round, but like rectangular the best. What about you?" He led the way through a narrow passageway that opened up to another room filled to the brim with hundreds more pieces.

Myla leaned in close to his shoulder as they browsed the first row together. "You're an enigma, Mr. Durand. At work it's a round table, but at home, rectangular. Quite mysterious as riddles go, and one not readily solved."

"King Arthur never had any industrial training, or his preference may have been assuaged to a more linear alignment."

He smirked and continued his perusal.

"Here's a hidden truth that may offset your penchant for sharp corners in a residential setting." She stopped following him and put her hands on her hips.

He swiped at some imaginary dust atop the closest piece, a clunky étagère. When he turned back toward her, his expression had gone blank. "What's the difference?"

"At home, a toddler can bang his head on sharp corners when learning to walk. You see, more than the king lives at home, and his heirs don't come automatically equipped with extras, like cautious balance and surety of step. It's a process, Weston. A safe home is a happy home." She passed him and locked her attention on a row of tables up ahead. She stepped up her pace, her interest piqued.

He soon brushed up beside her alongside a walnut burl conference table that could easily seat sixteen people. "I hadn't taken into account sharing the house, which is quite shortsighted of me. Thank you again, Myla, for bringing me a different perspective. You are more forward-thinking than I am."

His whisper-like tone sent a ripple of chills down her neck. She ran her fingertips over the burl grain, appreciative of its unique design. "A woman must think of the house as a home. It's both her prerogative and her responsibility." She glanced up at him and sensed his deep attentiveness, a cozy sensation. Her fingertips trailed to his forearm and traced a slight caress. "Plus, I truly think you need to hold one of these cats."

He burst out into a belly laugh. "You are preposterous with your relentlessness. That task will be a difficult cajoling, let me assure you." He rubbed his palm over her hand as though he had trapped her manipulative ways. "Let's look for the little cousin of this table, as I like the burl inclusion, don't you?"

She curled her lips into a smile and allowed him to hold her hand on his arm a few seconds longer. "Yes, I agree. The burl adds a level of sophistication. Trimmed with the right upholstery on the chairs, it would make a strong style impression."

"Oh, you know I'm all about style." He scanned the room and then lifted her hand to his lips and gave it a full-fledged kiss.

As much as she'd like to deflect the bold act, it hit Myla right in the knees. Or perhaps it was the way he looked at her afterwards, a magnetic engagement of the suggestive sort, but in a gentlemanly way, of course. "Let's find that little brother table. It may be just down the way."

"You're right. We must stay focused before someone beats us to the perfect specimen." He relinquished her hand and led her into the room. His gaze scanned over several rows as his hand gestured to dismiss each candidate. He soon paused at a table two rows in with a burl flourishing down the middle. "Take this one, for instance."

Myla nestled in beside him and gave the table her undivided attention. Rectangular, it easily sat eight people and had a middle seam for insertion of a leaf. "Look how the burl takes the light and throws it in every direction. Oh my, such a lovely scatter effect."

"Yes, it's lovely." Weston turned and placed a hand across her shoulder, almost a hug. "You seem to like what I like, Myla. What a relief." He dropped the brief embrace and resumed his inspection of the table.

A detail gained her notice that gave her a further affinity for the selection. "It has rounded corners. You might say that represents a compromise."

"I believe so, and the size is precisely what I had in mind. I like the beveled edge, too. It adds a touch of elegance without being overly delicate. Let's get some help clearing it from the others, so I can check beneath for the leg gable."

"And an extra leaf or two. You'd want the whole set, surplus or not."

"Good point. You want to go for help or stay here?"

"You stay and guard your selection. I'll run up front and get a salesman."

"Fine, but don't double back. Try squeezing through that corner up there, past the grouping of buffets." He gestured to the far corner.

Myla broke into a jog down the aisle, happy to hasten the process of the hunt. When she sidled through the tight opening, her gaze fell on a walnut breakfront that had been masterfully crafted. She memorized the setting to allow retracing her steps. A huddle of men stood near the warehouse doors, and she made a beeline toward them. A second piece caught her attention, and she stumbled, not looking where she was going. "Lord, I need to wear blinders in here. Help me focus and be the discerning helper that Weston needs, amen." She hailed a man near the register who immediately began walking to meet her. *What a relief.*

~

Weston tried to attribute his good mood to the aroma of fried chicken and the cabinet full of cream pies on the far wall, but knew better. The furniture warehouse had proven to be a veritable land of enchantment. Myla seemed to hang on his every opinion, oftentimes taking his arm as they moved from one selection to the next. Though he'd gained one more piece than planned, the breakfront did match the dining table. Plus, the resultant hug she'd bestowed—how celebratory had that been? He'd never received pleasure shared from someone else's delight, but it proved to be an overflow treat he could grow use to.

"These quaint servers are making me feel almost naked." Myla crossed her arms over her chest and clamped her hands over her bare shoulders. Her sleeveless top revealed slender arms curved in all the right places.

"Assign me the fault, as I thought four old blankets would suffice. Sorry to have asked for your contribution, but your blouse does serve a noble function to keep the breakfront's glass from cracking in transit. Let me applaud your resourcefulness, though we resemble paupers." He snickered and stuck a thumb under the ribbing of his undershirt.

She leaned across the small table. "You're catching a great deal of attention from the serving girls—your muscles, I mean." She waggled her eyebrows as yet another server passed.

He pressed his palms together and gave a Hercules flex that caused his upper torso to bulge. The tank shirt didn't hide much. He didn't know whether to thank the Good Lord that his stress reliever, the weight bench, also gave him a desirable physical attribute, or not. He tried to read Myla's reaction, but she had poked her nose into the menu.

"Please don't do that, Weston—not in public," she whispered under the page.

He couldn't resist the inference. "Oh, does that mean to wait until we're in private?"

Her eyes squinted into mere slits. "You're a stumbling block to their purity. That's what I mean." She glared over the menu.

"Oh, a thousand pardons. I need to recall my gentleman manners. Wait. I'll be right back." He rose from the chair and headed to the back of the restaurant. When he returned, he had donned a man's black frock coat, an obvious discard from some Yoder patron's wardrobe. "What thinkest thou of me now, Miss Templeton?"

"Quite Abe Lincoln-ish in style, but it does solve the exposure problem. Don't lose the handsome muscles, though." She looked up and batted her lashes as if to send the compliment across the table on a whisper of wind. A coy smile came to her lips.

Have mercy, she'd actually flirted with him…even after he'd donned his gentlemanly manners to guard against the improper. Maybe the coat made him more…approachable. He'd tease her and have some fun with it. "Isn't it enough to admire me for my brain?"

"And I do. But what a liar I would be if I didn't admit that a bicep flinching in the right capacity is like a seat cushion upholstered with woven leather—a cut above standard issue. Plus, think how handy the bulging pair will be when we unload the furniture." She fanned her face with the menu, but kept her eyes locked on him.

"Aha. A weekend lackey, that's what I am." He closed the jacket lapels as if to starve her of any further exposure to his musculature, a move that made him heat up to furnace-level hot. A buzz moved up his core as the tease ran its natural effect. To make matters worse, her foot rubbed against his under the table, an intentional caress. His pulse raced higher than the meringue on those cream pies in the corner.

"You've thrilled me with that breakfront," she whispered.

He grabbed her free hand and ran his thumb across her knuckles. "Once I lodge it in a more suitable house, you're welcome to come see it anytime you want." When her hand curled in his, he wanted to kiss it again. A large bowl of steaming mashed potatoes soon nixed that possibility. The platter of fried chicken arrived next, followed by a smaller bowl of green beans.

"My father might want his jacket back, sir," the server said with a shy curtsy.

"At the end of my meal," he replied in a sharp tone as he dismissed her with a nod.

Myla leaned toward him, her face full of secrets. "How fortunate for me to be the one who gets to ride with the gentleman after he surrenders the coat." Her eyes smoldered with interest through the steam of the potatoes. Soon, her other hand joined his.

Weston hung on every textured second like a man starved for attention. The chicken aroma soon did him in, though, and he remembered the need to say grace. "Let me pray over this fine meal. I feel like a man building his house all in a day."

She nodded and closed her eyes.

"Dear Father, who art in heaven, we thank you for this ample provision of our daily bread. To borrow the words of a lovely woman, this meal is a cut above standard issue. All honor be to you, Lord God, the giver of every perfect gift, amen." When he opened his eyes, Myla seemed to labor across an imbalance. "Here, come move closer beside me so we won't have to pass everything back and forth."

With a small scrape of her chair across the floor, she complied without a word.

He rose enough to steady her seat back as she settled down. When he adjusted her chair toward the table, he managed to scoot it another smidge closer to his own. He leaned in toward her enough to make the small gap separating them more personal.

"I understand weightlifters need extra protein to keep up their bulk." She slid the platter of chicken between them and handed him the serving fork. "Allow me to encourage you, Mr. Durand." She glanced at him sideways, her interest most evident.

"At this juncture, I hope I remember how to eat," he replied. The coat tightened against his chest as he attempted to draw a breath. He stabbed the fork into a crusty chicken breast and transferred it to his plate. A slender green bean soon appeared in striking range, and he nipped it into his mouth like a stallion taking a sugar cube.

Myla laughed, which sounded more like a purr.

He grunted his pleasure while the savory treat tantalized his taste buds. Why not press his good fortune? "I'll have another."

"Oh, I'm sure you will." She took another bean from the bowl. With her lips parted, she fed him the vegetable, her eyes never leaving his gaze. "Here's to the king of the home."

He chewed, swallowed, and cleared his throat. "Make that the home with rounded corners." He lifted his water glass and tipped it toward her.

Myla took her glass in hand and joined him, the glasses clinking over the chicken.

Weston hovered in the intimate moment, thinking he could kiss her right then and there. That should make the prim servers swoon in their tracks and melt a few cream pies, too.

"Darling, I think the potatoes are getting cold. We'd better eat now." She pulled away from his immediate proximity and began to serve the mashed potatoes.

Weston could hardly contain his elation. Why, he'd eat the whole bowl empty just to show the spuds who reigned. After all, she'd called him *darling*. The word still rang in his ears. Glory, hallelujah He'd shot from nothing to everything in a day's time. Plus, the progression held fried chicken, to boot.

Chapter 8

The lab phone rang and snapped Weston's train of thought right in the middle of his statistical evaluation. Installed late last week, its ring had a certain bite to it. He cuffed the receiver before it could sound off again. "Quality Control, Durand speaking."

"Weston, it's Duncan. I found something on my safety sweep of Hangar A this morning. It doesn't look like much, but I can't risk it. One of the engine covers on the XT-37 has been punctured. I want you to take a closer look before I jump to conclusions. Can you come over?"

"Yes, right away. Let me gather some inspection tools, in case I need to look further. I can be over there in five minutes."

"Great. I'll finish my sweep and double back. Meet you at the prototype then. Goodbye."

Weston returned the receiver to its base. The sting of having his productive morning interrupted needled him from the soles of his shoes up. His mind in logical mode, he gathered a magnifying glass, a grasping probe, and a sample bag for what he might find. Almost ready to exit, he doubled back and lifted a powerful ferrous magnet from its post on a pegboard. Puncture meant one thing to him—the turbojet's engine had been tampered with.

From Hangar C, he strode out into the sunlight of a Monday full of promise. He'd thought to find Myla on the shop floor and casually invite her to take lunch with him. They both needed to eat, after all. A 140 hovered at the far end of the taxiway, full of gumption to gain the sky. He could spend a full day by taking off like that, but it sure wouldn't be today. He approached Hangar A and could already see the tall frame of the safety manager standing beside the XT-37.

Duncan Reed motioned toward the left engine. "Thank you for your promptness, Mr. Durand. Everything we find is confidential from here on out. Try to work without drawing attention to your inspection."

"Fine. Show me what you've found." He gestured with the magnifying glass in hand.

"Right here, at the lower rim. It's a puncture mark, as I told you. I don't know if you can determine whether it was made intentionally—or by accidental contact."

He shifted closer. Immediately, the cover made him think of Myla. He had to shrug off that inclination. "Let's have a closer look, then. Too bad the lighting is so horrendous in here."

"Hold on a second." Reed stepped away and returned in seconds with a caged shop light in hand. He slid the power switch, and the naked bulb cast a bright, harsh illumination onto the cotton cover. The slice in the fabric caused the cotton to curl outward like a pouting bottom lip. He held the magnifying glass to it and glided the caliper in place. "Nine-sixteenths."

Reed slid a notebook and pen out of his pocket and recorded the data.

"As for intentional or not, I can only describe this cut as the result of a sharp blade, so that leans toward malicious intent. See here, the threads have been neatly severed." He leaned back to allow the safety manager a closer look at the inspection site.

"Blast the luck," he muttered. "I had hoped for a bird." A tendon flexed in his jaw.

"Not luck, sir. This is premeditated vandalism—or sabotage of an expensive engine—however you want to look at it. We'll need to take a cursory look inside the cover."

"Let me remove it, so as not to arouse any suspicion." Reed handed him the light. He pulled at the drawstring crimping the fabric's edge and soon had the engine uncovered.

With weighty dread, Weston stepped in front of the intake blades and held the light as central as he could manage to avoid creating shadows. Nothing but original design parts stared back. Reed's shoulder soon bumped his in an attempt to share the observation.

"You see anything? I sure don't."

"No, not anything obvious. Give me a second, though." He slid the magnet out of his back pocket. "I wanted to try this. I found a reference to using magnets when I researched that nondestructive evaluation topic you mentioned. Even as powerful as it is, the attraction can only affect the front chamber of the engine. I doubt whatever made that incision in the cotton could have gone very far, since we're dealing with a cut, not a shot blast."

"You're not making me feel much better about this."

"I'm an analyst, not a doctor." He passed the magnet parallel to the face plate in a quadrant pattern until he had completed a full sweep. The magnet failed to pull out any foreign material.

"Nothing?"

He pocketed the magnet and tried to peer in through the radiating assemblage of jet fan blades. "Nothing metallic, which would do the most damage if ingested." He shined the light into the chamber and tried to detect any inclusions.

"I want to order an upgrade to this cotton cover—or my nerves will be wrecked by the time this plane receives certification." Reed blew out a tense exhalation as though to prove it.

"You're playing right into the saboteur's hands, Duncan. Let's put the cotton back on and operate under the illusion of status quo. In the meantime, you can order a wire mesh from fabrication. We'll install it inside the fabric cover, as reinforcement."

"Yes, I like that plan of action better. I never pictured you as having a devious side though, Weston." He wrote a note and shot him a glance under his flat-lined brow.

"I'm all for countering with a guard that leads to defect prevention. I can barely inspect this contraption. Don't expect me to repair it."

"Point well taken. Can you get someone over here to sew up that cut in the cover? I want to put it back in place—you know—for the bird aversion." He gave him a grave look, one that didn't speak of bird watching.

"I think I can sweet talk someone into it at lunch today. Count on it, in fact." He handed the safety manager the shop light and walked back out into the sunlight.

"I used to be that sure of myself, Mr. Durand," Reed called.

He turned and regarded the man responsible for bringing him

to Cessna. Always the epitome of strength, he seemed vulnerable standing there in front of the XT-37. It could have something to do with the aircraft's price tag, or a nine-sixteenths breech of safety that bore the mega-bomb whisper of an explosion waiting to happen. He saluted his superior and turned back to hunt up a petite upholsterer who said yes to most of his requests for favors as of late. He'd sweeten the pot if he had to—and possibly if he didn't.

~

Stomach-down on the cockpit floor of a 140, Myla tamped her toes in protest of the personal banter. Every time they worked together on a four-seater, Miss Granger filled the passenger space with her latest rants. Myla looked over at her apprentice, and the young woman seemed too focused on the work at hand. "Get your stapler out and put in a line just under the seat edge next. I'll help you work the leather down."

Susie glanced up at her as she reached for the stapler. "Thank you for all the help, Miss Templeton."

"Call me Myla. Things aren't too formal out here on the shop floor." She resumed her work on the passenger seat when a sharp scrape occurred in the backseat area.

Miss Granger made a throaty growl. "Jeepers-creepers. I'll have to cover that. Guess I've got too much man on my mind this morning. He sure did cook up a nice pan of braised dove breasts, though."

"To whom are you referring, Miss Granger? I can't take a hint of what's sitting so heavy on your mind." Myla glanced over to Susie and rolled her eyes.

"Skip Sellers, the assembly manager out here."

"Oh, yes. He was your date for Open House, if I remember right." She punctuated her recollection with a staccato of stapler action that set the seat cushion into permanent mode.

"That's the fabulous day it all started. We've been out several times since then. I outshot him at skeet, so he had to cook me dinner. Can I say fabulous again? That guy has it going on."

"Sounds like he has you going, for sure," Myla replied. "It's nice to have something more than work going on, for a change. It tends to fill up a few empty places on the inside."

"Well said. Now, if I could just keep my focus instead of botching this installation." Another growl emanated from the back.

Myla stifled a laugh as she shared an amused look with Susie. A tug at her pants leg soon got her attention. She glanced back over her shoulder and found Weston standing at the top of the gantry peering in. From the smug look on his face, he'd been there long enough to hear some of their girl talk. "Hey there. What brings Quality Control up to our entertaining cockpit today?" She rolled onto her hip and dropped the stapler.

"Sounds like a small party in here, all right." He waggled his brow to further the tease.

"We try to whistle while we work," she replied. "Weston Durand, I'd like you to meet our new upholsterer-in-training, Susie Moore."

"My pleasure, Miss Moore. I think these Interiors ladies can keep you plenty busy."

Alice Granger shot through the split in the front seats and flashed a mock smile. "Howdy, Mr. Durand. Don't look for quality right now in my realm. I just pulled a boner when my mind wandered to Skip's company, but I aim to recover that part."

Weston looked at Myla and gave her the slightest wink. "Very well, Miss Granger. The laborer is the first line of defense against defects, and the best, if you ask me. Might I ask permission to borrow Miss Templeton here? We've had a cover problem on the XT-37 and some repair work is in order. Since it's so close to lunch, I hoped to ask for a two-for-one deal and steal her away."

Myla parted her lips and drew a breath. He'd been on her mind all morning and now, here he stood, asking for her company. What an amazing turn of events. Most of their interaction outside of the QC group seemed to be touch-and-go in the workplace. This encounter had more flair. Her pleasant reaction to possible time spent together filtered into a smile.

"Sure. Off you go." Miss Granger fanned her hand toward the cockpit door. "Susie and I have this covered. Myla's been hovering over our trainee all morning, anyway. Let's see what she can do on her own."

A word choked in Susie's throat, her eyes widening in a frantic stare.

"You're so right, Miss Granger," Myla replied. She reached for the young woman's arm and gave it a pat. "Knowing when to pull back as a mentor is a talent I haven't had the opportunity to develop. And you'll be right here if she has any questions. Thank you both. I'll see you after lunch." Before she could attempt to stand, Weston's hand dangled in front of her. She reached for it and accepted his kind help down the gantry.

"That went well, don't you think?" He beamed a smile down at her and tucked his thumbs in his pockets.

Myla unzipped her coveralls and stepped out of them. The day instantly cooled off. She bent to retrieve the suit and tossed it onto the pile of seat coverings on a nearby cart. "Maybe too well. Let's run away before the mean stepmother changes her mind." She nudged him with her shoulder and he obliged.

"Stepmother?" he whispered, his brow knit with the query.

"Call me Cinderella," she replied with a laugh. "I've just escaped my lock-up, and I'm running out to the ball."

"In that case, could you gather a needle and some thread along the way? Prince Charming has a snag in his jet engine cover." His cheeks dimpled with a wry smile.

Myla held his gaze for a step or two as they came out into the sunlight. The moment filled with magical innuendo like a slide down the rainbow. "I think I have what the prince needs, right here in my kit." She slid a finger down her neckline, until it rested over her heart.

Amused, Weston offered her his elbow. "In that case, let me escort you right to the problem zone. Be advised though, I cannot comment on the situation in public."

"Okay. Show me your problem, and I'll try to fix it." She put a hand through the crook of his elbow and followed by his side until they arrived at Hangar A. She spotted the hole in the cover right away. "Well, well. That didn't take long."

"To quote an expert—'it's springtime and the birds are nesting.'" He lowered his brow and gave her a look that carried a serious overtone.

"I'll get this remedied in two shakes of a cat's tail for you." She retrieved her stitching set from the kit and began to thread the needle.

Weston caught a laugh in his fist. His eyes sparkled as the personal joke struck a sensitive spot. "We're adding reinforcement in the form of wire mesh, behind the cotton," he said, his voice lowered.

"Aha. Looks are deceiving then. That's a clever approach, and it will stop whatever made this innocuous cut." She ran her hand up under the cover and sunk the needle in close to the opening. She advanced the needle up the cut until a series of even stitches marked the scar. When she tied off the knot and clipped it, she looked up to find Weston staring at her.

"Smart, proficient, and beautiful—truly a rare commodity." His approval radiated from his soft brown eyes.

Myla tucked her equipment back into her kit. She fingered the stitch seam, seeking a diversion. "You're about to invite me to eat lunch now, aren't you?"

"Business before pleasure," he replied, "and I believe our business has been concluded." He offered his elbow again, the more pleasurable aspect overtaking his expression.

This time Myla placed her hand around the base of his bicep. She amplified the welcome contact by rubbing her thumb over his skin until it skimmed the sleeve of his shirt. The muscle flex followed, like she knew it would. They stepped onto the tarmac under cornflower blue skies while his effect on her soared.

"Let's grab a sandwich and find a bench under a tree." Weston nodded to the back door of the cafeteria and pulled her in that direction.

Such a noble suggestion, why hadn't it occurred to her before? "That sounds great," she replied. "I want you to tell me more about that cut in the cover, but not enough that the bad guys will come looking for me." She shielded the sunlight from her eyes and gave him a tiny wink.

He laughed and pulled her tighter to his side as they approached the main building. Before he could grab the knob, the door flew open and several people filed outside, including the female test pilot who had flown them at the Open House. Weston held the door open and nodded to acknowledge her.

"Oh thanks, dearie. Wishing you clear skies," she said in a swanky Rita Hayworth imitation. She swung her hips as she walked out.

Myla almost choked on the fakery. She leaned behind Weston to hide her repulsion.

"Hey, wait up for me," a man called through the open door.

Weston drew her around to allow her to enter first, and she ran smack dab into the greasy tool salesman. With strong hands clutching her shoulders back, she veered in time to avoid direct contact.

"Wow, it's raining pretty women," Hague teased before breaking into a run to rejoin his lunch group.

"You wish," she muttered, eager to enter the cafeteria and snuff out the sight of him. She turned back in time to catch Weston's questioning look. "Can't stand that type," she added. The aroma of fried food filled the lunchroom as a gaggle of conversations tied knots in the air. "What are you in the mood for? Could we split a club sandwich?"

"Sounds great. Plus, a bag of chips to share and two sodas. You like the lemony kind, right?" He placed his fingertips on the small of her back as they walked up to the ordering line.

Pleased that he'd remembered such a little detail, it occurred to her that this was the type she could stand—more than stand, actually. "Yes, I do. Tell your gentleman he's being quite thoughtful today. What a break from the ordinary."

He seemed amused at the inference and bent toward her. "His head is full of romantic notions lately. It tends to fill up a few empty places on the inside, as you well know."

Myla gasped as her own words came back to make her heart flutter. At least Weston felt it too. What a relief. The clerk nodded, and he gave their order. All she had to do was stand there and look pretty. Thank goodness she had ditched the coveralls.

~

Weston crumpled the wax paper in his hand as Myla took a quick glance at her watch. Duty called, but he resisted the urge to switch gears. "I should let you get back."

"Not that I want to, but the wicked stepmother might come looking for me." She stood and brushed some crumbs from her pants. "Miss Granger is dating Skip Sellers from our QC group. Did you know that?"

He rose and joined her at the edge of the shade. "Skip mentioned they were going skeet shooting together. He's been a widower for seven years. It's healthy to see him going out."

Myla started out along the sidewalk. "She's changing, softening up I would say. Sometimes I miss the old Miss Granger, the one who didn't talk nonstop."

He laughed and came up beside her. On impulse, he picked a small violet from the shade of an elm and handed it to her. "Here's a small token of loveliness to benchmark a most agreeable lunch."

She accepted the flower and tucked it into her headband with a grin. "You'd better watch out, or I'll need to spill some of my giddy day to Miss Granger."

"That would turn the tide on her, now wouldn't it?" His smirk shifted into a lop-sided grin when he studied her face. "Oh, I almost forgot. Take a look at this for me." He grabbed for the paper and fumbled getting it out of his back pocket. "I had my first meeting with a real estate agent yesterday after church. He suggested these starter homes. Please take a cursory look and tell me what you think."

Her hand flew over her mouth. When she glanced up at him, her eyes held a question.

"Have I asked too much? You have such a knack for design, I really value your opinion."

"Fine, I'll look at them. You're flattering me beyond my capability though, as interiors are my specialty."

He turned sideways to gauge her sincerity. "Well, then consider these exteriors as clues to hidden treasures that lie within. I focus more on structure, not style." He handed over the paper as a lump formed in his throat. Had he forced her participation, or was she just being shy?

"Here's the one I'd look at first, the fourth one there. From the window arrays and gable placements, it should have the smaller extras that make a house interesting, like built-in shelving and alcoves. I'd place it under the cottage style."

"That one is my favorite as well. It's located in College Hill, another bonus. I'll call and see if I can set up a showing. Would you be interested in accompanying me?"

Her cheeks turned the color of a pale rose. "Surely you do flatter me, Mr. Durand."

"I don't recognize the value of rounded corners at first glance—and you do. Perhaps you'd see something that I would miss. If we both went, our assessments could complement each other for a fuller picture."

"Well, since you put it like that, I do have Saturday open, if that works for the agent."

"Let me call and set it up then. How swell. A-hunting we will go."

"Hi-ho the derry-o, a-hunting we will go," she replied in sing-song merriment.

He offered her his arm and when she took it, he leaned in to share a secret. "Just don't mention skeet shooting as you plan your hunt."

Her blue eyes sparkled at his toying. "Heaven forbid. No skeet, no Skip, and no mention of men in general."

"You're such a workplace survivor," he teased. "If only you knew how to keep your head down when danger lurked. Tisk. Tisk." He waggled his finger at her.

"If I knew how to keep my head down, we would have never met." She caught his finger and allowed it to skim her cheek before setting it free.

A sensation rumbled inside his ribs, and he snuggled her arm tighter against his side, which did nothing to quell the quake. *Heady stuff, this hunting.* How was a man to search out cracks and defects when much larger-scale persuasions engaged all about him? With an afternoon full of facts and figures, he'd soon be pressed to sort it out.

"Our time together is special to me. Thank you for inviting me to come along Saturday. I look forward to it." She stopped at the stairwell that would soon separate their paths. A breeze stirred and lifted her wavy hair off her shoulders.

"Don't make any other plans, as we could run all day looking at a host of houses." He let her arm go, but locked his gaze on her heart-shaped face.

"It seems I'm at your disposal, then. I'll expect you between nine and ten." She allowed her sparkling eyes to say the rest, until she turned and walked up the steps.

He opened the door to the corporate hall as the smelling salts of professional responsibility tried to displace the fragrance of romance. He sighed with a hapless release. "A beautiful woman, a cottage-style house, and tables with rounded corners. I'm out of my league here, Lord. Please lend me some timely guidance, amen." As he approached his office, he found that a tiny purple flower had adhered to his sleeve, a lilac's worth of assurance that divine help might be on the way.

~

He slammed the screen door to knock several moths away from the porch light. His sister greeted him in the hallway. "Hey, I got to go up flying today. What remarkable dividends it pays to make friends with a lady pilot."

"Great. Add her to your harem. Hope you got your paycheck, because we've got end-of-the-month bills coming due." She disappeared into the kitchen.

He followed, needing an update. "You got that hole poke done, right?"

"First thing this morning, though it screwed up my entire day's schedule. You're going to let me know what's next, aren't you? She looked up from the sink, expecting an answer.

"Stay away from Hangar A until I say when. Don't mess this up." He ambled to the fridge and took a look inside. "Did you buy any groceries this week?"

"I'll go tomorrow when I have more time. Want anything?"

"Yeah, a million bucks and a corporate apology. I'm still working on it, but even the Lone Ranger has the entire episode to get the job done." He grabbed the juice bottle and drained the dregs dry.

"Guess that makes me Tonto. Maybe I should darken my hair." She turned the faucet on to wash her hands.

He walked by and tugged at her braid. "Maybe lose a few pounds," he suggested. Before she could boil her typical reaction into froth, he stepped out back to head for the garage. The car's oil gauge was reading low. Maybe it was time for a change. The turbocharged jet flashed to mind and his blood pressure shot up.

He kicked the garage door open and reached for the string overhead. With a yank, a solitary bulb cast its light across the structure, dilapidated and surrendering to gravity like everything else around him. Somehow, the weightless feeling of soaring up in the clouds returned and snuffed out his general dissatisfaction with life. Things were about to get better, and not by happenstance either.

Chapter 9

Myla ran down the hall barefoot in response to the doorbell's ring. All her extra primping came down to this, as Weston's reaction this morning would speak volumes. The ringlets she'd put in her hair flounced against her ears. She ran her fingers through them to loosen the curls so they would seem more natural.

Water splashed from the kitchen sink. "Was that the doorbell, Myla?"

"Yes, Mother. I'll get it. I think Weston is here." She shifted the form-fitting waistline and let her fingertips float down the folds of the full skirt. Several shades of spring green, the dress loaned her a fairy-like feeling, though the cotton fabric made it light as a day dress. She crossed the living room and unlocked the door.

When she opened it, she couldn't have been more shocked. Weston knelt on the top step, petting the arched back of the next-door neighbor's cat. What's more, he seemed to be enjoying it. "Will wonders never cease?" She laughed and pulled a handful of curls back off her face. Only when the metal flashing of the threshold made her feet cool did she realize she'd forgotten to slip on her skimmers.

Weston stood slowly, his eyes locked on hers. "Look at you. What a vision." The cat encircled his ankles like an animal anchor.

"I'm trying to mimic the way Mother Nature dresses springtime. How did I do?"

"I see that when the grass greens, it makes the sapphire pools all the more blue, if that were indeed possible." He tried to step forward, but wore a cat on his loafers.

"Can you come in for a second? Without old Rally, I mean. Our day may call for wearing shoes, but it completely slipped my mind until just now." She gestured inside and enjoyed watching him extricate his feet from the pet trap. Once she turned to lead him in, her mother stood right behind her.

"Good morning, Mr. Durand. So good to see you again." She wiped her hands on her apron, looking like the epitome of domestic life.

"Mrs. Templeton, you're looking well. I trust that can be attributed to all your time spent in the garden." Weston reached for her hand and took it, giving it a cordial pat.

"My leaf lettuce is really outstanding this spring, but the heat is taking its toll. It turns bitter as the days lengthen and heat up. I'm afraid summer will be the absolute end of it. I guess I need more mouths to feed."

"Mother, I don't think we'll be back this evening in time." Myla put a conciliatory arm around her shoulders to apologize for making independent plans.

"Too bad I haven't introduced you to my landlord, Art Godfrey. He's hosting his nephew, a war veteran, this week. He's on his way to a new commission down in Independence and just commented on missing home-cooked meals at dinner last night. Poor Art fries everything. It's a wonder that old codger doesn't have one foot in the grave already."

"A war veteran? I should invite them for Sunday dinner. It would be my honor. Could you arrange it, Mr. Durand?" She fiddled with the tie on her apron.

He rubbed his chin. "Well, they might have made other plans, since it's already Saturday. Perhaps I should call and inquire. Would you show me to your telephone, Mrs. Templeton? I think I have a few minutes to spare, as Myla need to finish up her spring look with a pair of shoes for our outing." He glanced her way with a mischievous grin.

Buoyed by his attention, she decided to play the part of a lovely spring breeze. She gathered her full skirt and swirled on tiptoes in the general direction of the hallway. Before disappearing to her room, she grabbed the corner and halted. "Mother, I'll be happy to help you serve Sunday dinner if they accept."

"And I'll be much obliged to drive them over," Weston added

as he reached for the phone.

Her heart happy for the potential of another day spent together, she traipsed to her room to locate the renegade skimmers. On her way to her closet, she assessed her curls in the bureau mirror. Though she enjoyed the flounce, taming them back off her face might be in order. She slid a thin satin ribbon from a spindle that held the mirror, and then ran it under her hair. When she tied it on top of her head, she glanced at the effect and thought it made her cheekbones more pronounced. She soon located the cream-colored shoes and hurried back to the living room where signs of clinching the invitation abounded.

"Yes, I'll be sure to, Mr. Godfrey. You two enjoy your round of golf today. Goodbye." Weston replaced the receiver and gave her a nod. "They gratefully accept your invitation, Effie. Art wanted me to be sure and express his appreciation. It looks like you're entertaining a trio of bachelors tomorrow. Just tell me what time to have them here."

She seemed to bubble with excitement. "Well, we still have church in the morning, but I'll toss the salad before we leave. Let's say one o'clock. That will give me enough time to finish cooking the pork roast."

Myla put her arms around her mother and kissed her goodbye. "I'll get up early and make grandma's cinnamon rolls for our dessert. That's a true sign of spring in the Templeton household."

He put a hand over his heart. "Don't make me dizzy with anticipation. I can hardly remember the last time I ate a cinnamon roll."

"That's the beauty of family, Weston. We're the keepers of tradition and everything wholesome in this world, under the fear of God. Now, go have fun, you two. I've got to get my good china out and a thousand other things before tomorrow."

Myla slid her hand in his and tugged him toward the front door. "Remember, we have an appointment with the real estate agent. Let's not be late."

"Then I'd better keep my eyes on the road and not my housing assessment companion."

She led him down the stairs and released his hand to shoo Rally back into its own yard. When she straightened, his arm laced around her back in masculine strength. She allowed him to escort her to the passenger side and waited for him to open the door.

His hand traveled from her back to her elbow. "Why do I feel like the most fortunate man alive this morning?" His gaze searched her face for the answer.

"Spring fever?" She slipped from his grip and took a seat in the Pontiac. The day seemed to burgeon with potential like a flower bed bursting with blooms.

He closed her door and soon appeared on the driver's side. "I do have a bad case, I assure you." Instead of looking at her to validate it, he glanced in the rearview mirror and started the car. It jumped from the curb like a jaguar on the prowl.

"Let the house hunt begin," she teased. "Do you have the paper summary of potential candidates? I'd like to review that again on the way."

"Be my guest," he replied. "At least one of us needs to stay focused." He produced the folded listing and held it toward her pinched between two fingers.

Myla reached for it eager to take another look.

He grabbed her hand and held it hostage. "Promise you'll think out loud while we tour. If you like something, I want to know. Conversely, tell me what you don't like." His grip loosened.

"The agent should have these properties somewhat staged, since they're on the market. Still, I'm afraid reality will look much different than the magazine images I've been filling my head with. Let's pledge to look past the clutter for the potential that lies beneath."

"That's a deal. Myla, thank you for being here. It means a great deal to me." His voice turned husky. Suddenly, it seemed the traffic held all his interest, though his words hinted otherwise.

She reached with her free hand and absconded with the listing. "I'm charmed through and through with every aspect of it. Now, did you set up the appointment with Number Four here?"

"My advisor picked Number Four, so she gets Number Four." He suppressed the indulgent smile, but dimples dotted his clean-shaven cheeks.

She feigned steady interest in the list, but those dimples trickled down into her heart. Weston seemed particularly nice-looking today, or was she growing fond of his face?

"Aha. College Hill starts here at this turn-off." He steered the

Pontiac into the residential zone and kept its speed in check.

Children played along the sidewalk and dogs barked from the front porches. Myla sensed the vitality and took a deep breath as she rolled down her window. The breeze tugged at her hair. She touched the bow in her ribbon to make sure it had stayed tied.

Weston glanced at her and then focused on the road signs at the corner. "I want that ribbon," he said in a low voice.

She pursed her lips and gave him a coy look. "Keep your hands to yourself, Mr. Durand."

"Too late, my good Miss Templeton, as spring has already sprung. Now, help me watch for Perry or Harrison. I'm as lost in here as I can be."

"It's a hunt. Being lost adds to the adventure." She touched the ribbon again, to be sure.

~

Weston slowed the car to a creep and peered out the windshield at a cottage that showed its age. Had the picture misrepresented the house? "Lord, help us. This place is deplorable. How can this be right?"

"Let me check the address. Nineteen-oh-five North Perry is the address on the list." Myla looked at the property and grimaced. "Oh, no. See? This is nineteen-fifty. Keep going down this way. I'll watch for the porch numbers."

"Somehow, the windows out front looked right—but not the rest. I hope we haven't gotten our hopes up needlessly." He drove across a small concrete bridge flanked by a small park along the stream bank. Huge bur oaks pinned up the sky's canopy and somehow helped him regain his fortitude.

"These cottages date back to the thirties. The builder likely repeated the same ones throughout the neighborhood. Slow down and let me make sure the numbering continues in the same sequence."

"Yes, it does. See? There's nineteen-thirty-four. I think we're winding down to the right block." He leaned forward over the wheel to improve his perspective.

"That makes sense, as the north-south addresses start at zero on Douglas Avenue. We're three blocks away. How fun. We're between the rivers here. We shouldn't cross another bridge before we find the house." She propped up on the dashboard.

The oaks lining the road gave way to broad-leafed sycamores, and the grade began to slope downhill. "I'm afraid we might be heading for the next bridge, my dear Miss Templeton. Let's not be too discouraged, as this is only the first house on the list."

"But both of us picked it as our favorite." She sat up on her knees as if daring the house to show itself.

With a break evident in the tree line ahead, Weston slowed the car to get a better view of the last handful of houses rowed up along the curb. The second to last house held a familiar looking set of shed dormers centered on its roof. "Could that be it?"

"That's it," Myla squealed. She tapped the paper and pointed to the cottage. When she shifted to his side of the bench seat, she wore the elation of a child.

"Looks like you've gotten your wish, my friend. It's one house from the river—and just short of disappointment, I hope."

Her hands clamped the rounds of his shoulders. "You may have a view of the river from the back. How sensational! I can hardly wait to see."

He spied a man exiting the front door as he pulled to the curb, his view partially blocked by his exuberant helper. Her excitement contagious, he killed the engine and took her by the waist. "I'm glad I don't have to remind you to share your thoughts out loud. It seems you're a veritable babbling brook."

"Take me inside, Weston. I just have to see it. Such a darling front porch—with part of it shaded."

A hot flash made him drop a hand to the door lever. "Shade is good—for lots of reasons. Let's go meet the real estate agent." He popped the door ajar and checked for traffic before opening it all the way. "Kind of quiet around here, I'll give it that."

"Two positives—shade and quiet. I'll make a list on the back side of this paper."

"Once again, you're my capable note taker, Miss Templeton. Please do me the honor." He held out his hand for her and stood to sweep her out of the car. When she tumbled into his arms, he gave her an opportunistic hug.

Myla wrenched out of his grip, turning to see the house. She wandered into the yard and stood in the sycamore's shade.

The man beckoned from the porch. "Mr. Durand? I'm Lester Lange, your real estate agent. Please, come on up."

Weston shook his hand and shifted his footing to test the planks of the porch. They seemed sturdy underfoot, another good sign. Symmetrical sets of windows flanked the front door, an attribute he appreciated. "Thank you for your availability this morning, Mr. Lange. I've brought a friend, Miss Templeton, along with me. She is knowledgeable regarding interior design, so I solicited her expertise."

The man's eyebrows shot up into his hairline. "She makes a pretty good decoration herself, if you don't mind me saying so. Can you call her up here? We'll get started with the tour when you're both ready."

"She passed the point of mere readiness at the first bridge, Mr. Lange. Thank the Good Lord we didn't have to cross the second."

"This bridge crosses the Little Arkansas River, by far the tamer of the two. College Hill is popular, especially if you like a bit of architectural style with your function. So you say you're with the aircraft industry?"

"That's right." He turned, searching for her whereabouts. "Myla? Mr. Lange is ready to start our tour. Can you come on up?"

She broke into a jog, practically floating up the porch steps in a sweep of cotton. "Mr. Lange, it's nice to meet you."

"Thank you, please step inside." The agent opened the front door and led the way.

Myla started across the door jamb and slipped a hand back for him to take.

Weston threaded his fingers through hers and stepped into the cottage ramped to overdrive. With his crack-and-defect sensor engaged, he scanned the first room for drywall flaws that might speak of foundation settling for an aging house. No cracks were evident. Everywhere he looked, he saw nothing but well-placed features, including a fireplace with built-in shelves on each side.

Myla drifted to the far window and gave a subtle gasp. "You can see the bridge from here, Weston, and even some of the river upstream."

The agent leaned toward him. "Wait until she sees the back view. It's sure to please."

"Was this fireplace original? The brickwork is well done." He stepped toward it and knelt to peer up the flue.

"Everything is original with this one—all quality from the get-go. In fact, it's being sold by the estate of the original owner. They call that 'pride of ownership' in my business. It shines for this one, so well-appointed, it will sell itself. I believe it's been on the market four days."

Weston stood and beckoned to Myla, who seemed to be counting the shelves.

"Fireplaces can be dangerous to small children," she said in a low tone.

"They make wire mesh screens for that. Not to worry." He clasped her hand as the agent waited for them in the hall. They crossed to the next room.

"This is the formal dining room, complete with chair rail and traditional crystal chandelier." He extended his arm for their entrance, and Weston led the way.

"Might I see the chandelier illuminated, Mr. Lange?" Myla reached for the lowest dangle and made the fixture sway. It soon turned on and illuminated her face.

To test for ample space, Weston backed to the window overlooking the front porch and began to pace off the approximate length of his newly procured dining table. He added an extra step to move it away from the front wall. Even with a leaf inserted, the room provided plenty of space to accommodate the piece.

"This wall would hold the breakfront," Myla said. "You'd want to keep it out of direct light, so it's a good thing no windows were built along the western wall."

The agent joined them in the room. "Yes, a majority of the windows face either the front or the back. I've been in other models of this cottage that don't have that eastern window in the living room."

Myla clapped her hands under her chin in admiration. "Someone custom ordered it then—for the river view."

"I heartily approve," Weston replied. "Now, Mr. Lange, there can't be a kitchen far from the dining room, so kindly show us where." If it looked anything like Art Godfrey's outdated kitchen, he'd be sorely disappointed. He followed the agent down the central hallway until the space opened up on both sides. Light and airy, the kitchen boasted a continuous countertop on three sides. To the right, a nook held a small sitting area perfect for a dinette set.

Myla shifted to the windows facing out back. "Oh, goodness

me. Come look at this, Weston."

He approached the back door, gave the doorknob a jiggle test for durability, and finally allowed his gaze to wander outside. A small river meandered in a curve behind the house, visible for a block or more. The view would enhance his morning bowl of cold cereal, for sure. Myla seemed transported to another world. He decided to test her pragmatic mettle. "Would this water body pose an unwarranted hazard in your estimation? You know, for children playing outside?"

She stepped toward him, her eyes full of unrestrained admiration. "Who could oppose a section of river nearby, should God provide one? Between a sturdy fence and the watchful eyes of the parents, the potential hazard could be minimized."

He lost himself in those blue eyes and all the innuendo they contained. She'd passed his test and then some. In response to the magnetic attraction between them, he held out his hand to her, and she came closer. "This cottage seems to suit you, Miss Templeton. I dare say you've never looked lovelier than in the sunlight pouring through these windows."

"I'm so taken by it all." She looked into his eyes, her tone breathless with sincerity. She folded into him and tucked her face against his chest.

Unthinking, he bent and pressed a kiss onto the ribbon in her hair, while his arms folded around her in a hug. The embrace flowed over him like the river out back, liquid and full of life.

The agent cleared his throat from the far counter. "Miss Templeton? You might like to review the particulars of this kitchen. The working triangle is quite well-defined."

Ill-focused, Weston released her and stumbled behind her into the room. "What sort of triangle do you mean, Mr. Lange?"

Myla laughed and gave him a quick look over her shoulder. "Please allow me, Mr. Lange. You see, Weston, the triangle has three endpoints—ones that the cook must frequent to prepare the meals. The refrigerator, the range, and the sink anchor the triangle. One must be able to move quickly between the three. This house honors that arrangement, as you see I can make each endpoint with only a few steps." She went from the stove to the sink effortlessly to prove it.

He joined her at the sink to see what the view contained out that window. To his surprise, he saw another wing of the house that stood guard over a garden plot in the backyard. "Show us the rest of the house, Mr. Lange. I'm intrigued by this layout and pleased that the river view has been maximized."

The agent snapped his fingers and pointed back to the hallway.

Weston turned and beckoned to Myla. The house had him intrigued, all right. Maybe he should keep his hands to himself for this next part, likely the bedroom wing. He walked ahead out of self-preservation.

Mr. Lange paused momentarily and gestured. "Here's the first of two smaller bedrooms, one of which could pose as a study or craft room until the children come. Across the hall here is the second. The hall ends at the master suite. I'll allow you some privacy to view them all. Meet me in the kitchen, and I'll be happy to answer any questions before showing you the backyard."

Weston stepped into the front bedroom and assessed it for space. Perhaps his weight bench could fit in here. He memorized the space and went across the hall to compare the two rooms. They seemed identical, except this room contained his interiors expert. "Do you see anything objectionable, Miss Templeton?" He soon stood beside her at the rear-facing window.

"Look. The yard has a dedicated garden space. This is special, truly special."

He poked a finger in her back. "You didn't answer my question, darling. Is anything questionable?"

She looked sideways at him and then returned her gaze to the backyard. "You call me darling and expect me to remain objective?" When her bottom lip quivered, she bit down on it.

In no place to console her, his mind raced to finish the tour. "Let me view the master suite alone then. You might check it behind me—to see if meets your expectations." He pulled out of her proximity, certain that tears would be falling against that familiar windowpane in short order. He had dared to call her darling, yet he wouldn't take it back for anything.

To the right, the hall ended at an oversized door that gave the appearance of not having been original to the house. Perhaps it allowed for wheelchair access. He could only speculate. A tray ceiling centered the room with symmetry, though the addition of a private bath made it lopsided to the front. When he peered out the double window, there was the river again, casting its broad sweep over the landscape.

He made quick work of inspecting the bathroom, likely an addition that seemed a decade younger than the remainder of the house. He returned down the hall to find the agent, his questions lining up in a queue. He started with the bathroom addition which led to the demonstration of the original facility, now only a half-bath tucked into the crook of the hallway. Eventually, Myla reappeared and joined them.

"To the backyard then?" the agent asked.

"Yes, the backyard down to the river," he replied. He followed the man through the back door, trailing a hand for Myla to take. When her hand slid into his readily, he embraced what might be in his future. The air smelled clean as the thick grass soon padded his footsteps. He assessed the property and managed to hold periods of focus, until Myla would happen into view to distract him once again.

"This shed is handy," Mr. Lange said. He opened the door and revealed a collection of tools left behind by the owner.

Weston stuck his head inside and gave a cursory look. "I take it these tools come with the property?"

"Yes, the previous owner made specific mention of that." He closed the door and re-clasped the fastener.

Myla turned toward him so rapidly, her skirt billowed. "Oh, Weston! Here's the gate leading down to the river. Could we?"

He passed the question to the agent who shrugged his shoulders. "Okay. Please give us a few moments of private consideration Mr. Lange. Perhaps we could meet you back inside."

"I need to post the 'For Sale' sign out front anyway. You folks take your time."

Weston nodded his appreciation and headed for the gate. Myla ran ahead with her arms outstretched, looking like an actress from an MGM movie. Compelled by the scenery and driven downhill by the sloping riverbank, he abandoned his more critical inspection and followed her. A breeze traced the river's path, and the whole scene took on a dream-like quality.

By the time he arrived at the water's edge, Myla had bent over some tiny burrow, toeing it to test for occupancy. "So, about this house—I need you to tell me exactly what you think. Did you see anything of major concern? I found it sound and well-accommodating, but will balance my positive assessment with any detrimental observations you might have." He waited for her dallying to end so she could respond, but it seemed to have no end. "Myla, please. Don't make me call you darling again, just to get a rise out of you."

She swirled around so quickly, she came right out of her shoes. In less than half a dozen tip-toed steps, she came right up to him. Her chest heaved as her sparkling eyes searched his face. "It's fascinating here—and so captivating—to be with you. I'm simply enthralled."

Her mood transfixed him. The magnetism returned, this time with no agent lurking to hold them apart. He took her into his arms to discover her trembling like a willow tree, standing here by the river. With only one way out, he bent and drank in the sight of her as he placed an exploratory kiss onto her lips.

She pressed into it full of vigor and lengthened the embrace. The river flowed by, but time halted in a held breath. She started to pull away, and the exchange broke. A bird called plaintively from a nearby tree as she buried her cheek onto his.

He could feel her heart beating next to his, and then sensed her take another breath. The floral smell of her hair intoxicated him even further. He'd uncovered a sweet treasure out here on the riverbank, and he wanted to sample it again before the rest of the world broke in. He brushed his lips across her ear, and she came to him, allowing the second kiss with more ardor than before. He lifted her off her feet and twirled her, enraptured with the sensation at every point of contact. When he set her down, he moved his hands up the nape of her neck to stroke her hair.

She looked up at him, tears welling in her eyes. "Weston, I—"

He caressed her hair, moved by its softness. "Dear, sweet Myla—I'm falling in love with you." Her tears began to flow, so he tried to erase them with his thumbs. When he planted a tender kiss on her forehead, the trembling turned into an earthquake.

"I don't trust myself," she replied with a sob. In a split second, she tore away, grabbed her shoes, and ran up the lawn.

The ache of being left alone traveled up his frame as secondary punishment. He stared at his hands as though they had betrayed him. Or had it been his words of confessed love? A man doesn't kiss a woman like that and leave her to wonder about his intentions. He plodded up the bank and headed for the gate. When the real estate agent waved from the kitchen door, his concerns shifted to the matter at hand. *Should I make an offer on the house?* He wiped a hand across his chin and let out a groan. No one heard except the handy shed.

Chapter 10

Blessed by the church service, Myla planned to be nothing short of the perfect co-hostess. She had the cinnamon rolls cooling under the kitchen window, and the cheese-topped macaroni required ten more minutes to finish baking. She tugged at the belt of her favorite dress, a slim navy and white shift with red piping on the tab pockets. Her mother had mentioned several times that their out-of-town guest was a war veteran, including their morning prayer over toast and coffee. She'd even hung the American flag before departing for church.

Myla caught a glimpse of her reflection in a silver tray her mother kept propped on the buffet. Later, it would hold her cinnamon rolls, but for now it only gave a report on how well her chignon had held in place. She fought the first impression that it made her appear bookish. With a little extra facial expression thrown in, perhaps it could lend a different nuance. She practiced a smile and gave the dining room a cursory review.

The oven door squeaked closed, and something heavy banged on the stovetop. "Myla, can you come hand me that platter for the meat?"

"Coming, Mother. It looks like everything is right on schedule." She came back into the kitchen and retrieved the heavy-set platter. After she placed it beside the roasting pan, she reached for an apron and hastily tied it in place.

"Would you snip this string for me? I'd like to cut the pork roast before transferring it to the platter."

"Let me get the paring knife. I meant to tell you how nice you looked for church today, Mother. You're even wearing make-up."

"My face gets blotchy from gardening at times. I transplanted some volunteer tomato plants yesterday. They always seem to rash me out."

"Are you certain it doesn't have anything to do with company coming for dinner?"

"Saints alive, Myla. Courting is for young women like yourself. I'm just trying to keep from looking too outdated before my fifties set in."

She cut the string binding up the roast and handed her mother the knife. "At any rate, you look nice—and the food smells wonderful, both of which are sure to please." She turned to the sink and threw several utensils into a dishpan of soapy water. "You should show off your garden. Maybe Weston's landlord might catch the bug from your example."

"Vanity is a sin, like pride. But if someone expresses an interest, I'll be happy to entertain the expedition. Throw this string in the trash, will you? I may smell the top of that macaroni getting too toasted." She scooted to the side to free up the oven door.

Myla hurriedly tossed the greasy string into the trashcan and buried her palms into oven mitts. When she lowered the door, she drew the casserole dish out and surveyed the dish for doneness. "Please turn off the oven, Mother. I'll leave this on the vent to keep some heat on it, but it's ready. Maybe I should set the bowl of salad on the table."

"Yes, please do. Go ahead with the buttermilk dressing, too. I need to run to the back and tidy up my hair before the guests arrive. Tent the roast with foil in the meantime, in case they run late." She swept from the room in a whirlwind.

"So, it does have something to do with the company coming," she muttered as she reached for the pantry door. She found the foil under the wax paper and drew it out. Tearing off a sheet, her thoughts drifted to Weston. They'd never been together two consecutive days, so this would be interesting. She smiled as she tucked the foil along the rim of the platter.

Their visit to the house for sale had ended a bit unbalanced—attached and then detached—but he had expressed his feelings, and that made the moment by the river more than memorable. A satisfied coziness worked its way up her middle. The salad popped to mind. She hurried to the refrigerator and slid it from the shelf.

Once she'd delivered it to the dining table, she laid a trivet for the hot casserole dish.

She heard her mother's voice in the background, but needed to make quick work of adding the dressing to the table. She smiled when she saw that an old serving piece had been brought out of storage. The curvy gravy boat had seemed like a genie's lamp to an overly-imaginative little girl once upon a time ago. She ran a finger up its pouring spout as she walked it to the table. When she stepped into the dining room, there stood Weston, his gaze absorbing her domesticity in rapt silence. She felt the heat of a blush work up her neck before she could get the dressing into place.

Her mother soon broke the spell. "Myla, please come into the living room to meet our company."

She dipped her chin and walked around the table's length toward the front room.

"Here, let me make you perfect," Weston whispered. As she passed him, he tugged at the apron ties and dislodged her protective covering.

She gave him a tiny hum and followed the laughter coming from the foyer.

"Mr. Godfrey, this is my daughter, Myla," Effie said. She reached for her arm and drew her close to her side.

"Call me Art, and this is my nephew Reginald Brewster, my kid sister's son." He patted the man on the back and almost knocked him off balance.

"Just plain Reggie. Pleased to meet you, Myla. Weston had more than a few nice things to say on your behalf on the way over. And Mrs. Templeton, let me say what a lovely home you have here. Thank you for inviting us for dinner today. After yesterday's golf fiasco, we needed something to look forward to, believe you me." His eyes danced with merriment as he looked between his golf partner and his hostess.

Effie knit her hands together in a ball. "It's our pleasure, Reggie. I wanted to thank you for your service in the war."

Weston rejoined the group. "Looks like Myla's being quite the patriot today. Should we salute you as hostess?" He shot a teasing look in her direction while she feigned aversion by hiding behind her mother.

"Just follow orders young man, and you should make out all right," Mr. Godfrey quipped. "I did appreciate the American flag flying in the breeze as we drove up."

Reggie gave a bit of a bow, leaning on his cane. "As did I, ma'am. Patriotism has its place. After all, we fought halfway around the world to keep that flag flying."

Myla patted her mother's shoulder and felt the woman quaking behind her plastered-on smile. When Effie swiped the corner of her eye, Myla decided to take charge. "Let's all go into the dining room, shall we? The roast is ready to be served."

"This is when I say, 'aye-aye, captain,' isn't it?" Weston gestured at his landlord and the old man chuckled.

Effie blinked to collect herself and headed straight into the kitchen.

"Right this way, then. I'll show you to your seats." Myla led and waited for Mr. Godfrey opposite the buffet. "Reggie, you're there by mother's chair on the end. Mr. Godfrey, you're beside Reggie."

"What about me?" Weston stepped up beside her and ran his finger along the lapel of his Sunday suit.

"First, you'd better give me that jacket. I'll hang it on the hall tree and spare it the cheese sauce from the macaroni." Myla remembered to make her eyes more expressive and waggled one brow as a bonus.

He gave her a sheepish look and shrugged out of the coat. He handed it to her, but not without mouthing a message of thanks meant just for her.

A cozy flutter accompanied her to the hall tree. She'd run away from him only yesterday, yet he seemed to have returned for more fond attention. She hastened to the kitchen and donned the oven mitts to deliver the casserole dish to the table. Effie set the meat platter in front of the veteran, so she brought the macaroni around to Weston's place setting.

"You're spoiling me—but keep it up. I could eat that whole dish by myself." He gave her a sly look and fingered his fork like he'd make good on the threat. Instead, he stood and pulled her chair out for her.

"I'd hate to treat you like a yearling in front of the women, but you'll eat all of that macaroni and cheese over my dead body," Art

Godfrey said.

Reggie chuckled and rose to help Effie settle into her chair. "Please, allow me to say grace for this wonderful meal." When Effie nodded, he bowed and closed his eyes. "Dear Father, we thank you for the blessing of Sunday dinner, and all the American traditions that go with it. May the meal nourish our bodies, and may you continue to bless our nation, amen."

Myla didn't miss the look of pleasant surprise on her mother's face when she opened her eyes. Reggie gave her a private smile that soon caused her to blush.

"God bless America." Weston snapped off a salute that became a broad reach for the macaroni casserole.

Myla started the salad bowl around, her gaze settling on the genie gravy boat. Not that she needed to make a wish, but her heart had filled with a certain sentiment, one that God would have to grant. She claimed the verse to be the apple of his eye, right from patriotic Wichita.

~

Midafternoon in the Templeton backyard held all the idyllic charm late May could bolster. Weston leaned back on the porch glider and admired its two-tone aqua and white paint job. He closed his eyes as a robin sang a fluted warble from the tree casting its shade around them. The faint banter of gardening questions being asked and answered echoed up from deeper in the yard. If Myla didn't return soon, he might have to follow Mr. Godfrey in a post-lunch nap.

A second robin began to sing from the fence line, and it seemed the entire world possessed companionship except for him. Work needled into his thoughts. He sighed at starting the week with a solid day of radiography. He knew of no other way to detect flaws in that tail panel except to expose it to x-ray inspection down its full length. A tedious approach, but sometimes the situation warranted a closer look.

On the other hand, Myla served as pleasant distraction without further need of inspection. He'd known from the first time he'd looked into those blue eyes that something arresting lurked beneath. He sensed something building between them, especially after yesterday's kisses by the river. They needed to talk about the aftermath and what had compelled her to run away. More pressing, he needed to tell her about the house and pretend the two— kiss-and-tell and the show-and-sell—were independent events. God help him if they were. He'd asked for that discernment in repeated prayers ever since.

A door slammed and soft footsteps crossed the deck. "Hey, there you are. Are you giving my redbud tree a defect check?" Myla laughed and the glider swayed with her entry.

He reached out a hand for her without opening his eyes. "All I know is that it's good for shade. You caught me two yards short of a nap." Something silky tickled his palm and he reached further to find her. A plane flew by on the far horizon with the sound of a pesky fly.

"I thought I might like to give you this."

The silky wisp began to tighten around his thumb. Curious, he opened his eyes to see her hair ribbon from the day before being tied in a bow. He held his hand up and let the ends trail in the breeze. "What? Does this mean I'm caught or something?" He glanced from the ribbon in time to see her dimples press into place.

"Well, a woman has to leave a mark of color on a man. You know, like Maid Marion gives Robin Hood her scarf before he clinches the winning shot in the archery contest."

He leaned forward and held his thumb front and center. Maybe this would make the rest of what he had to say come a bit easier. He slid the knot of his tie loose and unfastened the top button of his dress shirt. With his thumb tied up, none of that came easy, but he wasn't about to be shed of her ribbon. "Okay, Maid Marion. Since I've had a head start on relaxation out here, you sit back, and let me talk to you a few minutes. Do you think you can oblige me that?"

She hummed and melted onto the back of the glider. Her hand dangled off his shoulder, but remained within reach. Her go-ahead nod came with a pleasant smile, as if nothing would suit her better.

"Good. I'll state my case then. You may think very little could have transpired over the last twelve hours, since you just spent the day with me yesterday—but that's not true. In fact, one might say a great deal of water has passed under the bridge since then. Please let me back up a little. Before Kansas, life was all about the business of obtaining my education. Seven years of scholastic rigor in the field of engineering can be a hapless plight, even for the diligently sought after bestowment of a PhD.”

Myla snapped her fingers to stop him. “You’re a learned man—one of great aptitude. Such aspiration must come at a cost—though seven years could be considered a steep one.”

“Thank you for being kind enough to say so. At the time, university life proved to be enough. But since my arrival in Wichita, I seem perched on the verge of my next step. Night after night cooped up on Mr. Godfrey’s back porch leaves me yearning for something more.”

“Hence, your need for the house comes due. It makes total sense, Weston. You don’t have to justify your quest for real estate to me. You have a steady job with more-than-adequate income and are set to make a good investment, one that builds equity over time.” Her fingertips scratched at the top of his shoulder as though to cajole him into her line of reasoning.

“If I’d have known you would be this easy to talk to, I wouldn’t have lost so much sleep last night.” He grabbed her trespassing fingertips with his hand, the one with the captured thumb. When her slender fingers laced through his, he placed her palm on his chest and leaned toward her. “I called the agent and put an offer on the cottage by the river.”

Myla’s eyes grew wide. Next, she tried to draw away, but couldn’t.

“I added a note to the previous owner, one that insured that I would pick up where he left off with the meticulous care of the house, the yard, and the garden. Plus, I thanked him for including the little shed out back, since I don’t own a yard tool to my name. But, I want it—every aspect of it—for the rest of me that’s not busy being an engineer. My current lifestyle is so lopsided it hurts, Myla. Believe me, there has to be something more than my career.”

Her chest rose and fell with several tightly-drawn breaths. She looked at him and dropped her gaze. “What are you asking God for, Weston?” she whispered. Her hand fell slack in his.

Torn by what to admit and what to withhold, he pressed his eyes closed. At such close range, an angel would have to drop from heaven to shield his intentions now. A breeze blew and the trailing ribbon tickled his wrist, an overdue distraction. He brought her hand up to his lips and kissed her fingers. “Everything,” he replied.

"I want every blessing God has intended for me. I want your company, Myla, but I don't want you tearing out of my arms because of my pursuit of it. I'll apologize for the kiss if you want me to, the second one more than the first—if one act can carry more guilt than the other."

She shifted on the glider, making it sway with the motion. "No, Weston. No guilt and no apology. I wanted the affection—but wasn't ready for how you made me feel. Perhaps we could show some restraint—to honor God and each other."

Her admission brought a watershed of relief with it. "Absolutely. Restraint would be in order. So, I might kiss you once, but not twice, on any given date." The thought of such a peaceable solution began to pour through him like a glass of cool water. Quantification he could do. Engineers excelled at numbers.

Her brow furrowed. "Date? Will there be dates?"

"Of course, there will be dates. A man doesn't allow himself to get tied by such a constraint as this satiny yellow ribbon and not want to date. Maid Marion has left her color mark, has she not?" He set her fingers free.

She touched his jawline in a soothing stroke. "I would like to say yes to that next date, as soon as you ask, of course."

He should have taken her in his arms right there, notwithstanding her mother's presence on the garden pea row, only a stone's throw away. Yet, she wanted restraint, and he would accommodate her request. It was the Christian thing to do. He lowered his chin as her fingers departed. "If God allows me the house—I think we should celebrate that good news."

Myla laughed and clasped her hands under her chin. "That's perfect! Call as soon as you know, and we'll plan to celebrate the success of your real estate transaction. I'll give you carte blanche to call anytime at all." She held out her empty palm, an open offer.

"Oh, I'll take it all right. That and a cinnamon roll." He lunged for her to take possession.

She squealed, allowing the hug before popping to her feet. "A cinnamon roll I can handle. Not to break our newly forged rule, but how about two?" She dangled her hand back for him and stepped toward the kitchen door.

"Yes, two—but wrap one to go. I'm restraining myself, remember?" He swung his hand into hers and soon beat her to the door. He opened it and gestured her in, and then gave her a hungry glance. He'd take the cinnamon roll, the river cottage, and the carte blanche, all rolled up into one—with a blue-eyed woman sealing the package. It smelled, tasted, and looked like a dream, even if he mainly had permission to kiss her fingers.

~

Duncan Reed stormed into the lab, in his hand a clutter of wrenches. "I don't know if I can live like this for another month." It sounded like his throat contained the Sahara Desert.

Weston pushed back from the testing table. He recognized a troubled man when he saw one. "Please—have a seat. You didn't find all of those this morning, did you?"

"Ha! These came from Hangar A alone. I never made it anywhere else, but saw four more items left on the shop floor on my way in here." He sat with a harrumph and held the tools out as if they'd been exposed to radiation.

"Let me take those off your hands." He reached for the misplaced FOD candidates and gave them his passing scrutiny. One wrench seemed particularly out of place. "Hey, look at this one—my father owned that line. Why, these haven't been manufactured in years." He handed it back to the safety manager and tapped at its label embossed on the handle.

Duncan leaned forward in the chair. "Why did I find it on the assembly floor then? Most of our tools are state-of-the-art."

"Good question. Someone might be bringing tools in from home to use, but that piece wouldn't be considered superior. For one thing, it weighs a ton." Weston turned and placed the rest of the violators on the lab table. All appeared dulled by considerable wear.

"Something seems off here, but why would anyone deliberately leave behind a bunch of wrenches? It's like we're being toyed with. I have greater concerns than tool pick-up duty. I hate to make an end-of-day cleanup mandatory, but that looks like where we're headed."

"Skip Sellers reports that his men have been compliant with the shop floor de-cluttering effort, at least for the most part. Why would the mechanics in Hangar A have such a different mindset? I'll have to give that some thought." He held out a hand, and Duncan plopped the antique tool into it. Weston's suppositions traveled down several lanes of development, all nefarious and knot-tying for his stomach.

His guest swiped hand over his face. "Somebody's planting these tools, right under our noses. We need more surveillance and heightened security, but it won't be done by me. I'm stacking worry on top of worry here lately. Honest to God, I've reached my limit." A sigh chased his statement.

Weston leaned back in his chair with the knowledge they had both arrived at the same conclusion—the tools were not happenstance. Someone had been in over the weekend and left the contraband right where they least needed it—Hangar A near the XT-37 prototype. The truth thundered across his ears as if RCA's Nipper had suddenly gone tone-deaf. When a ringing followed it, he knew his blood pressure had elevated. "Well, you mentioned a month's time earlier. Is there some relief coming our way after that?"

Duncan ran his fingers through his hair and sat straight up. "Relief? Not unless you call the labor of childbirth relief, which it isn't in the least. That comment was a cloaked commiseration. I'm sorry, I should have told you upfront. We've had a complication with the pregnancy. I'm out of my mind with worry."

"Not the baby, I hope and pray."

"No, the baby's fine. The doctor used an ultrasound device to check on it—right there inside her womb. Something called a plug dropped out too early. Now, Lorna Rae will have to stay in bed the last four weeks. Thank goodness our friend Vivian can get little Trudy to the bus stop and back each school day."

Weston sensed the need for a rescue of sorts. "See, you can depend on your friends to rally around when you need them most. Maybe God is guiding you down a path that leads to trusting him more. Count on me to pray for the baby's well-being through it all."

Duncan rose to his full height, his face chiseled in stone. "I can't lose Lorna Rae—not after all she's become to me. If you really want to answer a prayer, you'll discover how to get us out of this FOD mess. I'll take whoever is leaving these tools out and hang him on the bent propeller that sent my consecutive safe-day record shattering on the shop floor."

"Then hang him high, Mr. Reed, as I'm right on his heels." He stood and offered his hand as an assurance.

The safety manager shook it with a slight hesitation. When he looked up, he seemed vulnerable—as though the FOD had already struck its mark and precipitated some collateral damage. He gathered the tools and made his way to the door with a lanky stride. "I may have to take leave from work if Lorna Rae needs me."

"No question. I'll be here, guaranteed. Let's plan for me to accompany you on the morning inspection round, just to witness how you conduct the floor sweep."

"Next week. Count on it." He hefted the lab door open and walked out, his knuckles turned white gripping the problematic tools.

Weston paced toward his desk, potential solutions popping into mind, each with subsequent dismissal. His mind wandered to Lorna Rae's predicament. He couldn't picture the affable woman rendered to bed rest for an entire month. Duncan's mention of ultrasound came back into focus, and the analytical side of his brain ran with it. An image from his latest industrial radiography journal flashed to mind. He tore open the top drawer and produced the magazine. In seconds, he found the advertisement. A man stood with a strap around his neck that cradled a portable gage which allowed him to test the pipe right in place.

"Yes, I think I've got it. Glory be, I can sweep those Continental-Teledyne jet engines with this baby and not take out the first fan blade. Let someone dare to try something now."

With his brain working a mile a minute, his fingers fumbled with a simple pair of scissors to clip out the order form. Some hero he made, crashing onto the aviation scene like the Lone Ranger with the tail wag of Rin Tin Tin. He glanced over at the section of the 195 he'd been inspecting and recognized the connection. "When did radiography become the cure-all of the moment?" he muttered. Focused on the remedy, he strode out the door heading for the procurement office with his latest request, resolute it represented one they could not deny.

Chapter 11

Though hot, Myla had sincere gratitude for the gardening gloves that saved her fingertips from direct exposure to the loose dirt her mother had scrounged up with her hoe. Such mindless work allowed her to daydream as she plucked another errant chickweed plant from the carrot row. All her daydreams seemed to float toward the same scene where she stood by the river in a desirable man's arms. The figure Weston cut in his Sunday suit at dinner had been memorable also. She had no regrets for planting the surprise kiss on his lips while pretending to feed him the cinnamon roll during a private moment in the kitchen that afternoon.

When he'd tried to kiss her goodbye at the curb, she'd held up one finger to remind him of their deal. Restraint now had a cat-and-mouse endearment to it, one that might work to her advantage on occasion. How hard could it be to catch an analytical man off-guard? She snickered at the ploy and tossed the latest weed into her cull pile.

A shadow soon blocked the lowering sun. "I had better start the watering round, or we'll be late for prayer meeting this evening." Effie plopped her gloves on the nearby bench and turned toward the spigot off the garage.

"I'm almost done here anyway." Myla shoved a thumb under a small rosette and plucked the unwanted plant from its footing. She stood, collected the weed pile, and headed for the trashcan. When the first spray of water exited the hose, it arched into a rainbow under the glinting sun. Too bad the okra row didn't enjoy the prismatic show, though it looked like the water would be well received.

Her mother whistled an old show tune and paused as she walked by.

"Glad to hear you're so lighthearted, Mother. It wouldn't have anything to do with that nice Mr. Brewster, would it?" She gave her mother a playful look over her sunglasses and tossed the pile of weeds into the can.

Effie waggled the garden hose, and the rainbow seemed to dance. "Did you know he was right there in the heat of the attack on Pearl Harbor? Reggie was stationed at Hickam Air Field at the time. They awarded him a medal for downing two Japanese airplanes amid the bombing mayhem. Thank God someone could fight back."

"Yes. Plus, I thank God some of the men walked away that day and lived to tell about it. He seems like a nice man. Weston told me he's headed to Independence to save the regional office over there. He's a whiz at managerial stuff."

"Well, I find that much to his credit. He takes good care of his Uncle Art, too." The water fell onto the tomato plants next, one stalk at a time.

"Guess he could always come back on the weekends to visit Mr. Godfrey, say if he had another reason to make the trip worthwhile." She collected the hoe and soon found her mother's gloves. Maybe it wasn't fair to hint of romance, if she wasn't interested.

Effie pulled at the hose. "I don't know about that."

A sharp whistle sounded from the side of the house. "Hey, anybody home back here?" Weston appeared over the hedge, his arms crisscrossing in the air.

Myla's heart leapt into her throat. "Hello, there. We're just finishing up the garden work. Come on back." She clapped the dirt loose from her hands and adjusted her headband to trap some wayward strands of hair. When Effie glanced her way, she gave her a quick wink. Soon, a second figure passed through the gate's arch, doubling their company. She stepped back to shut off the water, prompting her mother to look up.

Reggie Brewster gave them a wave.

Weston trotted down the garden path, his back straight and his shoulders square. He looked like he could conquer the world. A mile-wide grin soon broke out as though to hint that he already had.

Myla tried to quell her pleasure. "To what do we owe this midweek invasion?"

Her mother walked up beside her and extended her hand to Mr. Brewster. It dripped water, so she quickly dried it on her skirt.

He accepted her greeting with a smile. "Good day, Effie. Hello, Myla. I'm just a tag-along today. When this young rooster crowed about heading over here, I threw myself in the Catalina to come along."

Weston drew a long breath. "I had to come tell you as soon as I knew."

Effie patted the man's hand without releasing it. "Thank you, Reggie. I'm pleased that you did. It's so good to see you again."

Weston tugged on her elbow to shift closer. "Myla, I thought you might like to hear."

Reggie leaned into the huddle and gave a slow wink. "I think it's time to celebrate."

Myla could hardly separate the two men to decipher any sensible meaning from either one. She stared up at Weston and knit her brow. "Celebrate what?"

"They accepted my offer on the cottage by the river," he replied with haste. "It's going to be mine within a month's time. I couldn't wait to share the news with you."

She attempted to trap her gasp with her hands and earned a taste of the garden's dirt. Though spitting wasn't too ladylike, at least she deflected it away from the visitors.

Reggie laughed with a deep baritone resonance. "It looks like she's spitting happy for you, Weston. Maybe you should sweeten the pot with the offer for those milkshakes now."

"Milkshakes?" Effie asked. She glanced from one man to the other.

Weston dropped his hand from Myla's elbow to her waist. He gave her a look of pure delight. "Would you come celebrate the acceptance of my offer with me at Dairy Delight? We could raise a frosty glass to God's good favor."

She mulled it over for a second and shook her head to play hard to get. "I'd have to click my chocolate dip-top to whatever you order, as a milkshake won't suffice for me this evening." She allowed a tight smile to curl her lips and flashed him a mischievous look through her lashes.

He growled like a bear and swept her into his grip. He tossed her over one shoulder and made an about-face up the path.

Between bursts of laughter, Myla craned up to see her mother take Reggie's elbow and follow them toward the house, something she never thought she would see. "Will wonders never cease?"

"I sure hope not," Weston replied. When his footsteps pounded the wooden deck, he lowered her to the back door.

"Give me a minute to freshen up. Be right back." She held up one finger and pursed her lips over the top of it.

"I can hardly wait," he replied. "Meet us out front by the car."

Myla let the screen door slam behind her as she rushed to her room to change her blouse into something a bit more feminine and a lot less sweaty. Weston Durand had acquired a house—and could scarcely wait to tell *her* about it, much less celebrate it. Her heart had already begun the applause, but she'd save the encore until after the dip-top, a yummy plan.

~

His sister wiped the kitchen counter a second time and gave him a weighted glance. Not even the box fan made a difference with the heat tonight as the end of May slammed smack into summer. He raised the soda bottle to his lips and wished it was something stronger.

She threw the dish rag into the soapy water and it splashed halfway to the table. "Did you hear me? I said next week marks the seventh year of losing Momma. It seems a lot longer than that, doesn't it?"

"When the years drag on through the land of making due, it can seem longer. Maybe I can celebrate by reaching my bonus quota this month. We could use the commission money to buy something for her grave." He shoved his legs straight under the table and stretched. The ride up to Hesston had about toasted him in the heat. At least sales were good at the farm implement manufacturer. He liked being in the bonus zone. It motivated him, for sure.

"Can't we throw in an act of rebellion? Plastic flowers seem kind of tame." She up-ended the basin and a cascade of greasy dishwater raced down the drain.

"Want to make another cut in the engine cover? You could shape it like a seven and make it our little jab back at the company."

"Can I toss a tool back there this time? They'd never find it until…well, you know."

"Why, Elizabeth Jean. You sneaky little saboteur, you. I'm aiming for the fourth of July for the big bang, so hold off on the accidental metal deposit for now. Just make the cut, okay?" He stood and gave her a sympathetic pat on the shoulder as he passed by on the way to his room. "I've got a hot date with the lady pilot this weekend, so things are falling into place."

"Accent on the falling—and I can hardly wait." She plopped the dish rag on the dinette table and tried to wipe the glitter out of the Formica finish.

"You know, you should try to date someone. How about one of those guys you're always tossing snack crackers to at the plant?"

"I guess it wouldn't hurt to drop a few hints for payback. A dinner out would be nice." She tossed the rag over the faucet and dried her hands on the tea towel.

"See. Now you're talking. You have two days before the weekend starts. You'll be over there on Friday, right?"

"Like clockwork. Yeah, let me see what I can do."

He walked into the back hall thinking about his date with the lush-lipped pilot. He hoped she was the burger-and-onion-rings type, so he could save his commission for what he really wanted. Man, he truly needed that bonus. He'd have to look for someone working a specialty area and try to talk up the possibility of some new tools. With the development of those fancy jet engines, that shouldn't be too hard.

~

Weston allowed the Pontiac to creep toward the curb. "That's my cottage, the one with the shed dormers over the front porch."

"Say, what a nice location," Reggie replied.

Weston caught his gaze in the rearview mirror and gave him an appreciative nod.

Myla looked over the seat. "Mother, you should see the backyard. It's my favorite feature. There's a garden plot all lined out and everything."

"Oh? Do you think I could see it?" Effie asked. "I mean, would it be trespassing?"

"Let's risk it, shall we?" Weston replied. He slid the gearshift into park and killed the ignition. Before he could play the part of the perfect gentleman, Myla had thrown her door open and exited. He lost her in the lengthening shadows under the sycamore.

"Here's the gate on this side." Myla swept around the west end of the house and disappeared behind the foundation plantings.

"Someone's excited for the exploration," Effie said.

Reggie came around the back bumper and opened the door for her with a smile. "Maybe I'm getting a glimpse of what she looked like as a girl." He pointed at the gate with his cane.

"That's right," Effie replied with a laugh. "Always full of energy."

Weston stopped along the front sidewalk. "I'd better catch up to her. In case she runs into a hostile fox squirrel or something." He broke into a run and shot through the gate only to find her kneeling by the back stoop. "Hey, did you lose something?"

She rose with the sweetest smile on her face. "No, I found something, or at least the remains of something—this herb garden. These dark leaves are mint." She held up a tiny leaf toward him.

"Good discovery. I bet I'll be surprised like that at every turn, especially as each different season rolls around." He rotated his gaze around the expansive backyard as the scent of mint wafted over from the steps. When he moved closer to her, he heard her giggle.

"This is so unbelievable—that this will be yours, I mean. I can hardly get over it." She shook her head, which sent her wavy hair in accentuated motion.

Reggie cleared his throat as he brought Effie toward them. "What? No mad squirrel back here? And I had braced myself for a skirmish." He waggled his cane as a threat.

"No, just this sweet herb garden by the back steps," Myla replied. She gave the leaf to Effie, who sniffed it right away. "Come over here, Mother. Take a look at the garden plot and tell me what you think of its potential." She tugged her away from Reggie, and the two women walked off, arm-in-arm.

"So, did you take out a fifteen or a thirty-year mortgage on this?" Reggie hitched his thumb toward the back door.

"Thirty. That's quite a commitment, right?" Weston dug at his knit collar and didn't get much relief for the lump in his throat.

"Sobering, yet doable. The way this community is committed to aviation, I don't see your job going away anytime soon. There's something to be said for that kind of stability. A man can raise a family in the midst of it." Reggie pushed his thick curly hair over the top of his ear. "Unfortunately, insurance doesn't allow that kind of putting down roots. I've had to take the rambling as it came, but I've always met the nicest people along the way."

"Wichita is friendly like that. I'm glad you've got your uncle here, so you have a reason to come visit." Weston glanced over at the women as they navigated the rim of the garden area.

"Yeah, to see Art and maybe Effie, too. She's agreed to escort me around the Wichita Gardens on Friday. I have to ship out Sunday to make the Monday morning meeting in Independence."

"But it's Memorial Day. Won't they be closed on Monday?" He stepped toward the garden, and the war veteran soon followed.

"Sakes alive. You've just bought me one more day in Wichita, Weston. That might be just what the doctor ordered. My, won't Art be tickled?" He laughed as Myla rushed up.

"Mother has a packet of bush beans tucked in her pocket from our gardening work. Let's get them planted and give the garden a running start. Could we?" She gave him a sideways glance that begged for immediate approval.

"I guess we could—"

"Let's run to the shed and get a shovel. Mother's lining off the row straight as an arrow." She tugged at his arm and smiled.

Reggie motioned with his cane. "I'll help Effie keep her bearings linear, captain. You go conquer the shed, and get the little lady what she wants."

Weston looked at Myla and lowered his brow. Unable to stave off her infectious enthusiasm, he allowed her to pull him along. Her sheer scarf caught his fancy, swirled with pinks and yellows. He might have to take that thing off and enjoy the bareness of her slender neck. The shed afforded a bit of privacy where he could launch his attack. She wouldn't even see it coming.

"Come on, slowpoke." She threw the latch and let the door squeak open. "Oh, there's the shovel—up on the rack."

"Help me out by getting that hard rake in the corner, will you?" He reached for the shovel and angled out of the doorway.

"Anything else?" Myla turned with the rake, her eyes dancing with excitement.

"Yes. I need a flag to mark this territory as mine—so I'm choosing your scarf. Do you mind?" He readied his fingers as she shook her head. He made slow work of the untie job, his gaze locked on hers. He slid the scarf off her neck and looped it around the shovel handle. "So lovely, my Maid Marion."

"Are you going to make your shot, dear Robin Hood?" she whispered.

With no need for discussion, he bent and captured her lips in a dark corner of the musty shed, earthy and sensual all at the same time. His hand clamped over the scarf, the flag marking his territory. He merely needed to claim it. He would, once his rationed embrace wore off. Planting beans had been a marvelous idea, the beginning of a bountiful victory garden.

Chapter 12

With a rare day up in the Interiors office, Myla settled in around the cut-outs for the Western Durango custom order and began to fit the seat segments together. The hand-punched throttle cover lay on a counter nearby, her first precision effort of the day. Not yet eleven o'clock, Friday seemed interminable in length. She could attribute that to a lack of plans for the holiday weekend, though Weston had hinted toward a possible outing. Maybe not knowing had lent the morning a sense of imbalance. She shrugged off the feeling and focused on her task.

When she decided to baste the seam to ease the stiffer woven leather into compliance, she shoved back from the table and walked toward the sewing room. Drawn to the window over the supply nook, she searched through a strewn mess to locate the curved needle she needed. Outside, the weather looked abysmal, with dark gray clouds hovered over the facility. When she found the card of graduated needles, the wind buckled against the building and rattled the window pane. She returned to the work station, her sense of imbalance shifting to general unease.

Though the weather had brought soaking showers in late April, May had been tame for a Midwest spring. Every day seemed fair because she was falling in love, and her affections vaulted through a cloudless sky. She thought of Weston and wondered what airplane part he might be crouched over inspecting in his lab. She guided the basting thread through the eye of the needle and left a long tail dangling behind it. The second she touched the leather with the needle tip, the window pane clattered in protest of the wind.

Someone approached her from behind. "This storm's going to be a whopper," Susie said. She rolled her shoulders to limber up from her morning bent over the sewing machine.

"Did you see the forecast? I wonder if we'll get much rain."

"Yeah, the weatherman said it might get *bumpy* today. I don't think he uses that phrase too often."

"We just staked the tomato plants yesterday. That cost me two pairs of old nylons."

"Your garden should be fine. It's the trees I worry about. There's a reason the prairie is treeless, after all." Susie wrung her hands in a knot and gave a glance out the window. "Looks like the men are closing up Hangar A, Miss Templeton. Guess it's for the best to protect the expensive aircraft inside."

"Oh? They haven't had to do that yet this year. It must be getting worse out there." She dropped the needle and pushed back from the table. "Let me take another look." She returned to the supply nook and planted her nose against the window pane. An eerie green hue had filtered into the darkening gray, a color that typically meant wind gusts. The second door to Hangar A pinched the opening to a small gap that soon filled with men escaping the building. A tiny pellet struck the glass, and she jerked back in instinctive response. "Uh-oh. Here comes the hail."

"My mother taught us not to trust a storm bearing a curtain of hail." Susie's voice dropped low as she spoke the passed-along portend.

Myla turned and put her hands on the young woman's shoulders to offer some reassurance. "What do you say we try to get as much done before lunch as possible? Then, if the storm breaks over the facility, we'll toss in the towel and hunker as needed. Is that a deal?"

Susie nodded as the pitter-pat of pea-sized hail pelted the window pane.

"Okay. Tell the others to stay away from the windows in the meantime, just in case."

"I will, Miss Templeton. We only have an hour, anyway." She walked back to the sewing room, her hands still knotted at her stomach.

Myla exhaled and took her seat. The needle seemed cold to the touch when she picked it up. She selected a starting point and pushed the tip into the thick leather. With a bit of pressure, she punched through the thickness and made her first pass. To tie the complementary side piece to the woven leather, she plunged the needle tip into the supple, smooth leather.

A piercing tone sounded from the far end of the building, followed by a mild exclamation from someone in the sewing room. Seconds passed. The tone faded but then grew louder again. Recognizing the tornado siren, Myla stood, the skin on her neck taut to the point of discomfort. "Ladies, let's head downstairs. Everybody, file out of the office. You know the drill. When the siren blows, we go."

The first worker appeared, and she motioned toward the door. Two more clustered together, their hands clasped in commiseration. Susie came last, her knuckles pressed under her chin. "We didn't make it to lunch, did we Miss Templeton?"

Myla put an arm around her shoulders and flipped off the light as they exited the room. "No, we didn't quite make lunch, but that's okay. This is just a precaution, that's all." A line had already formed at the top of the stairs, an unavoidable bottleneck in the evacuation plan.

Susie looked at her with fear in her eyes. "I feel the urge to pray."

"Yes, but pray with your eyes open, so we can keep moving, okay?" She gave her shoulders a shake and soon found the back of the line. "Remember folks. Use both sides of the stairwell, as all roads lead down to the storm shelter right now. Pass the word along, will you?" A wide-eyed man from accounting accepted the mission and flashed the okay sign. He shouldered between two lines of employees and shouted through the doorway.

Progress soon improved. Myla locked elbows with Susie to keep the exodus advancing. As they rounded the landing, Weston popped into mind. "Lord, keep us all safe right now, even the men who closed the hangar doors. Please don't let anyone be out on the runway in this, precious Lord. We don't need to lose a life—or a plane."

"Amen," Susie whispered, her gaze riveted on the person in front of her.

At last they entered the lower room, a mechanical basement filled with pipes and heating ductwork. Progress had to assume single file through the first section, so Myla slipped her hand into Susie's to pull her along. Soon, the room opened up to larger caverns of space between the working components of the office building. Laborers filled every nook and cranny.

Men from the assembly shop floor began to arrive wearing their trademark coveralls. One or two made humorous remarks as they filed by, but the atmosphere held a somber tension. Something made the floor rattle above, causing Susie to squeeze her hand until it hurt.

A broad-shouldered man worked into the middle of the main passageway. When he cupped his hands to his mouth, a pit formed in Myla's quivering stomach. She recognized Mr. Reed, the safety manager who kept the daily track record on the blackboard. Poor man, he'd barely gotten back up to a month of consecutive safe days, and now the tornado sirens were mocking his tally. Things didn't look good.

"May I have your attention please?" Reed raised his hands demanding quiet. The babble hushed while the storm rattled against the south wall. "We have the latest news from the National Weather Service. A reliable source called in the presence of a funnel cloud on the ground west of the town of Clearwater. The service predicts it will take a northeast path which directly aligns with the eastern portion of our facility. We'll have to stay put for now and ride this thing out."

"Dear Lord, that's Hangar C where Weston's lab is located," Myla said. "I hope he knew to evacuate."

Susie shrugged her shoulders, her eyes clouded with worry. A late flurry of workers entered, filed past them, and searched for a space to alight. A slender man knelt off Susie's far shoulder and settled in beside them. As he ran a hand through his wet hair, he turned and gave a low whistle.

His presence punched Myla in the midsection. The refugee was Hague Amherst. *Why not Weston, Lord? Where is he?* She moaned and leaned her head back on the concrete wall.

The tool salesman wiped his face with his palms. "Man that was close. I barely made it out of the parking lot. Not to poke fun of Chicken Little, but I do believe the sky is falling."

Myla looked at him over Susie's head. "Is it still hailing?"

"Yeah. What started out as pea-sized had worked up to nickel-sized by the time I ran inside. Had to leave all my tool orders in the trunk and make a dash for it."

Forced to redirect her gaze, the sight of him made her stomach churn anew.

Susie sniffed. "People are more important than things, anyway."

"That's right," Myla added. "We prayed for protection for the labor crew and have to trust God to lend it."

Hague caught his face in his hands again and blew out a breath. "That's a healthy attitude, Myla. It makes me want to ask forgiveness for the impish prank I pulled on you earlier. Given the dire situation we're in, do you think you could offer a jerk like me some forgiveness?"

Susie tried to stop the whimper in her throat as she glanced between the two of them. The southern wall shook again and ductwork rattled overhead. Four more workers shuffled by in single file and kept going down the way. Their coveralls were soaked through and through.

That he'd even aired their private little secret grated against Myla's last nerve. Her chest began to overheat. The prickle soon worked up her neck to her cheeks. She'd pledged to bury that brusque encounter in her memory and not let it resurface, yet here sat the perpetrator, asking for a clean slate. She'd rather give him the business end of a sledgehammer.

Susie crimped her fingers with a squeeze. "Forgiveness would be the Christian thing to do, ma'am." Her eyes pled for them to be reconciled and done with the issue, as if returning her concern to a tornado had any spiritual merit.

"I'm young and sometimes foolish," Hague admitted. "Especially around a woman who's the higher side of good looking." He gave her a crooked smile and then hung his head.

Myla let go of Susie's hand and laced her fingers together. That should keep her from punching the insincere galoot with his feigned flattery. She wouldn't fall for that ploy. The building shook against her back, and her ears popped.

Susie slammed her palms against the sides of her head. Fear rode her expression.

"Pressure's dropping," the salesman said. He squeezed his eyes shut and then gave her a direct look that held a plea.

"Oh, all right. I forgive you for the trespass earlier. At least the tools were high quality."

Hague worked his jaw and buried his tongue in his cheek, seeming to struggle through the moment. He extended the hand of peace across Susie's knees and held his empty palm straight up, begging hers.

Myla knew touching him was wrong, but given the setting and the storm creeping up their entrance drive, there might be more important matters ahead—like survival. She whispered a prayer and slid her hand into his where it found a warm reception.

His grip wrapped around her fingers. "Thank you for restoring my faith in humankind." His tone teased, but his eyes hinted of deeper sincerity.

Distracted by the passing of several more latecomers, Myla allowed the hand-holding to continue a bit longer than comfortable. A man passing by shook his wet hair and sprinkled them. Before she knew it, a pair of lips pressed against her knuckles to seal the absolution.

"I really mean it," Hague whispered. His words hung in the air like a tantalizing lure.

Susie's eyes grew wide, a front row witness to the suggestive transaction. The entire building seemed to quiver as a shadowed figure knelt right in front of her.

"Am I missing something here?" Weston asked as he clutched an armload of bulky equipment. His gaze traveled from Myla's face to the tool salesman and back again. One eyebrow arched as though to demand a reply.

"Not at all. Thank God above you're safe," Myla replied. Embarrassment heated her neck as she sorted through her predicament. Too bad Hague still held her hand in his.

"I'm plum falling apart down here," Susie replied. With that, she rocked forward right into Weston's chest where she buried a sob.

He cradled the young woman in one arm while adjusting his equipment in the other. The unmistakable sound of metal striking metal sounded overhead.

"Direct hit," Reed shouted. "Everybody down on the floor!"

Weston bent forward, his elbow breaking the hand-to-hand connection as he sat Susie back on the concrete and covered them both.

Myla accepted his chivalrous action as the shield of protection she'd been praying for, though she suddenly felt unworthy. With tears burning her eyes, she buried her face into his shoulder. A heavy box settled on her lap, and then his arm swept around her waist to draw her closer. Though it pressed the air from her lungs, she clung to him in tight desperation, unashamed to wipe her tears on his rain-soaked neck.

Weston turned his face toward hers, his breath in her hair. "Keep telling me you love me, Myla," he whispered in her ear, "because I really need to hear it right now,"

She pulled back far enough for him to see the liquid sincerity in her eyes. Despite the awkward situation earlier, she had no doubt to whom her affections belonged. The lights flickered off and on which generated a collective moan across the basement. In seconds they went off for good, and a searching kiss soon slid onto her quaking lips. She gave the exchange her due penitence. Confession was good for the broken soul, and hers felt shattered to pieces.

Susie wept aloud and a pair of arms pulled her away under a murmur of comforting words. At least Hague was good for something. The roaring sound of a train passing whipped by the building as Weston broke off his embrace.

"I thought you'd never get here." Myla pressed her cheek to his and tried to still her racing heart. She withdrew for his reply, but only by inches.

"I'm here now, and that's all that matters." His finger traced the curve of her neck as though to ask if that was enough.

Myla knew of only one answer, and brought it to him on her lips where it exploded in a forbidden second kiss, a deliciously breathless violation that made her forget all about her lowly place as a storm refugee. The sensation of being one with him filtered over her in the dark, a mysterious blend of touch and tangible want. Her stiff-armed resistance now trounced, it left her exposed. Vulnerable in a dark, threatening place, she didn't mean the basement.

Chapter 13

Weston cleared his throat and passed the agendas to his right as Rich Yost took a seat on the QC circle beside Skip Sellers. He nodded at Myla as she joined the group, watching her ready the notebook without any verbal reminder. "Good morning to all. I thought we'd get started today with an ice breaker. Let's try some word association. I'll toss out a word or phrase, and you give me the first answer that pops into your head. This will put our thoughts in motion, and then we can tackle some QC concerns."

"Plus, it will give Ernie Pike a few extra minutes to join us," Skip said. A tease twitched his mustache.

Weston placed a finger along his jawline. "Ready? Here goes the first one—impressive."

"Mickey Mantle's homer," Skip replied.

"Detroit Lions," Rick Yost added.

"How about Rosemary Clooney?" Ted Halyard asked. He waggled his brow to accentuate the connection.

Myla crossed her ankles. "Sunset over the lake."

Weston fought back a little smile on that response, as he had shared that scene with her during their Memorial Day canoe float on Lake Afton. Their balanced embrace on the water had been more impressive, though he'd concede the sunset to her, since she dare not mention the rest. "And here's my answer—a trained workforce. Next candidate—continuous improvement."

"Plain common sense," Skip said with a nod.

"Yeah, gotta have it," Ted added.

"Find a better way," Rich replied. "From my perspective, now that the tornado took out the paint shop, it's time to re-invent our department."

Weston leaned forward in his chair. He appreciated the link back to what they were trying to accomplish. "Good one, Rich. Nothing like a clean slate to make us re-evaluate, right? Anybody else?"

Myla glanced up from her note-taking. "New ideas, the more, the merrier."

"True, an influx of never-been-tried ideas certainly keeps the 'continuous' aspect alive." Weston held up as Ernie Pike walked into the room eating a doughnut. "Good, now the gang's all here. I'll throw out the last term, and I'd like you to share whatever comes to your mind. It may not seem important now, but it could be meaningful later. Here's the word—seven."

Myla's head jerked up, a question knitted across her brow. Her head tipped as if to send a private inquiry.

"Seven's the lucky number," Ernie offered. He pointed half a circle of pastry into the air.

"It could represent a boy's age or a man's anniversary." Skip rubbed his chin and seemed unsure he'd hit the target.

"Okay, let's survey the aircraft out on the floor for sevens," Ted Halyard suggested. "There's the L-19, the 140, the 195, the XL-19B, and the XT-37. Hey, there's your seven, Mr. Durand, the new jet for the Air Force. Don't they keep those jets over in Hangar A?"

Weston played down the connection, sure Duncan Reed would not appreciate having his latest jet defacing incident broadcast around a group of idea hatchers. He held his peace and tried to catch Myla's gaze when she looked up.

"Well, seven is considered the perfect number in the Bible," she offered. "It's supposed to be a symbol of completion, like a group of seven items…or seven years…or seven judges."

"Okay then. We've had everything from a seven-year old birthday boy to perfection. Seven can be more than a number. It can be a shape, a symbol, or a quantification. Have any of you heard? The tornado last week was on the ground for seven minutes. In that particular case, seven represents a duration. I hope this exercise expands your mindset as we venture into the QC aspects of our meeting today." Weston glanced down at his agenda. "Old business is up next. Does anyone have a follow-up on anything we've already presented?"

Myla raised her pen to request the floor.

Weston couched his pleasure and gestured toward her.

"I'm pleased to announce the first ever Western Durango interior has been installed in our debut custom-ordered 140. We had to re-train the upholstery crew in the process, but an upgrade certainly merits the effort." Her cheeks blushed at the self-defacement, but her eyes shined with the triumph.

"The impact of such aesthetic improvements will fall beyond quantification," he reasoned as he glanced around the circle. "But can you imagine how this rancher will feel every time he slides into that cockpit to go up? Our first QC success falls somewhere between pride of ownership and pride of craftsmanship. I have to ask you, Miss Templeton, how does it feel to you personally?"

She fiddled the pen back and forth before meeting his gaze with hers. "I feel like I made a contribution, something beyond what had been previously achieved. Proud might not be the right word. I'm satisfied with the accomplishment. Yes, that's much closer."

A small fire ignited in his mind like a nerve had just connected two important thoughts. "Then, accomplishment is worth the re-training…in the end. Is that what you're saying?"

"Yes, in fact, you should expect a bit of consternation to tackle something new—or that road would have already been traveled down by someone else." She bit her pen cap as Skip nudged her shoulder and nodded.

Weston paused to let her analogy work its way through his structured thoughts. Beyond her upholstery success, Myla had escorted him down another untraveled road, one of a more personal nature. Perhaps his bit of consternation had been watching another man kiss her hand, sleazy devil though he was. At least that trouble fell behind them now.

Skip straightened in his seat. "I've got another follow-up, boss. Are you ready?"

Weston pointed his index finger at his main QC supporter and shot at him like it was a loaded gun. He blinked in an effort to get his mind back on track.

"You all know we've been on rigorous cleanup duty to

maintain order on the shop floor in Hangar C. Left behind items have reached an all-time low, our surplus materials now have extra storage on the back wall—at least what the tornado let us keep. And, for bragging rights at the monthly managers' meeting, we've had the lowest number of violations per safety inspection than any of the other hangars." Skip sat back and crossed his arms over his middle.

"That's pretty dad-gum good, Skip," Rich offered. "Not perfect, but getting there."

"I don't know how you arrive at perfection, fellas. There's always the human element, and that comes with a major flaw attached." Skip shook his head. "Forgetfulness, absent-mindedness, and don't-care attitudes are just a few of my problems, but I think the key is motivating workers to do a good job for the company."

Weston had to jump into this conversation. "Can I add mal-intent to the problems that might surface in the work force? Most of the violations are because we don't mean to slip up, but do. Let's not rule out foul play from the arena of possibilities. Suddenly, we leap out of the realm of quality control and venture toward threats of safety—and possibly even security."

He glanced to his left and saw an incredulous expression on Myla's face. Perhaps he had ventured too far. "I think our time would be best served if we move on and leave the dark side of the human psyche to Dr. Freud. Let's move forward with the agenda to new business where we can think forward as well. Are there any pressing resolutions on the horizon?"

Rich Yost dumped his face into his palms. "There's the slight matter of my paint shop being wiped off the face of the earth. What should I recommend to the top brass? It's almost a relief that it's totally gone, as the inadequacies got twisted and hurled into the ditch over on Hoover Road right along with the hull of the building."

"Great observation, Rich. So you have to start over from the ground up. This is when you can ask, what would I do differently? Then, the architect can design something that better accommodates parameters such as ventilation, air temperature, paint residue, and so on."

Myla raised her pen again. "So, can the continuous

improvement paradigm also include these quantum leaps of adjustment? I mean, a total re-build is not like a tweak in scale or cost."

Weston appreciated the question, almost more than its source. "Remember we said that CI must work to improve every facet of operations, plus increase our competitiveness by developing our resources. That seems all-inclusive, despite the scope of the improvement. A majority of our success may be gained from improving existing processes."

"But it wouldn't exclude the option for wholesale improvement, like rebuilding the paint shop," Rich added, his expression less despondent.

"I gotta cut in for a piece of this debate," Ernie Pike said. He gestured toward Rich and noticed some doughnut icing on his hand. He licked off the evidence of his indulgence and tried to suck in his gut. "When Tools & Fixtures requested a separate building to house our department, we got turned down right away. They told us it was cost-prohibitive."

"Yeah, Ernie, but Rich has to have a paint facility." Skip raked his fingertips through his mustache. "Those Bird Dogs alone are coming down the assembly line twenty at a time. There's something to be said for keeping up production rates."

Weston liked this direction. "Yes, efficiency is also quality control. Any chokepoint becomes a problem for the entire process."

"And affects our delivery to the customer," Ted added.

Ernie grumbled under his breath and hitched around in his seat. With his thumbs tucked into his belt, he circumnavigated his entire girth, a generous trip. "Well, don't kill the messenger, guys. I'm just reporting what I heard at the coffee pot when I picked up my morning doughnut."

"Do you know something about the paint shop you'd like to share, Mr. Pike?" Weston hoped to add some legitimacy to the man's eavesdropping delivery, though it felt more akin to a set-up. He held his palm up to invite the disclosure.

Pike hung his head and then looked up at Rich Yost through his bushy brow. "Word is Operations wants to move the paint shop over to Pawnee Plant. That's what I overheard."

Rich shot to his feet stupefied, his hands clamped over his ears.

"They'd have to freight every last plane over there by rail, fully assembled and everything," Skip said, his eyes wide.

"That doesn't seem to make a lick of sense," Myla replied. She shook her head and shot him a piercing look.

Weston tossed his agenda on the nearby table. His meeting had taken a turn toward the discombobulated, not a routine short-circuit. Maybe catastrophic events had a domino effect, as dealing with the tornado's fallout sure seemed unavoidable at this juncture. He had a trump card, so perhaps he should play it. "Rich, this is a perfect opportunity for mistake-proofing at the senior level. There's a chance we could nip this ill-advised option in the bud. I have an open-door invitation to the VP's office. Let's go down there and talk through this, as the QC circle has been working on other viable options since our first meeting. He'd have to consider that at face value, since he knew that hiring me would not be giving the continuous improvement process mere lip service."

Rich straightened his shoulders and gave him a nod. "Thank you, Mr. Durand. I believe I will go along with you for that upper-level encounter."

Skip clapped his hands together in approval. "And remind them of the 'common sense' aspect of continuous improvement while you're in there. The Pawnee Plant is the last place that new paint shop should go."

Myla laughed, cutting the tension in the room. She scrawled one last line into the notebook and held it up for submittal.

Weston stepped over and took the notebook with a sly wink. His intentional brush of her hand meant something more. "I guess I should say 'meeting adjourned' until next month."

"I can hardly wait for the follow-up on this particular case." Skip nudged Myla, his eyes full of mirth. "I may have to step into the QC lab and get an update later in the week."

Weston allowed a smile to curl his lips. "Open door policy— for anybody at anytime. I appreciate each of you and your participation in this Quality Circle. Now, Mr. Yost, let's go spread some continuous improvement around the admin wing."

"Nobody needs it more," he replied, already headed for the door.

Weston managed to hold Myla's gaze a second longer. She'd been a gift to the group, in more ways than one. And to him…yes, a gift, tied with a yellow ribbon right to his heart.

~

Myla pulled her hair back to better focus on her inspection of the leather seat. Susie's installation ability had made progress, but had not fully arrived at the difficult points, like covering curves and applying the piping trim to cover her stapled seams. Upholstery had its craftsmanship. Apparently, the knack had to be acquired.

For the third time that morning, her thoughts turned to Weston. Friday had arrived and they still didn't have any plans for time together over the weekend. That didn't sit too well with her, as she had nothing else planned. She tugged a wrinkle out of the corner cover and eased the extra material toward the crevice of the seat. Almost ready to leave for the next cockpit, she spied a tiny awl in the floorboard, accidentally left behind by her trainee. She sighed and scooped up the tool. This would have to become an object lesson for Susie, so she could learn to conduct her final sweep as a matter of habit.

Myla backed down the gantry, a string of corrective words collecting in her mind. When she rounded the nosecone, she found Susie in front of the next Bird Dog engaged in conversation with an attentive Hague Amherst. As though a repellent had been sprayed in the air, she pivoted and headed the opposite direction. There was no way she would be dragged into an encounter with the tools salesman today. She gave herself five seconds to come up with a better plan. Before she knew it, she had stopped in front of Weston's QC lab. Reminded of his open invitation, she squeezed inside the cracked door.

An eerie glow radiated from the rear of the lab. While she allowed her eyes to adjust to the murky lighting, she made out Weston's silhouette centered on a machine back there. "Weston? Is this a bad time?"

"No, not at all. Come back here, I want to show you something." His chair screeched as he shoved back a few inches to receive her.

"What is that bluish lighting under there?" She reached for the chair back and found her hand intercepted by his.

He pulled her around front and the chair wobbled. "Here, take a seat and let me show you. This is a fluorescent penetrant technique for defect detection. I have a panel from a section that Skip ran a tail tapping on. We're having a gentleman's disagreement over which method is the more accurate test. He holds that the tapping—though rudimentary—is fairly diagnostic. Here, let me shift the light to incandescent."

Myla saw the test article transition from a wonderment of blue-glinted color to plain silvery metal under regular light. She pulled back and looked at Weston, who had crowded her chair by leaning against the test array. "You're using special lighting to see the defects?"

"Correct, it's black light." A tiny smile played across his face. "Watch again, especially in this area marked by the red tape. Do you see it?"

"Yes, I'll hold my focus there. Go ahead and switch the lights." She held her head still and dared not blink, as she wanted to detect the difference. The room light flicked off and in the next second, the bluish light came back on. The marked area turned out to be a lengthy scar that ran like a small creek right across the panel. "Oh my word. This is amazing. Tell me, did Skip catch this crack in his tail tapping technique? It's as big as the Rio Grande."

Weston leaned closer. "No, I'm afraid he missed the whole thing. It's a manufacturing defect that should have been caught before becoming part of the aircraft. I have no qualms having pulled this section out, now that I've made this discovery."

"What else can you detect under here? This is fascinating." Her tone bordered on breathless, excited over the technology. He may as well have opened up another world to her.

"The small dots there that pit the surface are porosity defects. We have to keep those to a minimum, but this piece is not that bad. The fluorescent penetrant also detects sand inclusions and shrink cavities, as well as larger anomalies like this crack. One day when these Bird Dogs have some service wear on their frame, we'll likely have to test for failures to keep the aircraft safe over their lifetime. I hesitate to project that far ahead, because I have enough work at the present." He gave a small laugh, and his hand found the top of her shoulder.

She covered his hand with her fingers, but kept her gaze fixed on the test material. The scene etched its way into her memory. Weston had shared his work with her as though an intellectual equal. His work entailed so much more technical precision than hers, yet the whole realm held a depth of fascination—or perhaps it was the man at the controls.

"Had you dropped in for something specific, Myla, or should I simply consider myself the most fortunate man at the plant today?" He moved toward the apparatus and touched the light switch. "Oh here, perhaps you'd want to check me for pitting or inclusions while this contraption is running." He popped his head over the tail panel. The bluish light shone behind his profile.

Something moved in her chest, a sensation not unlike staring at the galaxy and being inspired by the starry array. There stood a genius of a man asking her to inspect him. She wouldn't have to search too hard on this one. "You're amazing to me, Weston Durand." The words slipped out coated with velvet, like the darkness surrounding each star.

"Have lunch with me then, and let's make some plans for this weekend. I'm moving my furniture into the cottage early. Perhaps you could be my placement consultant." With a click, the bluish light disappeared and the ordinary illumination returned. Fortunately, it still featured a most extraordinary man.

"Susie left a tool in the last cockpit she installed in. I found it when I came behind her for my inspection." She produced the awl to prove her claim.

"So you came to me for that?" He held out his hand. "Mr. Reed would better serve as your point-of-contact for left-behind tools."

"No, I came down the gantry and had one of those moments. You know, if you turn right, it takes you into a situation you don't want. So you go left, and avoid it for something much better." She took his hand and shot him a coy glance.

"Which means I beat out what? The snack room? It *is* my lucky day." He gave her a toying look, but didn't surrender her hand.

"Yes to your offer for lunch, and double yes for the furniture consult. We should do more of this working together thing. I think we make a pretty impressive team." She stood and angled for the door.

"Pretty, yes," he repeated. "Impressive, double yes." He reached for the doorknob and seemed to linger in her proximity. "But now that you've seen my fluorescent penetrant technique, I may have to swear you to secrecy."

"Of course. My lips are sealed." She teased him with a slow wink as she turned forward expecting the door to open.

Weston made a whistling sound under his breath. "You had to mention your lips, didn't you?" In an attempt to shove the door open, he leaned into her, his nose grazing her ear.

She closed her eyes, and the allure of the bluish light flashed back to mind. Spellbound, he led her out into the hubbub of the shop floor content to see only what she chose to see, the object of her affections profiled in a fluorescent aura, right where he would remain for instant retrieval.

~

With lunch break over, Weston rounded the balcony stairwell and wondered how he might preserve his heightened good mood. Myla had been a tonic for his end-of-week dread, and now he felt a carefree lift in his step. Glancing toward the rear of the hangar, he spotted Skip Sellers strolling into the snack room. Skip might appreciate knowing about the reversal of mindset on the paint facility relocation. He released the railing and headed to the snack room.

Light-spirited, he decided to hail the fellow circle member with a friendly salutation. He popped his head inside the door. "Fancy meeting you here," he called in a playful tone.

The snack room service lady straightened from her task and put one hand on her ample hip. Her eyes roamed up and down his frame. "Same for me—only double it," she quipped.

A man chuckled behind her. Skip stood up after grabbing his bag of chips from the vending machine. "Which one of us are you really looking for, Mr. Durand? I've got a few minutes, but I can't speak for Bette here."

With his face heating from the situation he'd thrown himself headlong into, Weston stepped into the room to get things straightened out. "Sorry, Bette. I didn't realize you were here when I spotted Skip stepping in. Please accept a thousand pardons on my part."

"Story of my life." She gave him a hooked smile and man-handled a stack of moon pies out of the rolling crate she'd been tending. "The weekend starts in four hours, and everybody's still looking right past me."

"Try Hangar B," Skip suggested. "The men are really thick as thieves in there since the paint shop guys have been crammed in. That's more chances per square foot, right?"

"You're a true gentleman, Mr. Sellers. I'm heading that way next." She emptied the top of the crate and turned to straighten up the shelf display.

Weston gestured to the door and rolled his eyes as the man approached. They walked out shoulder to shoulder to lengthen the escape.

"You 'bout walked through a muddled mess back there. I hear she's on a manhunt."

"So it appears. Thank the Good Lord above I'm a taken man."

"So am I. Alice Granger and I have become…well, an item." His mustache danced to one side, and the corners of his eyes crinkled.

"Funny how that can happen, if a man's smart enough not to put up too much resistance. Can you spare a few minutes to join me in the lab? I have an update on the paint shop switch."

"Sure thing. You'll have to tell me how top secret this thing is though. If I slip and share it with Alice, she's likely to blab it from here to Haysville. Poor gal, she laughed and cried through 'I Love Lucy' giving birth to Little Ricky last night. I think she misses having a family."

Weston cleared his throat and pushed the lab door open. The tail section still sat under the detection apparatus, so he thought he'd give an eye-opening lesson on accurate defect quantification. "First, let me give you a closer look at this tail panel I've inspected. Come on back here." He led the way and offered the floor supervisor the chair.

"All set. Let her rip, Mr. Durand." He clamped his knuckles together in his lap and focused straight ahead.

Weston killed the overhead light and toggled on the black light. He held back his commentary, until his friend got an eyeful of the penetrant lines.

"What in tarnation is that scratch up the panel? You're not telling me that's a defect, are you?" He leaned closer and used his fingers as a caliper to measure the fissure.

Weston switched the light supply and allowed the red tape to guide the man's rudimentary measurement. "I don't have to tell you. That's the job of the fluorescent penetrant. I don't believe your tail tapping gave you the honest assessment this procedure can. Think about the difference.”

“Can you take a look at the surface of the tail right where it sits with this?” Skip motioned for the lights off and soon got the bluish light back. “I’ll be jiggered.”

“Yes, I can use Magnaflux for this type of surface detection, but we’d have to go with direct current for deeper inspections. But, my deepest bag of tricks is what I’ll be able to test with my new portable radiography gage. It’s an x-ray machine. You know, like taking x-rays of metal. I’m practicing on the turbojet engines over in Hangar A.”

“No wonder they picked you to be the preacher man for continuous improvement,” Skip replied with a laugh.

Weston chuckled and switched on the room lights. He headed for his chair, buoyed by the camaraderie. “Somebody’s got to keep up, right? When I negotiated my contract to come on board here, I made it conditional on my attendance to the annual conference of the American Industrial Radium & X-Ray Society. If I ever got cut off from that kind of technical information exchange, we’d grow outdated in a heartbeat.”

“Going from props to jet engines is no baby step. I heard the DeHaviland Comet might be having more than its fair share of crash landings across the big pond.”

“Yes, I’ve heard that, too. They’re suspecting pressurization issues. I am quite certain the test pilots would appreciate someone getting to the bottom of that with a workable solution. Speaking of solutions, you might be interested to know the Bird Dogs may not have to travel over to Pawnee Plant just to receive their paint jobs.”

His face turned expressive. “What? Did you buy Rich Yost a decent night’s sleep with your visit to the VP’s office?”

Weston chuckled again. “We simply went in there and laid it out. Even by rail, that kind of handling so late in assembly would be catastrophic from a quality control perspective.”

“So what did the VP say about the proposal? Was it a viable approach?”

“He admitted the option was currently on the table. When Rich mentioned the wingspan on the Bird Dog, the VP got kind of sheepish. It seems management may have miscalculated.”

“What? They forgot the fuselages already had their wings on?”

Weston nodded, his face animating with the truth. When Skip snorted, he thought the lab door might blow open. "It was one of those precious moments you wish you could bottle and sell. I'd call it 'Confounded Capture' or something of that nature."

"How about 'Knucklehead Stew?' That's more like it. Wow, you can add that to your list of QC improvements, Weston, right after the Western Durango—your first success. Say, you haven't mentioned how that, ahem, partner project is going." He waggled his eyebrows.

Weston leaned back in his chair. "We're seeing each other with regularity. In fact, Myla's helping me place the furniture in my new house in College Hill this weekend."

"Sound pretty domestic to me," Skip replied. He smoothed his mustache as if to make his eyebrows lower. "Alice and I split time at both our houses, but I see that running its due course to a joint end, if things continue to work out."

"She likes the cottage," he quipped. His fingers found a pencil abandoned on the desktop and began to tap it. "I'm trying to make Myla fond of an old tool shed out back."

"Good move, though most women prefer the kitchen. Maybe she'll warm up to it—in time. Hey, thanks for the defect demo. I think I'll phase out the tail tapping, for now anyway. Let me know if you want to train anybody with that x-ray machine. I might give it a whirl."

"Great." He now had a second ambassador of improvement. *What advancement.*

Chapter 14

Weston lengthened his stride to keep up with the caffeine-driven safety manager as they headed for Hangar A. The morning seemed too young for such high angst, as Monday hadn't clocked in past nine yet. He clutched the portable radiography gage to his side, his primary weapon at cracking the sabotage case with the XT-37's jet engines.

"Hope you didn't mind the call at home last night." Duncan looked back over his shoulder and cut his next stride short to allow the gap between them to close.

"No, not at all. Since we had most of my furnishings already moved to the cottage on Saturday, I didn't even have my weight bench to keep me busy. The closing is in eight days, and I couldn't be more ready. I don't even think I'll miss Old Man Godfrey's cooking."

"I remember that feeling, only I got the house, the spouse, and the adopted child all in the same month. Maybe that's what I'm paying penance for now, the crash course in starting married life with one fell swoop." He pointed to a hangar door sliding open and changed his bearing.

Weston toed the line between caring and meddling. "Is Lorna Rae doing all right this morning?"

"She had a spell of disappointment when the doctor decided for the inducement, but both of us want what's best for the baby. With me at home, she won't have to worry about taking care of Trudy, or trying to get a meal on the table. She can follow orders and stay in bed."

"I can have Art Godfrey come over to do the cooking if you'd like." He grinned and let it drop to the tarmac when his escort grimaced at the idea.

"Even I can burn an egg with the best of them," Duncan replied. He glanced at him sideways, his demeanor lightening a shade.

"Land sakes, do you realize you'll be a father again by Father's Day? That's amazing."

"If you're trying to ease my angst, please stop. You crack-and-defect guys sure know how to search for the weaknesses, don't you?" Duncan kneaded his hands together as he stepped into Hangar A.

Weston made a crackling sound through his teeth and passed the radiography gage's wand down the length of the man's arm to conduct a mock scan.

"Very funny, wise guy. Try to focus on the XT-37, okay? We'll clear her engines first, and then I'll take you on my typical rounds searching for FOD items left lying around. Did you have the seven stitched closed last week?"

"Fixed and as good as new—if you like needlework," Weston replied. "I'm growing fond of it myself."

"That's what happens when you date an upholsterer. Lorna Rae hooked me with her cakes which have fewer sharp edges, but many more calories. Oh, here's the plane just like we left it."

Weston approached the left jet engine and surveyed the cover. "Let me run the scan with the cover intact. I need to establish a procedure that's repeatable with as few steps as possible."

"Right. We can always remove the cover, if we think the x-ray shows something, and delve deeper from there."

"I set the gage to the housing thickness as per Continental-Teledyne's specifications, so I should be ready." Weston turned on the mechanism, and the radiography gage began to hum.

Duncan stepped back from the aircraft and observed in silence.

With a keen focus on the monitor, Weston scanned the length of the engine. Only the designed structures appeared to be present. He turned off the gage and examined the engine cover with a critical eye.

"Everything okay here?" Duncan raised his hands to mimic the length of the engine housing.

"Top notch. Let's do the right side." He stepped around the nosecone as the safety manager lagged behind. He took the extra seconds to repeat the cover inspection and noticed a difference right away. "Mr. Reed, may I confer with you?"

The man's facial features tightened. "How can I help you?"

"Well, I noticed the left side cover had been cinched with a square knot, and this one is a half-hitch. Would you have tied it like that? I mean, either is fine to do the job." He pointed the wand at the seal while Duncan inched closer to inspect it.

"That's not how I left it…and no one else has authorization for removal. Unless, of course, your seamstress took it off doing the repair work—a logical explanation."

"No, Myla does the mending with the cover intact. To tell you the truth, I think those punctures were meant to fool us. I'm not going to get too worked up about this tie deal, until I run the scan and see what results we get." Weston rubbed a finger over his brow and positioned along the intake of the jet engine.

Duncan took two steps back and crossed his arms.

Weston turned the on dial and allowed the machine a few seconds to resume operation. He passed the wand over the intake blades and traveled toward the rear. Only inches into the inspection, he halted at a transverse process that had not been present on the other engine. He led the wand forward and came back again, this time tracing the diagonal rod as it tipped up into the combustion compartment. The hairs on the back of his neck began to stand up. "Duncan, come get a look at this." He exhaled and waited for another pair of discerning eyes to join his. Feeling the man press against his shoulder, he nodded and led the wand back over the anomaly. "We may have an inclusion here. The other side lacked any transverse process. I don't remember one in the schematic, either."

"It looks to be approximately four inches long. Do you think you can get to it for the extraction? I'd hate to have to call Continental-Teledyne and ask them to send a rep over." Duncan's mouth flattened into a grimace.

"Let me try my magnetic probe first. I've been working to improve that technique, since we're trying to make a go of nondestructive evaluation. Let me go retrieve the probe from my lab. Maybe you could pull the cover off in the meantime."

"Hit the trail then and get right back. I'll try to look nonchalant, though I feel anything but. Leave the x-ray machine here, in case we can't clear the object."

Weston reached for the strap around his neck. "Good thinking." He set the gage on a nearby table and broke into a trot across the tarmac. By the time he'd crossed the expanse between hangars, he had a nice lung-burn going, not to mention how his dress shoes pinched his feet. The day rubbed against the typical mold already and would likely shatter the norm in every way. In rare cases, quality control could buck up that way, like a jackass avoiding the gate. Duncan's personal situation with the baby's inducement only crimped the situation like a vise, but it couldn't be helped.

Once inside Hangar C, he shoved a shoulder into the lab door and raced inside for the probe. He found it hanging on his pegboard organizer, a short-lived victory. He grabbed it with both hands and retraced his steps across the tarmac.

Duncan had the cover off and folded over the back of a chair. "Can you talk me through what you're attempting with that?"

Weston positioned the probe at the intake and forced all the air from his lungs. When he inhaled, his hands began to shake. "Well, since the object is angled, I can pull the heavier, downward end through the bottom of the intake chamber—if it will respond to the magnet at all. That's what I'm banking on. Then, all I have to do is navigate it through the bottom two blades."

"That task requires the hands of a surgeon—but you're shaking like a leaf. Here, give me the probe." Duncan motioned for possession and soon had it.

Weston shot him a wide-eyed look, unsure of where the safety manager was leading.

"Father God, lead us to the outcome we need, and guide Weston's hands while he uses his training to accomplish this task. Help us protect others. In Jesus' name, amen. Okay, now you're ready." He handed over the probe, and the heavy magnet bobbed on the far end.

This time when he lifted the probe into place, not one tremor shook its length. He selected the two blades by educated guess and slid the apparatus inside the chamber. Once a three-inch portion had disappeared, he began to maneuver it around, side to side. He felt the contact before he heard the metallic clink. "I've got something attached."

Duncan moved closer to the engine intake and positioned his hands like a catch basin for the mystery object.

Bent and listening for obstructions, Weston retracted the probe with precision. When it hitched, he angled it with the slightest nuance and tried again. He blinked his eyes, readying for visual contact. In seconds, he began to see the tip. "Get ready to pinch it in your fingers, Duncan, in case I lose it coming through the outer housing." He pulled back and waited as two inches of the object showed clearly.

Duncan slid a finger beneath the probe and soon gripped the intruder. "Good boy, come to daddy and let him have a nice, long look at you." He palmed the four-inch object.

"Looks like a nail punch like you'd use for finish carpentry work," Weston said.

"It's solid metal though, and big enough to wreak havoc inside this precision combustion chamber," Duncan replied. "Good work on getting this extracted, Mr. Durand."

"Thank you. Let's have a look at the tool catalogue in my office. If we can figure out exactly what it is, then we might have a clue as to who might have left it."

"First, we have to replace the cover, and then we have to take the long way back, so I can show you my FOD inspection route. Even with this complication, my time at work remains short-lived, and there's nothing I can do about it." Duncan handed him the trespassing tool and snatched the cover off the chair. In one motion, he slung it back over the top of the engine intake and cinched it with his typical square knot.

Weston stepped closer to the hangar door to allow the sunlight to illuminate the tool. Just above the cross-hatched handle, a faint scratch in the finish glimmered in the light. Though difficult to make out, he thought he saw a T mark the handle. He'd get the magnifying glass on it back at the lab and take a closer look. A wayward thought prickled into his conscious as the safety manager beckoned him onward. *Good God above. It couldn't be a leather punch, could it?*

~

Myla watched her boss as she climbed the gantry beside her.

They would share duty in the four-seated 140 today, where she'd stitch the back two seat covers into their permanent positions. Miss Granger acted as animated as she'd ever seen her, most likely attributable to her fellow QC circle member, Skip Sellers. Why, goodness, the woman had almost grown tolerable.

"And then he promised me we'd go if I wanted to, so I said yes, I did." Alice shifted her tool pack to the side of her coveralls and bent to enter the cockpit.

"Where is the Sedgwick County Fair held? I've never been." Myla ducked in behind the woman and squeezed past her with an armload of sewn leather covers.

"West down the highway in Cheney. It's not a bad location, as long as it doesn't rain. Hand me two, will you?" She grunted as she dropped to her knees and faced the pilot's seat.

"Hey, maybe Weston and I should check it out, too. We're always looking for fun spots on the weekend." Myla separated two covers out and pushed them forward on the cockpit floor.

Her boss's dimpled knuckles soon covered hers. "If you come out Saturday while we're there, pretend you don't see us, okay?" Her eyes darted down the gantry steps as though to check for an eavesdropper. "It's Skip. He's acting all ill at ease at the craziest times. I think he's trying to tell me something important, but he's getting all knotted up inside."

"Could he be ready to pop the question?" Myla pressed her lips into a circle to keep the secret between the two of them.

"Tell you the truth, that's what I've been wondering. A girl doesn't want to get her hopes up needlessly, but we might be close to something like that. Gosh, here I am babbling on like a school girl. Let's get to work instead of daydreaming what might be. I'll find out at the fair—and I expect you not to see me there."

"I'm already looking right past you." Myla giggled as she pulled the stapler loose from her belt and selected her first candidate from the two remaining covers. As she fit the curves of the leather over the padded seat frame, her thoughts wandered to Weston and their weekend together at the cottage. He'd asked her opinion on every aspect of the furniture arranging and taken pains to settle each piece to her liking.

The kiss he'd stolen after inquiring about curtains for the eating nook certainly bore revisiting, as he seemed so playful and attentive for the remainder of the day. Could they be headed for a question of their own before too long? She tried not to hoist the possibility against Miss Granger's expectation by the month's end, but it fell into the range of credible options—or should she say pleasurable?

Alice cleared her throat up front and let go a string of stapler shots. "Guess I should mind my own business about this, but I think she's mighty young."

Determined not to fall behind, Myla straightened her cover and began aligning the seams for closure. "Who's that, Miss Granger?" With one last tug, she set the first staple and followed with several more down the back edge of the seat.

"Our little Susie, that's who. I think she has a beau. Haven't you seen her all smiles around that traveling tool salesman?" Instead of waiting for a response, the woman employed her stapler again.

Myla rocked back on her heels. That declaration caused her no uncertain amount of concern. Maybe she should pry and see what the boss lady knew. "That guy is just in and around trying to make a sale. Are you sure Susie is affiliating with him for some other reason?"

"I passed her on the gantry last Friday, and she smelled like Aqua Velva, not Juicy Fruit. I think they'd been cuddling on break, though I didn't witness it. I'm her boss, not her mother. I can't keep my eyes on everything. Plus, I don't want to seem like the hypocrite, since I'm dating somebody from work. I'm just saying she's young. That's all."

"And young women are prone to making mistakes, if I can fill in the blanks for you," Myla replied. She pulled out a length of trim piping and reached for the glue to set it in place over the staples.

"Uh-huh. Young and foolish. They go together like peanut butter and crackers." She grunted again and moved to the passenger side.

"Maybe I should have a talk with her—find out what she'll confide to me. I think this all may have started the day of the tornado. Drat it, I sat right beside her in the storm shelter and could have put a halt to it, if only I'd known they'd turn into an item."

"She's an innocent babe-in-the-woods, and I'd wager he isn't as inexperienced. I hate to see her get led into something over her head." The stapler added its staccato opinion.

Her insinuation set loose a memory of Hague Amherst's stolen kiss in the backseat while searching for the missing bonus tool. Soon, Myla's cheeks burned with anger. Miss Granger had a reason to be ill at ease. She would have that heart-to-heart talk with Susie, the sooner, the better. She tugged at the supple leather and banged a staple into place right through the expensive covering into the back of the seat. *If only issues of the heart could be pinned that easily.* Lord help her, she only confessed to being an upholsterer, not a fashioner of hearts.

~

Weston forced his eyes to search out what he didn't want to see. With Duncan Reed's shoulder next to his, he couldn't find a way out of the inevitable. They turned the catalogue page from large awls to smaller hand-held tools. He suddenly felt claustrophobic.

"This is close. The cross-hatching on the handle to improve grip looks about right." Duncan leaned closer to study the description. "It says the punch can be used for anything from setting nails in wood to tacks in upholstery work—a versatile four-inch punch."

"This is the Snap-lite Tool line," Weston added. "It could match another manufacturer's line better, but it seems close, if it's not the exact one."

"I believe we have a Snap-lite vendor here, at least once or twice a month. Maybe they have a copyright mark embossed on it. Did you say you had a magnifying glass?"

Loathe to produce it, Weston made slow work of opening the desk drawer and retrieving the hand lens. His head said one thing, but his heart screamed another. Both seemed on a collision course with reality, as four inches of cast iron didn't lie. He placed the magnifier on the desktop instead of handing it to the safety manager.

Duncan glanced at him with a furrow in his brow. He took the lens and began examining the slender tool. "Hey, there's a marking down by the handle, but it's scratched in, not embossed."

Weston planted his face in his hands to shield himself. "Can you make it out? What does it say?"

"I can definitely make out the letter 'T' but the other part looks like a squiggle—or a sine wave. Let's stick with the 'T' for now. I'll try to generate a list of employees with the last name starting with 'T.' I can leave it for you to cull through. I'm in the office until Wednesday. After that, I'm on leave through the baby's birth."

Weston's mind whirled through possibilities a mile a minute. One thing for certain, he needed that punch. "Can you leave the tool with me? I might be able to run a penetrant test on it and better read that marking."

"Sure thing. I need to leave everything with you, quite honestly. I might not be back for two weeks." Duncan straightened and handed him the magnifier.

"That would be through the Fourth of July break. I hope Lorna Rae doesn't have that much of a complication."

"You have more problems than she does, as her equipment upkeep is nominal."

Weston tried to swallow, but it turned into a gulp. "Thanks for trying to cheer me up. I should have stuck with quality control and left this safety stuff to you and the birds."

"My bird is a stork, and he's about to deliver. I'll get you that list by tomorrow."

Before Weston could formulate another objection, the lab door swung open and an animated Skip Sellers surged inside. "Hey, sorry if I'm disrupting something. I just found this posted in the snack room and thought about your antique tool dilemma." He shoved a flier onto the desktop and it fluttered down in front of him.

"Snap-lite Tools?" Weston asked. The last thing he needed was another finger pointing in that direction. The sleazy tool salesman came to mind kissing Myla's fingers.

Skip pressed his thumbnail against the bottom of the advertisement. "See here? You can get a five percent discount by trading in your used tools when you buy the new ones. How nice of them to take the worthless stuff off your hands." He harrumphed so hard his shoulders quaked. "That's probably where the old wrench came from you found in Hangar A."

Duncan moved around to study the flyer. "Good work, Mr. Sellers. You might be onto something. Mr. Durand, I'll try to dig out the name of our Snap-lite Tools rep and get that to you tomorrow as well. By the way, how did you do on your FOD sweep today, Mr. Sellers?"

"Zero violations, Mr. Reed. I think we're beginning to get a handle on this thing."

"Bravo. Now, if only Hangar A would mimic your success, then I wouldn't have a monkey on my back." Duncan drew a heavy breath and walked out of the lab.

"Did he say monkey?" Weston propped his brow in his hands and stared at the flyer. The 'S' of Snap-lite curled like an asp. "Mine feels more like an ape, and he's none too happy." His stomach started to heave, and Mr. Godfrey wasn't even in the kitchen cooking.

Chapter 15

Myla knew the conversation had to transpire, and Tuesday offered a beautiful June morning for it. She glanced over at Susie who was busy unfolding a bolt of leather to begin a cutting task. Since the alternating summer vacation schedule had left the sewing room short of staff, they'd agreed to pull off the shop floor today and stockpile some material for later use. *The fewer interruptions the better.* The tight space would work in her favor as well.

Freedom of movement came as a real treat, since the coveralls required for hangar work were hot and bulky, not to mention unflattering. She fanned her face with the to-do list and searched for her favorite scissors. Susie soon brought the bolt of upholstery fabric over and plopped it onto the table.

"Oops. Sorry about being so clumsy." The young woman blushed and covered her mouth.

"That's okay. My fingers are stiff from all the installs. I'm looking forward to today's change of pace." She regarded her helper and spotted a yellowing bruise on her neck under the tip of her blouse collar, the kind fast girls took home after a weekend of carousing. A leaded pit dropped into her stomach when it occurred to her it might be too late for their little talk.

She turned back to the counter to collect her demeanor. "Susie, I've been meaning to chat with you about something. Now seems as good a time as any." Myla tossed the scissors onto the table and came back for the pattern pieces. "Want to pick which pattern piece you prefer?"

"I'll take this one." Susie selected the middle of the seat

cushion, leaving her the flanks and the backs, a fair trade-off. "Hope I haven't done anything wrong, Miss Templeton. I'm trying to keep up with you and Miss Granger, but it isn't easy being the new girl, believe me."

"Oh, no. I didn't mean talk about work. I wanted to chat with you, friend-to-friend, about men. Since all three of us in installation seem to have boyfriends this summer, the time is right to get the truth out there. Without meaning to be a spoilsport, I wanted to let you know that some men can't be trusted." She picked up her scissors and tapped her chest right over her heart.

The young woman stared at her wide-eyed, her fingers hovering over the leather. "What do you mean by that?"

Myla nodded to the pattern piece to encourage her back to her task. She centered the seat back pattern and began the cut-out, her keen eye reducing waste as she made the cut. "Men are not all the same, Susie. What you see on the outside—say good looks—may not reflect what's on the inside, like an insincere heart. Some men play games, like flirting, just to get a woman in their arms. That's why for years, I kept my stiff-arm defense up and tried to hold them off."

"That doesn't sound like something a girl can keep up for long," Susie replied. She took her scissors and traced out the seat pattern, scoring the leather with the blade tip. She snatched away the paper and made her cut along the crimped line.

"It served me well and protected me—until discernment led me to realize that I was ready for something more. Even now, I fight the urge to run away from the physical part. I guess it became ingrained in my character. Anyway, you have to watch out for yourself in these relationships. I saw Hague Amherst giving you some attention on the shop floor Friday. I know from experience he's the flirty type. Plus, he's much older than you are."

Susie paused long enough to adjust her blouse collar. Her lips twisted as she finished the cut-out and stacked it on the counter. "Hague claims he's just misunderstood. But he likes our group, because we're friendly and don't put on airs about being better than others."

"You mean better than a traveling tool salesman? We're not supposed to judge others, right? So, I don't. But don't confuse empathy with romantic interest, Susie. I'm only trying to protect you from the possibility of a wolf in sheep's clothing. Get your stiff arm up and protect your reputation while you get to know him a little better, that's all."

The young woman's bottom lip began to quiver as she set and scored the next piece. "You act as though he's out to get something. Sometimes, two hearts are simply looking for each other, Miss Templeton. I was scared in the tornado, and he made me feel safe. That seemed real."

"Real—or possibly opportunistic? A tight space in the dark could lead to a number of outcomes." She started her next piece, recalling Weston's look of concern right before the lights had gone out that day. Was she a hypocrite for having given him a kiss then and now lecturing Susie about self-control? "Well, it all comes down to what a man harbors in his heart. You have to be sure, before you let down that stiff-arm guard. I hope you understand."

"Excuse me for a few seconds." Susie sniffed, darted around the table, and ran out of the room, her hands clutching her throat.

Myla leaned over her work, her palms pressed to the table as a sigh deflated her lungs. Her prim lecture had turned into a train wreck in short order. Maybe Susie didn't need her interference—or perhaps she was too late to make a difference.

Someone harrumphed at the doorway. There stood Alice Granger, larger than life, looking none too pleased. "Is this your recipe for making up a shortfall? I'm doing the work of both of you on the shop floor, and you send her off in tears like a school girl. I suggest you shift in high gear, while I try to coax Susie back on the job."

"Yes, Miss Granger. I'll turn up the production rate." Myla doubled the fabric and began to cut two seat flanks out at the same time. Her scissors jammed, and her hand soon ached at having to power through the stubborn thickness.

When Susie walked back in, she didn't look up while she set her nose to the proverbial grindstone. That could be construed as another method of stiff-arming the enemy, since productive hands never played in the devil's workshop. *Some comfort that lent now.* Myla tossed two more pieces onto the counter and pulled another length of fabric off the bolt. After Hague Amherst's sleazy smile flashed to mind, she knew she wouldn't apologize to Susie. Her warning had fallen right on target.

~

Trapped in a corner, Weston had the sensation of falling from the surface of the earth. None of this seemed his true concern. He'd found a methodology for testing the jet engine, and now, he wished the blasted technology had never been invented. Propellers he could deal with ad nauseam. He glanced up, not realizing that Duncan Reed waited for his reply.

The man's expression softened. "Trust me. Once this blows over, you can pick up where you left off, but for now, I cannot leave you in charge knowing you might have a conflict of interest—personal interest. We must have your agreement on this matter, or I'll appoint someone else, someone with less understanding of the situation. I don't think you want that."

Weston glanced down at the employee list Reed had delivered, the laborers with a legitimate connection to Hangar A underlined in ink. It stole his breath to read Myla's name as a suspect, which set off a major battle between his logical self and his emotional being. Funny, his gentleman side seemed to be playing the coward on this issue. The dissonance played out in mind-numbing paralysis at the moment.

"Okay, I'll take your silence as acceptance—for now." Reed drew a long breath and checked his notepad. "Did you speak with Skip Sellers regarding the role of neutral employee liaison? That aspect is important to several members of the administration."

"Yes, he'll do it as a favor to me. He mentioned my paradigm of continuous improvement. Now, it seems he surpasses me in sincerity, and I'm the laggard. Ironic, isn't it?"

"You want quality control to catch on at every level, right? That should be cause for celebration then, as you're igniting the workforce for the betterment of the company."

"Forgive me, while I pause to count the cost, Mr. Reed." His despicable tone had not been intended, but he did register the deepening furrows on the safety manager's forehead.

"Back to the schedule for this afternoon. The restriction meeting will be in your lab at four o'clock. I'm having security escort the staff of the upholstery department out, so it doesn't seem like we're pinning one person with the suspicion."

Weston stood up behind his desk, a dwarf in front of the hulking visitor's frame. "I appreciate any sensitivity we can include with our investigation. I'd like to protect Myla as much as possible. They all have strong employee records, without a mark against them. We don't really know who planted that punch inside the jet engine casing. This part of the investigation is preliminary, until you can figure things out."

Reed stuffed his notebook in his pocket and gave him a stern look. "Until *we* figure this case out, Mr. Durand. You're a resourceful man, with equipment that enables you to peer beyond the surface of things. If you could figure out how to countermand the mal-intent of the criminal mind, you could crack this case wide open."

"Cracks are the enemy in my line of work, Mr. Reed. I'll search for my own suitable analogy for this mess. It looks like I'll be spending plenty of time alone to make a run at it."

Duncan Reed headed for the office door. His jaw flexed as though he had to bite back a parting comment. He grabbed the door post and turned back. "Since you claim to be a Christian, Mr. Durand, this might be a good time to practice your faith."

"You mean like not hastening to judge one's brother unjustly?" The question hung in the air between them, taking on an air of insubordination he hadn't intended.

Reed nodded and released the door jamb. "See you at four o'clock in your lab. No consorting whatsoever until then."

Weston sank into his chair, his knees aquiver like off-balance bowling pins that refused to drop. He rubbed his temples and began uttering a prayer of protection for Myla, though they all needed coverage, every last one of the known players—and possibly one or two of the unknown. Maybe the guilty party would simply raise a hand and accept the consequences of their thoughtless action. He added that to the prayer, but it only felt half-hearted.

The scene of Hague Amherst kissing Myla's hand replayed in his mind, bringing a mouthful of poisonous bile with it. At the sound of a sharp snap, his eyes flashed open to reveal two pencil halves, one in each hand. Much greater breaks would be imminent. One huge separation could take all his personal plans and dash them onto the cliffs of what-might-have-been, a shoreline he never saw coming.

He could almost feel Myla's stiff-arm defense already, like the one she'd given him at the drive-in movie during the romancing-in-the-waves scene. This one seemed to grab him right around the throat, though. "Once kissed and once missed" resurrected itself like a demon-creature between them. He hated being the "missed." He hated it with an ever-growing passion.

~

An odd feeling itched over her shoulder blades as Myla followed the security guard into Weston's lab. She glanced at her boss and quirked her brow, but the woman's bulldog expression gave no clues. Susie followed her so close, she'd already stepped on the back of her shoe twice. Once Myla entered the door, she spotted Skip Sellers and relaxed enough to take a breath. A half-circle of chairs faced Weston's desk, where the safety manager sat grim-faced.

Weston had his back to the group, fiddling with something on the rear counter. He glanced over his shoulder, but didn't seem to see her.

Myla took the end chair, and Alice Granger sat next to her. Susie alighted part-way in the third chair like a tiny bird. The atmosphere grew tense. No one spoke a word. Skip shifted his stance and moved a step behind Miss Granger's seat. Before she knew what was happening, the security officer exited and pulled the door closed.

Duncan Reed cleared his throat. "Mr. Durand, are you ready to begin?"

"Almost," Weston replied without turning around. A metal plate reported against the countertop. In seconds, he brought a small tray toward the group. He nodded and placed it on the desktop, a paper napkin covering its contents.

Mr. Reed picked up something that looked like an agenda and tapped it on the desktop. "This is a preliminary investigation which may involve your upholstery group, Miss Granger. We've asked the three of you in here today, because you're the ones typically out on the assembly shop floor. There has been a breach of security this week, and we wanted to disclose the object at the center of it, to see if you might be able to help us further the investigation."

"Go ahead, Mr. Reed," Alice replied. "We're out here working like everybody else. We've got nothing to hide. Our installation work speaks for itself."

Skip Sellers made a throaty noise as though he approved of her comment.

Myla looked up in hopes of catching Weston's attention. Perhaps he could wink to her in support. He might as well have turned into a dressmaker's manikin, he seemed so stuff-shirted and expressionless, standing beside Mr. Reed. Her professional bearing unhitched just a bit.

"The violation in question involves this item." Reed lifted the tray and removed the napkin. When he lowered it to eye level, a small punch rolled forward.

A stitch crimped Myla's side. The tool looked like one from her Snap-lite set. She crossed her arms and felt her waist for the tool pack, finding it secure and zipped tight.

Susie leaned forward to get a better look. "I may have used that particular tool."

Mr. Reed leaned over the desk, almost trapping Susie in his long shadow. "Since this tool has been marked, presumably by its owner, it will be easier for us to trace. Mr. Durand has brought the insignia up on his surface inspection machine, so we can verify the markings."

Myla glanced over at the fluorescent penetrant apparatus, the one that had regaled her with its galactic abilities only last week. Now, it seemed like a vise, squeezing out her breath.

Weston chose that moment to drop his manikin act. He reached for a photograph and handed it to Skip, who surrendered it to Alice.

Myla had no difficulty seeing the emblem highlighted by the penetrant despite its being framed by her boss's stubby fingers. The photograph bore the two letters of her initials, the ones with which she always marked her tools. "Might I examine the tool? I can confirm what the surface inspection revealed, if I could take a closer look."

Weston started to advance and seemed to freeze in mid-step. He gave a message-riddled look to the safety manager and gained a nod. Now with permission, Weston lifted the tray and handed it to her, his gaze diverted to the floor.

Though his disregard hurt, Myla reached for the tool, determined to aid the investigation. "It's a midsized punch, similar to the ones I recently ordered from Snap-lite Tools. I have my set right here, if you'd like to examine it."

"Yes, that would be in the best interest of all concerned," Mr. Reed replied. "As to the identifying mark, what is your determination?"

Myla fisted the punch while she unzipped the tool kit and produced the full set. She handed it to Weston, but when he acted like his shoes had been nailed to the floor, Skip intercepted the case and passed it to the safety manager. The nerves down her arm jangled. Her pulse began to bang against her eardrums.

With a flip of the case top, Mr. Reed exposed the tool set to the scrutiny of all. Like an eight-year old with a missing front tooth, the set had a gap in its array. One of the punches was missing. Reed held it closer to the three upholsterers to make it more obvious.

In a daze, Myla unfurled her fingers and held the punch up to look at its handle. Still partially stained with fluorescent dye, the shank above the crisscrossed handle bore the mark she'd put there herself. It read "MT" as clear as day. "Yes, this tool is mine," she managed, her throat as dry as August.

Reed made a notation on his agenda, the motion of his pen carrying a threat akin to eviction. The room fell quiet for several condemning seconds. The air grew impossibly thick.

Myla sank into a quagmire of circumstantial dread. She had to own up to the tool. Honesty was the best policy. Her mother had taught her well. A slow movement in her peripheral vision distracted her attention.

Susie rose to her feet. "Please let me repeat. I think I used that tool." She rolled her hands into a ball and rubbed her knuckles. "I won't sit here and let Miss Templeton get in all kinds of trouble on my account. Sometimes, I'm careless with our tools and leave them lying around."

Miss Granger stood and put her arm around the smaller woman's quaking shoulders. "We'll stand united in the accusation then. We all use those punches, as a matter of fact. They can come in quite handy, especially when an awl is too big for the job. Tell me, since when is it a crime to leave a tool laying around a cockpit by mistake? You're making a federal case out of it this time, for no apparent reason."

Reed responded by flinching a tendon in his jaw.

Weston's face turned red.

Skip shuffled his feet behind them.

Myla rose to her feet. Awareness overtook her, an inch at a time. It wouldn't have caught anyone's attention had the punch been left in the cockpit. No, it would have to be found in a more guarded location, one where it could cause a lot more trouble. She squeezed her eyes closed. In the darkness, the jet engine covers popped into mind. *Heaven in a hand basket.* They were suspecting her of staging a FOD. She stepped forward until she stood directly in front of Weston, leaving him no room to ignore her. "You found the leather punch inside the XT-37's jet engine, didn't you, Mr. Durand?"

His eyelids lowered in a leaden blink. The front of his shirt rose with an inhaled breath. His mouth hung open for an infinitesimal second as though he struggled with a response. "Yes, I did. I also have a job to do on the shop floor. Unfortunately, at this juncture, our two jobs have collided, Miss Templeton."

Myla clamped her gaze on Weston, the man she thought she knew. The friend she knew, the one who had declared his love on numerous occasions, would have come to her rescue by now—or at least have offered her some manner of consideration. Instead, she got the manikin.

Mr. Reed shot to his feet. The desk chair screeched across the floor as if to yield him added authority. "For the next two weeks while I'm out, I'm asking Mr. Durand to step into the lead for this investigation. Because of this, I'm requesting voluntary cooperation from the Interiors Department regarding a number of restrictions."

"Such as what?" Miss Granger boomed. She planted her heavy arm across Myla's shoulders. She now protected both her employees in true mother hen fashion.

"First, your access outside of your office and sewing room is restricted to Hangar C. If anyone on your staff is found in Hangar A, that blatant act will represent the grounds for immediate dismissal. Legal ramifications will likely follow."

"So we only work on the Bird Dogs for two weeks? That might just be a recipe for success, Mr. Reed. We'll have to catch up on the A-195's by October though. What else do you have?" Miss Granger widened her stance as if bracing for the next round.

Myla's brain had gone numb. The sensation soon spread to her heart, though she still could feel a trickle of sympathy for Susie. For Weston, she felt nothing. Neither shock nor the pain of separation bubbled up. He had known she'd be led in here a suspect, and he'd acted as though it meant nothing to him. Her speech earlier this morning to Susie echoed back in her ears. *Men have an insincere heart and cannot be trusted.* In repulsion, her stiff-arm fortitude popped back into place, rigid and unforgiving. She clamped her jaw tight to seal it.

Reed consulted his notes. "Secondly, for the sake of the investigation, we're asking you not to confer with any other employees. We are setting Mr. Sellers in a neutral position of employee advocate, as requested by the vice president's office. Please channel any concerns and/or correspondences you may have regarding the investigation through him."

Skip stepped forward and tipped an imaginary hat. He nodded and worked his mustache around a bit. A least his eyes were honest and clear.

Miss Granger gave a low growl. "Is it just me or does anybody else sense that the fox is guarding two separate hen houses with this set-up? Come on, we all know each other here—some better than others."

Reed cleared his throat and pretended to check the paper. "Yes, Miss Granger, you've jumped right into number three—conflict of interest. Ordinarily, I would be here to provide some demarcation between personal and private affiliations, but due to my unavoidable leave of absence, I have to defer my authority to Mr. Durand."

"And I've asked Skip for his support as a quality control liaison," Weston added, "to which he has agreed." He gave the man a strong nod of affirmation.

Indignation rose up Myla's spine. Her nerves tenuous at best, she'd heard enough about quality control and continuous improvement. She stood two steps away from losing her livelihood, a survival platform if ever one existed. When she grabbed at the missing tool to take possession, Weston clamped his hand over hers to deny it. She struggled against his strength which only drew them closer. Her fortitude faltered. "I'm truly sick of hearing this cockamamie mistake-proofing rhetoric, Mr. Durand, because you're about to make a whopper."

Weston looked deep into her eyes, while he peeled her hand open and withdrew the errant tool. "Poka-yoke, Miss Templeton," he whispered with a tilt of his head.

Myla balled her fist to knock the Japanese smirk off his face when a heavy hand jerked her away from Weston. Miss Granger tucked her in what felt like a wrestler's hold and gave her a sweltering look.

"So my next-to-the-last point is no consorting shall take place between any of the parties involved in this investigation. While we're making links with who could have perpetrated this act, we don't need any confutation to exacerbate the strained relationships." Reed gave Weston a long stare.

At that point, Miss Granger's jowls hung open, her pending county fair proposal hung out on the line like rainy day laundry.

Myla put her arm around the woman in solidarity. "Don't worry, Mr. Reed. That curtailment shouldn't be any great hardship." She sliced a look at Weston and saw the authentic hurt on his face. *Too late to bring in the gentleman now.* She heard Susie sniff and realized she had no tears for the situation, none at all.

"Lastly, we insist that you be walked out of the facility daily," Reed added. "I've arranged for security today, but in the future, you'll have to call them over when you're ready to depart for the day."

The gut punch of being deemed a potential criminal struck Myla with air-sucking force. Her ribs could have touched side-to-side as the air rushed right out of her lungs. The policing treatment shook her from head to toe. Had it not been for Miss Granger's steel grip on her shoulders, she would have melted in a puddle right there on the lab floor.

"What about lunch?" Alice asked. "Should we isolate ourselves and eat in the Interiors office? I wouldn't mind that."

Reed bent and scribbled a note on the paper. "Thank you, Miss Granger, as I had not thought of lunch. Yes, that seems fair treatment, if you don't mind."

"I don't mind anything for two weeks," she replied. "But don't try me much beyond that, as we have work to do in several other hangars. We're not the ones you're looking for. You have two weeks to figure that out. Ready, ladies?" She turned toward the door, her head held high. Susie draped over her left arm like a deflated dirigible.

Myla had but seconds to leave the scene a victor. She pulled at the waist of her coveralls to realign her dignity. When she spotted her tool set on the desk, she motioned for its return.

Mr. Reed scooped it up in one fluid sweep and planted it right in her palm. He nodded and dismissed them to the security officer.

Though she felt the weight of Weston's gaze from the periphery, Myla chose to disregard him in an act of self-preservation. He could have given her that missing punch, especially since he'd already taken a picture of it in his penetrant scan. Maybe he thought the errant tool might end up inside his precious jet engine again. The mere thought of it boiled her blood. She passed through the lab door and followed Susie down the walkway.

Weston didn't trust her anymore. A tiny ache deep in the center of her chest produced the first tears in her eyes. Though they threatened to drop, she willed them back, until she made it to the parking lot where it began to rain in an emotional cloudburst. How could such a tiny punch shatter a heart and poke a hole in her future like that? She wandered to her car inconsolable.

What had Weston told her? Poka-yoke—to avoid error. She remembered his introductory speech to the WC circle where workers would put up guards on their saws to keep them from cutting too deep. She needed a guard in place now, though the cut already seemed too deep to repair. Much too deep, and it was only Tuesday.

Chapter 16

Weston regarded the roster in front of him in search of a security breach that had led them to this miserable point. More than employees came and went from the aircraft facility. That pulse of extra activity injected a layer of chaos into his review. Engineers detested chaos, and he was no exception to the rule. His stomach growled in protest of having skipped breakfast to make more time for the morning's research.

He skimmed down the vendor's list and found the tool salesman. Even if his access proved legitimate, Hague Amherst still represented their best lead to perpetrate the tool sabotage. Weston needed to prove that suspicion by examining the schedule of his visits to the plant. The tornado had struck on a Friday, trapping him down in the basement with the staff. Since he'd detected the FOD on Tuesday, that timeline didn't exonerate the tool salesman from guilt.

The strewn tools represented another matter altogether, as they happened with much more frequency than once a week. He scratched his head and continued reading down the list of names to see if Snap-lite Tools sent anyone else out. It could be a tag-team effort, after all, not just one man. By the time he read through the lengthy 'W' entries to end the list, his eyes blurred with fatigue. When his stomach complained again, he stood for a time-out. He patted his front pocket to be sure he had coinage and then headed for the snack room to turn human again.

Filing down the balcony steps, he tossed a wave at two mechanics from Skip Sellers' crew. The shop floor echoed with noise, the kind that meant mass production of airplanes. He allowed the rivet-setting staccato to accompany him to the snack room. Relieved at finding no one inside, he approached the vending machine to select his late breakfast. When peanut butter crackers seemed too bland, he opted for the double-decker moon pie on the top row and slid his coins into the feeder slot. The mechanism twirled and hurled the treat with such zest, it bounded right out of the machine and slid to the rear wall.

A mutter of complaint under his breath, Weston stooped and traced the path of the snack through a year's worth of dust. Its wrapper gleamed against the tile molding at the base of the back wall, a boardinghouse reach. He fished his arm past the leg of the vending machine and wiggled his fingers until he made contact. Eye-level to the floor, he happened to glimpse a bundle tucked behind the drink cooler.

Suddenly both thirsty and curious, he drew out the moon pie, dusted it off, and stepped toward the soda station. One glance over his shoulder assured his privacy. He dropped a nickel into the soda cooler and angled the cola bottle out. The penny dropped on purpose. In chasing the copper coin, he got a closer look at the bundle. Wrapped in cloth, it looked to be about eighteen inches long. Though its ownership could be questioned here in such a shared public spot, he determined to inspect it, on borrowed terms if nothing else.

Once he grabbed the hidden cache, his imagination soared into the upper atmosphere. Its weight seemed considerable for such a compact package. Headed straight for the lab, he adjusted his grip on the cold cola which squished his breakfast pie the slightest bit. An unbalanced load, he wanted to have it all. He'd almost made it when Skip Sellers appeared from around a Bird Dog nosecone and tossed him a wave.

Without a spare hand, he nodded toward the lab door and, in seconds, the shop floor manager joined him.

"Say, what do you have there?" He shoved the door open and gestured inside.

"I don't know yet," Weston replied. "Close it, will you?" He knelt beside the desk and let the bundle roll onto its top. He set the drink down and tore at the cellophane wrapper on the snack with his teeth.

"Didn't your mother ever tell you not to do that?" Skip teased.

"Can't help it—I'm rabid with hunger." He bit into the double-decker and hummed.

Skip's eyes danced. "Thought I'd come see you before paying my liaison visit to the upholstery team today. Got any messages you want me to relay?"

He held up a finger to buy time since the chewy marshmallow filling between layers may not have been exactly fresh. He worked to swallow and needed a sip of drink. In his haste to gain the hidden package, he'd forgotten to jack off the bottle cap.

Skip stepped up. "Here, allow me." He twisted the spur-edged cap, and the soda burped with the carbonation release.

Weston took a long sip before clearing his throat. "Okay. That's better. I don't know what to make of this package I just found behind the drink cooler. How about we take a look?"

"Suits me." Skip pocketed the bottle cap and widened his stance.

He pulled at the fabric ties which soon proved to belong to an old-fashioned apron. As the bundle fell loosened, a stash of well-worn wrenches spilled out with a clatter.

"Holy mackerel. If I'm not mistaken, those look the same vintage as the ones Mr. Reed has been finding over in Hangar A."

Weston squinted, attempting not to look past the obvious. "These might represent the next round of strewn FOD fodder meant for Hangar A."

"So why are they stashed over here?"

"Easier? Safer? More invisible?" Weston took another giant bite out of the moon pie and worked on developing a nefarious scenario while he chewed.

Skip fingered a couple of the tools in silence. His Adam's apple worked up and down as he glared down at the cache. "Seems pretty premeditated, doesn't it?"

He nodded, swishing down another swallow of soda. "I've been thinking, if it is the tool salesman, he might have an accomplice. Say he's locked in his regular route, one that puts him here on Fridays. But we've found the tools on different days, so that part happens when he's not around."

"Don't forget, the cuts in the jet engine covers didn't come on Fridays either. I think you're onto something." He rubbed across his mustache and peeked at his watch.

"Look, I know you want to get out there and check on the women, but we've got to keep this accomplice thing mum for now. Don't mention this tool stash to anyone. I'm going to photograph the whole bunch and then put them back."

A furrow dug into the man's brow. "Return them? Are you crazy?"

"That way whoever hid them there won't know we're onto them. When these particular tools show up on the floor of Hangar A, we have confirmation that the two are related."

"Best roll them up the way you found them then. I'll go spend my time with the innocent folks caught in the crappy middle of all this mayhem. Got any messages to send?" Skip raised an empty palm at him.

Weston leaned his head back and took a long drink from the soda bottle. Myla's eyes had held disbelief and a searing speck of something else on Tuesday when the investigation came crashing down on them all. He'd only managed to offer her some cryptic advice at that point, which seemed to irk her even further. Perhaps he should tone it down a bit, especially since they were not supposed to be fraternizing in Duncan Reed's absence. "Guess you can tell them I'm in cold pursuit of the case." He raised the soda bottle and quirked a sneaky smile.

"Oh, they'll love that one," Skip replied as he exaggerated a frown. He shoved his hands into his pockets and headed for the door.

"Mum's the word on everything else," he insisted. His guest nodded and exited the lab door. He opened the top drawer and produced Reed's Instamatic camera. With a flash, he captured the evidence and worked to roll up the apron just like he'd found it. As he headed for the door to re-deposit the cache, he pulled a Cessna cap off a hook and hid the bundle beneath it, in case any passers-by might take an interest in blatant sabotage.

~

To ease her stiff knee, Myla extended her leg onto the gantry. Her once-pleasant work had turned into continuous dread. Her fingers hurt from chronic upholstery tugging, because Alice Granger had turned into a demon-possessed taskmaster. They'd done more work in two days than they usually accomplished in four. Poor Susie could barely keep up, though she didn't utter one word of complaint.

Alice grunted as she pulled out of the cockpit. "I'm finished back there. Let me go check on Susie for a minute."

"Okay. I'm on the final seam here." She picked up the stapler and eyed the placement of the first anchoring shot.

"How's my favorite crew getting along today?" Skip called from the bottom of the gantry. "Working hard is my guess."

Alice made the gantry wobble and soon a pair of hands grabbed the rail. "Now, that's more like it. When you see a lady in distress, you need to provide assistance."

"Pardon my lapse of chivalrous behavior, my fair lady." His teasing tone earned him a glancing blow on his muscular arm.

"Well, don't let it happen again," she replied. "I gotta go check on the kid over yonder. You can stay here and talk to Myla." She gave his shoulder blade an amicable tap and motored up the line to the next aircraft.

Myla ran a series of staples to finish out the seat cover and scooted to the edge of the cockpit. As much as she'd like to stay in a righteous huff over their treatment in the company's investigation, staying mad at Skip was not a possibility. To her surprise, he had climbed midway up the gantry and sat sideways on a step waiting for her.

"Are you doing all right?"

Myla collected her loose tools and zipped up her kit. "I've been better. Miss Granger plans to keep our noses clean by working our fingers to the bone." She eased onto the top step and gazed around the shop floor. "How is he?"

Skip fingered his mustache as if counting his words. "Making progress. Some venues have opened up."

"Well, he's not going to find any more evidence pointing to me. That tool was stolen and planted, just as sure as I'm sitting here."

"Uh-huh."

"That sleazy tool salesman Hague Amherst is deep into this. Make sure Weston knows that, will you?

Skip nodded and pulled a bottle cap out of his pocket.

"Here's something else. I think Susie made be dating the guy. I walked out from a cockpit and saw them together last Friday. She happened to be using my tools that day. He probably pilfered it right there and then. If I'd only known to watch, I wouldn't have gone the other way and ended up in Weston's lab. What a wasted effort that turned out to be."

"If it helps any, he's mighty subdued over this thing, too. None of us saw it coming, except maybe Mr. Reed." He flipped the bottle cap into the air off his thumbnail and made a game out of catching it.

Myla pressed her fingertips into her temple. "At any rate, Hague will be back around on Friday. I'm planning to set some bait to lure him into a trap."

"What kind of bait is that?"

"The bare-skinned kind." She unzipped her coveralls and blew a breath down her blouse.

"Don't go carousing with the devil now, Miss Templeton. That guy's a wily one."

"That's why I have to decoy him away from Susie. She's our weakest link right now. My ploy aims to outfox the wolf and take the pressure off her, so we don't make any more mistakes. Plus, I might gain some insight as to his motivations."

"I don't think Mr. Durand—"

"Skip, our Quality Control manager seems to hold me in little regard. Why should I give his wishes a second thought?" Irked, she let out a long exhalation.

Their staff liaison sat on the gantry mulling over her last acrid comment. "Well, he said to tell you he's in cold pursuit of the case. Take that for what it's worth, but the man does deserve some credit." At that, he flipped the bottle cap up again, twice as high as before.

Ready to have things turn her way, Myla snatched the bottle cap in midair. "Tell him this for me—hot bait is better than cold pursuit. Please give him this." She unzipped the kit and soon found an equal exchange, the bottle cap off her brand of justice, Sun Dew soda. She planted it in the palm of the go-between, knowing it would stick right between Weston's ribs, pain intended.

~

Weary from the day, Weston rocked back in his desk chair and took stock of his progress. He now had glimpsed a stash of tools that could be related to the FOD clutter used to pock-mark the floor of Hangar A. He had surface-tested two wing flaps, and they'd come through the penetrant scan beautifully. Skip had proven to be a trustworthy go-between, having delivered his message to Myla and brought hers back.

He eyed the Sun Dew bottle cap and allowed his thoughts to detour toward Myla. Where he'd use reason and logic to approach the investigation, she'd chosen a more emotional route for discovery. He was dull cola brown to her splash of lemon-lime, but the world needed logic like she needed him. The thought of her offering bare-skinned bait to lure Hague fell outside the limits of acceptability, though.

Skip had made a good argument for having the Bird Dogs rotate out the completion end of the assembly line. That way, he could keep the Interiors crew working in cockpits right off his office balcony. Skip could use the balcony for a viewing post to keep an eye on things come Friday. Plus, he could see everything transpire from right in his office chair, though the prospect held little positive compensation.

The weariness settled into his forehead in a low throb. He fingered the entry in the phone book and dialed the number one digit at a time. Even the receiver seemed heavy in his hand. He'd have to up his reps in the weight room tonight. When the connection clicked, he sat straight up. "Hello. Is this Midwest Food Distributors?"

"Yes, how may I help you?" a woman asked.

"This is Weston Durand from Cessna. I'm re-evaluating the vendor access list for our main facility off Hoover Road and K-42. We wanted to make sure we kept your route representative on our updated list. Can you assist me with that?"

"Yes, Mr. Durand. Let me look that up for you."

"I think her name is Betty or something like that," he added.

"Please hold a moment, sir."

Weston scanned the vendor list, but it lacked anyone named Betty. Skip had been pretty sure of that when he'd reported it. He closed his eyes and could see the plain-faced heavy-set woman as though she stood there in the room with him. The connection clicked open and he could hear a rustle of papers in the background.

"You're right about the name, Mr. Durand. That route belongs to Bette Rondale. She conducts every stop south of Kellogg, actually. That puts her in your neck of the woods two to three times a week."

"Can you spell that for me, so I can get it right on my list?" He reached for his pencil, which sent the bottle cap spinning.

"Sure. That's B-e-t-t-e, like Bette Davis spells her name. For the last name. That's odd. I thought it was Rondale but here it reads 'A' hyphen R-o-n-d-a-l-e. I never noticed that before."

"Oh, well maybe that extra 'A' is why I can't find her on my current list. I'll be sure to include it from now on. Thank you very much, ma'am. Have a good day." He swung the receiver back on the base and wrote down the hyphenated name. As the 'A' spawned another idea, he flipped forward in the phone book and found Hague Amherst's listing at 1406 Beckemeyer Street. He might just pay Mr. Amherst a drop-in visit, or at least give him the time of day for a friendly drive-by. He'd wait until dusk to give the salesman every opportunity to be home.

Weston pulled out the official record he'd been keeping on the investigation and wrote in the day's findings that included five worn tools and a possible snack-delivering accomplice. The onus fell on him to connect the two. He'd need more than three traded-in wrenches and two crooked screwdrivers to accomplish that.

He closed his eyes and touched the bottle cap, allowing its spurred edge to prick his fingertip as a reminder of Myla's painful position. He'd watch over her. God would have to watch over them both. He recalled the Bible verse that clearly said to flee from evil. Instead, they were courting it. Or at least one of them had gone a-courting. His stomach soured, making the possibility of finding a fast food bite to eat fly out the window with the scolding caw of a crow.

~

Myla turned in the mirror and viewed her profile that featured her latest selection. An off-the-shoulder blouse would be fitful to work in, but once she unzipped the coveralls, it would do nicely for skin bait. She had bought that blouse to interest Weston in her feminine features. Now, it had to be employed for lesser pursuits. She inhaled and sucked in her ribs, the draping lines of the chiffon collar glancing off the tops of her shoulders like Venus de Milo posed in sleek marble. She was the model of temptation. The thought made her frame shudder.

Footsteps padded up the hallway. "Myla, dinner is ready."

"Coming, Mother. Just give me one minute to change clothes." She shrugged out of the blouse and hung it back on the hanger. As she gave it one last inspection, she sighed and put it in the closet alongside her more innocent apparel. *Where in the world can I hide my stiff-armed protector in that thing? Lord, have mercy.* She grabbed a cotton shirt and slung her arm into it. When she stepped into the hall, the first tiny tinge of fear crept down her spine.

Chapter 17

Weston paced the distance from Hangar A to his office in record time. He had wagered that the old tools would not show up as FOD threats on a Friday morning, and they hadn't. In fact, everything looked primed and set for a productive day all around the XT-37. Father's Day was Sunday, which should put everyone in a good mood.

He flipped up the light switch about the time the phone started ringing. In three steps he had the receiver in hand. "Quality Control. Durand speaking."

"Weston, it's Duncan. How's your morning going?"

"Clean as a whistle, chief. Don't worry about things here. Are you keeping Lorna Rae off her feet this morning?"

"Time is up waiting for the baby to come naturally. She goes in this morning at ten o'clock to start being induced. She acts happy about it, though I'm a bundle of nerves. I called to ask for prayer, mainly for the baby and Lorna Rae."

"Count on me to pray. I'll spread the word around to my QC circle members, too. Do you think you could call me back by the end of the workday with news of the baby?"

"Let me add you to my list. Say, did you find out anything else after we talked yesterday?" His voice lowered and seemed muffled.

"When I did the drive-by at dusk, the snack company's delivery truck sat in the side yard. It looked like the regular parking spot, as the grass was rutted with repeated use."

"Good eye. They're in this together then. Since the tools didn't reappear on the floor of Hangar A, you might make a quick check to make sure they're still stashed in the snack room. You should try to interface with that distribution woman and learn more about her."

"Well, why not? Especially since my own girlfriend isn't speaking to me. I'll come up with something short of swabbing her with fluorescent dye and running a surface scan on her. People analysis is way out of my expertise. See what you're forcing me to do?"

A laugh reverberated down the phone line. "I've been through the same painful adjustment. Thank the Good Lord that I had Lorna Rae to see me through it back in those early days. Consider it your rounding out process in the meantime, Weston. I need to go. If you don't hear back from me today, pray all the harder."

"Will do, Duncan. I'm happy for your family. You're making the right choice to be there. Don't worry about us. I'll talk to you the first of the week, if not sooner. Goodbye." Weston lowered the phone, thinking how much the safety manager stood to gain in the next few hours. In comparison, all he would accomplish boiled down to surface scans and surreptitious activity on the shop floor. Neither inspired him much. To make good on the request for inspecting the snack room, he pivoted and left the office in obligatory haste.

Activity on the assembly floor appeared sluggish. He inspected several aircraft right in front of his balcony and could see they still needed finish work in the cockpit. He'd have to thank Skip for carrying through on that. He started a mental list of tasks to be done as he whirled into the snack room to peek under the drink cooler. When a figure straightened at his rapid approach, he froze stock-still. The snack distributor had beaten him to the room. In a quandary, he blurted out the first thing that came to mind. "Fancy meeting you here."

The woman turned to see if anyone else was standing behind her, her expression questioning his reception. "I uh, well, I come here a lot."

"It's Bette, isn't it? Happy Friday, Bette." He gave her a smile and a salute as he stepped toward the vending machine.

"Golly. Please excuse my mess. I'll be done stocking the machine in just a few minutes. A little early to be snacking, isn't it?" She grinned and ripped open a box of square nabs.

"I'm moving into a new residence and the kitchen cabinets are still bare. I need to get domestic over the weekend and hit the grocery store. How about you? Any weekend plans?" As soon as he asked, he feared it may have been too forward of him, so he tried to recover. "I mean Sunday is Father's Day, right?"

"No, not for some of us anyway. My parents are both gone now. I won't be doing anything this weekend, but getting off my poor aching feet. I might try to catch the baseball game on television. The Yankees are having quite a season."

"Aha. America's pastime. My father has been begging me to come back home and go fishing with him. It's such a long drive though." He pretended to study the rows of snack food, lost as to his next move.

She approached and got the peanut butter crackers all aligned in a proper row. "You should go while you still have your old man around." She shirked her shoulders and went back to unloading the box. Cinnamon rolls came next. "Hey, do you like these?"

Weston wrinkled up his nose in response. He'd never cared much for the filmy icing slathered on top. He tapped his chin with an index finger, reluctant to make his choice.

She brought the load of buns and dealt them into the slots with remarkable precision.

"You're pretty good at that, like a poker dealer."

"Thanks. Say, I don't know your name." She dug into the box and lifted out the next treat. A load of moon pies skittered across the table.

Like a kid in a candy shop, his face animated at the chocolate temptation. "I'm Weston, from Quality Control. Guess you could say I'm a fan of how neat you keep this place."

"Well—that's sure to be my best compliment today," she replied in a teasing tone. "Do you like these?"

"Oh, yeah. That's what I came down here for, a double-decker moon pie. See, you've figured me out, and we've only just met." He started to wink and made it a blink at the last second. *Good grief.* He was terrible at this kind of thing.

"Then here, this one is on me." She shoved the treat toward him across the table.

Stupefied at the prospect of receiving her kind favor when he was actually conducting surveillance, Weston froze in place.

"Really, go ahead. I do it all the time. Shucks, if I had a nickel for every messed up snack I'd ever given away, I'd be on vacation in the Caribbean by now. Ask the guys in Hangar B."

"No, I can't accept this, Bette. Besides, these aren't messed up at all. They look just fine." He held both palms out to demonstrate his refusal.

She tipped her head as though to accept his decline. A split second later, her fist walloped the moon pie with a powerful blow. Knocked well out of perfection, it now sat a lot closer to a pile of crumbs as far as condition went.

In an attempt to hide his mortification that a civil woman could act that way, he reversed his repulsion and made a grab for the less-than-intact snack. He tugged a crooked grin into his cheek and gave her another salute. "Thanks for this…and the Father's Day advice. See you next week, Bette."

"Okay, Weston. Good luck with that grocery shopping."

He exited without looking back, fearful that she might volunteer to accompany him and show him the ropes. Instead of chastising himself over his cultural ineptitude, he replayed their conversation in his head to isolate what he'd learned. Both her parents were dead. That might be worth noting. He swung the pulverized snack between his finger and his thumb while diverting to the admin wing where the coffee blend didn't burn a hole in the pit of his stomach. He still didn't know if the tool cache remained, but he could certainly confirm that later. Right now, he had to eat breakfast, maybe using a spoon.

~

At odds with her clothing all morning, Myla pinched through her coverall to adjust the drooping shoulder of her blouse. She centered the back panel of the pilot's seat and started the rapid-fire arch of staples to hold it firmly in place. She'd no more than reached for the glue bottle when someone started striking the gantry rail down below.

"Myla, I've messed this one up big time," Susie called. "Can you come lend me a hand?"

"Yeah, give me a few seconds here." She drew the glue track and found the piping to trim out the seam. With more haste than Miss Granger required, she slapped the line in place and anchored the tailings with a staple on each side, beneath the seat and out of sight.

When she pulled out of the cockpit, a slight breeze played across her skin. Out of dire necessity, she unzipped and dropped the coveralls to her waist. She drew a breath and threw her head back in a lumbar stretch to feel human again.

"Don't start posing now," Skip called from below, his tone playful. He nodded back toward Susie as she stood waiting with hands on her hips.

"I'm simply roasting today. Guess I forgot what June could be like." She slid down a few steps on her rump and glanced around the hangar.

Skip scuffed his shoe. "He's not here yet."

"Who? What makes you think I'm looking for someone?"

"Because your bare-skin bait is out, that's how." He harrumphed and paced down the shop floor.

Embarrassed, she hoisted the heavy coverall back into place and pulled the zipper toward her chin. At the bottom of the gantry, she looked up in time to see Weston's back as he entered his office. How much of that exchange had he seen and heard? With the new planes being hauled right in front of his office, she couldn't do much about being in plain sight.

She walked over to Susie, who motioned her up the stairway. "How bad is it?"

"I left a wrinkle in the seat that won't pass Miss Granger's inspection. Lord knows, I'm trying hard." Susie huffed and followed her up the gantry.

"I've told you before. You have to stop this from happening from the first tuck you position. If it's off, the entire cover will be off." She knelt in front of the botched installation job and tried to determine the least amount of ripping out required.

"Show me that trick leveraging the tool again, will you? I got that to work once or twice before, but I've forgotten the hand placement on it."

"Okay, but what you really need to focus on is the alignment aspect. Get right in front of the seat if it helps you square up visually." She emphasized the last few words, not meaning to run out of patience with her trainee. She tore at the left seam until it loosened enough for resetting. With fabric to work under, she took out a leather punch and rolled it like a tightening rod. The wrinkle flattened to smooth, supple leather, just what the customer would want. "There you go, Susie, one perfect seat. Now, stitch up this seam again and you're done."

"I'll pay you back some day, I promise." She switched places and got right to the seam.

Myla tossed back her sweat-drenched hair and wished she'd worn a headband to hold her bob off her face. She slid down the stairs and headed back to her aircraft, ready to tackle the back seat. In half an hour, she could have lunch and cool off under the shade of a black locust tree between hangars. That left her just enough time to finish the job.

Someone stepped into her path. "Hey there. Glad to see you made it through that tornado last week." Hague Amherst smiled and tucked a package into the crook of his elbow.

"Hello, Hague. Yes, all is fine and dandy now, except the far end of Hangar C. Once the new fiscal year begins next month, they'll fund the rebuilding project on that portion. Is that Susie's new tool set you're toting around there?"

"Yeah, she wants the same set you bought. I think there may be some admiration going on there." He winked and glanced around.

Myla cringed, her finger playing with the tab of her zipper. "Listen, can you give her a few minutes? She's fixing a mistake, and I need her to get it right."

"Sure thing. Want me to come back around?"

"No, I've got a few minutes to kill, if you want to hang out."

He combed through his unruly hair. "You bet."

Myla sat on the gantry steps and let the coverall down enough that it draped across her arms. She fanned her face and shook her hair. "So, have you been busy this week?"

He squatted and leaned against the stairs beside her. "They're slowing me down by adding that Hutchinson route to my regular territory, but I'm killing it with sales. I'll make my bonus two months running now. Extra money is always nice."

"I'd be horrible at sales. Guess it pays to have the right skill set." She blew down her blouse and shrugged it further off her shoulders. The breeze caressed her neck as a set of rivets pounded from close by. "You ever thought about settling down to one location like the plant here?" Finally, she'd managed to get one of her intentional questions posed.

"Not a chance, baby cakes." He glanced around the hangar with disdain. "No, this isn't for me, not by a long shot."

She needed to drag this out further. Maybe she'd play her desperation card next. "I broke up with my boyfriend." She closed her eyes and pictured Weston standing like a manikin. "He's such a stuffed-shirt white collar type. What was I thinking?"

"You look hot today, Myla, and I don't mean weather hot." He smiled and his gaze held the smoke of masculine attention. "I know you shot me down the first time, but I've got better manners than that. Think about giving me a second chance to prove it. I'm definitely interested."

"Thank you, Hague. I may need a couple of weeks to get over this guy. How about you stay in touch? Can we leave it like that for now?" She stood and resisted the urge to bolt.

He rose and came around the gantry rail to face her. With his free hand, he reached for her coverall front and lifted it back up onto her bare shoulder. When she managed the other side, he tugged at her zipper pull to close the coveralls. His motion came slow and deliberate as his gaze seemed to lick her skin. When he released the tab, his fingertips brushed against her neck.

"Such a cool jerk," she said, lowering her lashes.

"Hey, that's what my sister calls me. Can't be all bad, right?" He backed away, his palm splayed out, feigning innocence.

She smiled and nodded toward her assistant. "Maybe not. Keep it short with Susie. She's behind schedule." She backed up the steps, watching until she saw him nod, and then turned and retreated to what she felt comfortable with—supple leather. Immersed in her work, she failed to hear the visitor approach up the stairs until a shadow fell across the pilot's seat.

Skip leaned into sight. "Hey, Miss Templeton. The boss wants you up in his office when you get this seat done."

An irritation surfaced as she pulled the cover into place. "Miss Granger is my boss."

Skip cleared his throat as a few seconds ticked by. "Bring Alice if you want, but I think this might be a meeting of the more personal nature."

Caught in the aftermath of her bait-and-inquiry session with Hague, a spitfire correctional confrontation with Weston might count as the last thing she wanted. "We're not supposed to consort, you know."

"I told him much the same thing. He said he had something of yours to give you. Besides, it's lunchtime. Maybe we could call a ceasefire, it being Friday and all."

"Miss Granger thinks I'm eating with her back at the office."

"I'll escort Susie over there instead. Don't worry about us." Skip looked left to right as though an ambush might be lurking. "He's struggling with the load right now. Could you please go up there, like he's asked?"

"Oh, all right. Just this once, I suppose. Would you make sure that tool guy isn't hanging around Susie for me? I told him to keep it short. He had a new set of tools to drop off."

"You mean more tools to lose?" He snickered and exited the cockpit.

"Fine and dandy," she muttered. "I'll take my sweet time about it. Duty first and all that." In fifteen minutes, she'd done all the stapling and trim work the job required. The two rear seats looked perfect. She'd done an exemplary job, so why were her knees quivering? She swept the cockpit floor with her gaze and gave all four seats a final inspection.

Her feet clanged down the stairs while she took off her tool kit. She locked it around the gantry rail like usual and looked up above the balcony at her destination. Her next breath hitched against her ribs as a traitorous backlash coiled through her. She'd spoken it, and now she was about to live it—breaking up with her boyfriend. It came with a stab, even if she'd caused it.

In the long run, she'd been trying to help Weston. Perhaps that could serve as some consolation late at night when she had no one to wrap their arms around her on the back deck glider. She sighed and made the ascent. A prayer came forth, though she hadn't conjured one up.

Myla lowered her shoulders and entered the office. Dark, she could see the bluish light of the penetrant apparatus remained on in back. "Weston? Are you in here?"

Something moved to her left. "I'm here."

She backed up against the door, a hundred thoughts springing to mind all at once. Shouldn't she turn on the lights to get this out in the open? "Skip said you wanted to see me?"

"That's right." He moved closer, his breathing shallow.

A prickle of anticipation ran through her. "You have something of mine?"

"Yes, I do, your bottle cap."

She felt the words more than heard them, he had moved so close. With a tug, her zipper headed down and a cool sensation swept over her as the coveralls peeled off her shoulders. Her mood shot from defensive to something deeper. A fingertip traced the edge of the chiffon and halted near her heart. A second went by until she felt the poke of the bottle cap freefalling down her cleavage. She needed to say something. "Hague Amherst has a sister. You should find her."

"Exactly what did you say to him?" His hand slid up her neck where a knuckle skimmed her jaw.

"I called him a cool jerk. He laughed and said his sister always called him that."

"You two were mighty cozy there on the gantry, which seems odd to me, since he knows I'm in the picture." His hand grew weighty where it rested against her collarbone.

"I told him we'd broken up—as a ploy to keep him engaged in conversation, nothing more." She could plant a kiss on him at this range, just to prove it. Her heart pounded.

His hand evaporated from the surface of her hot skin. "I see. That's it, Myla. I'm taking you off the case. No discussion. Stay clear of Hague Amherst. He's on a slow course of self-destruction. I'm not letting him take anyone else with him."

"Especially me?" Pushing through the hurt, she wanted to hear him say it.

"Most especially you. Love is not some trinket you dangle in harm's way. You have to protect it, Myla." He sounded as though he'd backed away.

Needle pricks shot down the back of her neck. She'd been guilty of toying with his affections, but wouldn't do it again for the world. Her chest grew leaden. "So we're not breaking up?" she asked, her tone tinged with hope.

A chair scraped against the floor as Weston sat in front of the penetrant scan device, a black silhouette. Seconds passed. "You may be dismissed for lunch now. Remember, you're off the case while still a suspect. You know what guilt-by-association is, I presume."

Pained by his allusion, Myla grabbed the doorknob and tried to exit before the first sob broke loose. She ran down the balcony and headed straight for the Interiors office to share her pathetic lunch with two other spinsters in coveralls who seemed better equipped at maneuvering around in this man's world than she did.

As she passed, the new hangar door seemed to mock her, so she gave it a swift kick which only added pain to her list of regrets. Late June greeted her with ninety-five degrees radiating off the black tarmac like a real no-man's land, perfect for her situation. She dropped the coveralls to her waist. If this was hell she'd walked into, she planned to walk in fully exposed.

Chapter 18

Weston knew this stream as a boy. It ran as clear today as it had twenty years ago. A gossamer monofilament line arced halfway across its width and made contact with the surface without a splash. His father had the right touch. With a mere flick of his wrist, the cast found the perfect spot, oftentimes with a fish lurking nearby. "Happy Father's Day, Dad."

"Thanks, Son. You made that come true by walking in our front door yesterday afternoon. I haven't seen your mother that happy in ages. Plus, I'm getting a chocolate cake out of it, too." He twitched the line, and it angled toward a shady patch.

Despite some graying around his temples, his father looked like the same man who had driven him to his first day of elementary school to start his run at higher education. He had capped the journey by attending Weston's graduation at Iowa State. A long history of trust melded with high expectations had forged between them. Now, he needed fatherly advice again.

"Dad, there was an accident at work back in May I wanted to tell you about."

"Oh, anybody hurt?"

"At the last second, I had to rescue a young woman trapped in harm's way. We both got hurt—but it could have been worse. I limped for a few days with a cut on my right calf. For her part, she had to take a few stitches in the hip."

He nodded and flicked his wrist. "Is she anyone special?"

"Yes. I think I'm falling for her, Dad. Her name is Myla Templeton. She's beautiful and creative. Her upholstery work is top-notch, and she's even started an innovative line of interior design for the aircraft cabins in a western theme. She's helping me at my cottage, arranging furniture and such."

"So her opinion matters to you?"

"It does. She matters a great deal. I'm trying to understand my strategy, if you will, as I seem to be undone by her proximity, many times at the wrong moment. Right now, there's been an act of sabotage at work, and I'm in charge of the investigation. Unfortunately, I detected one of her tools planted as a hazard inside a jet engine which places her as a prime suspect. We all know it couldn't have been Myla, but the safety manager slapped a 'no consorting' limitation on us during his leave of absence. I'm struggling through that sanction, no denying it."

"Best to concentrate on the long term at times like that. When a fellow says, 'no you can't' then you have to ask 'when can I?' and work toward that mark. It sounds like the solution to your problem is to find the real culprit."

"I think I'm hot on the trail with a suspicious tool salesman who may have a handy accomplice. He's on and off the site as part of his delivery route. My biggest problem is I don't have a motivation to pin on him, not to mention little circumstantial evidence. Like a darling hindrance, Myla has thrown herself in the mix, flirting with the guy to gain information."

"You don't need that kind of help. She doesn't realize how unpredictable that kind of riff-raff can be. How'd you counter that?"

Weston pretended to check his line and fought back a guilty smile. "She tried to set some skin bait to lure him in. You could say I nailed her on it afterward and forbade any further involvement in the case."

"Good tactic." He released his rod with one hand and scratched his forehead beneath the brim of his hat. "If you can keep her out, I mean. Women can be headstrong. She does have her innocence to protect."

"In more ways than one. This guy's a greasy Romeo. He probably has a filly at every site he visits. I've spotted him a time or two with one of our female test pilots, roaming the tarmac like an alpha wolf hot on the scent. In truth, I've doubled my weightlifting regiment every night, worried it might come down to me against him."

"Outthink him, son. That's your real weapon. Collect your evidence and find the chink in his armor. Maybe he doesn't have a wise old dad to give him good advice like you do." He chuckled and began to reel in his line.

"You're right. I'm getting to know the possible accomplice—his sister. She mentioned the parents were both deceased." He walked up the bank toward his father as the water agitated between them.

His father pulled back and set the hook with a grin. "Want to bring him in, Son?"

"No, you go ahead. It's Father's Day, after all. Besides, you need the bragging rights." He laughed, waiting for the fish to clear the water's edge before he slapped Weston on the back.

The fish gleamed in the sunlight and his cares took momentary wing. "I'm glad I came home, Dad. It's good to talk like this."

"Once you split the investigation wide open, Mother and I would like to come see your little house on the river and meet this young lady. But, I can venture—if you like her, we like her, too. No question." He unhooked the bluegill and tossed it back into the water.

"Aha. You've gone catch-and-release on me, huh?"

"Well, now that I know romance may be in the offing, I want my grandkids to have fish to catch some day." He wiped a hand down his dungarees and then slapped his arm around Weston's shoulders. "That part, in particular, is going to make your mother elated."

"Look at me, playing the part of a good son. Guess that means your investment is paying off." He grinned, though the stink of fish slime grew stronger by the minute.

"It sure does. Plus, you're buying dinner tonight, now that you have a great salary after all those years of scrimping by at the university." He gave him a jostled hug and released him.

"Don't forget I close on the house this coming week. That's when I have to cough up the down payment and sign for the thirty-year mortgage." He shook his head as though it was a heavy load to assume all at once.

His dad threw a hand in the air in protest. "Bah, ask your mother for a cough drop and get on with it. I don't know a man worth his salt that hasn't taken on a mortgage responsibility of some sort. The financial commitment keeps you honest."

"And reporting to work regularly." He picked up the familiar tackle box and pointed back up the path. "Let's go see if Mom has that cake baked yet. She might like to ride around the country some on our way out to dinner."

"That's thoughtful of you, Weston. I hope Myla appreciates that about you." He tugged down his hat to match the declining sun.

"I can only hope so too, Dad. Hope and pray, that is." He stared at the unkempt grass along the edge of the path, his thoughts skidding through technicalities in the sabotage investigation. There had to be something more. He just needed to look closer to find it.

~

Myla immersed herself in the sewing job. Yards of cream-colored glossy cotton, accented with small geometric links overlaid on it, stretched across the dining room table. She'd known it as soon as she'd seen it in the fabric store yesterday. This would make ideal curtains for the front two windows of Weston's cottage. The gold would tie in the gilt of the dining room chandelier and the off-white would contrast with the dark walnut wood. She had measured to include a top casement to gather the curtains on the rod, but now considered whether clip-on rings might be a better choice to allow for proper pleating.

So immersed in the project, she'd lost track of the time. The sun had fallen behind the cottonwoods in the distance. The effect muted the lighting in the room. She stood to flip on the overhead light when the doorbell sounded. Her heart leapt into her throat, as drop-in guests at the Templeton residence were few and far between. She switched off the sewing machine and walked to the front door. She brushed loose threads from her pants before pulling the door open.

Reggie Brewster tipped his cane at her. "Hey there, Myla. Is your mother home?"

"Why yes, Mr. Brewster, please come in."

"I came to town to celebrate Father's Day with Uncle Art, and thought I'd stop by to see Effie so we could catch up a bit." His smile rose from his lips and crinkled his eyes with genuine pleasure.

"I think she's knocking around back in the utility room. Let me go get her."

He held up a finger to halt her and shifted his weight onto the cane. "First, let me say that your father was a noble man for serving in the military and giving his all for his country. Days like today bring back the empty hurt of such personal sacrifice. I can tell you, he'd be honored to know you and your mother have made a real go of it here in his absence."

"Thank you for saying so, Mr. Brewster."

"That's Reggie—if we're going to be friends—and I hope we are. That's part of what I've come to talk to Effie about, but I can't go spilling the beans yet. Point me toward her, will you?"

She snickered and gestured toward the kitchen. "Positively do not look in the dining room. I have the place in a wreck right now. I'm sewing some curtains for Weston's new house."

"Well, that's mighty domestic of you. I mean that in a nice way. Rest assured, he'll appreciate it." He approached the back with measured steps as though not in a hurry. "If I had to speak the truth, I think that young man has a bad case for you, young lady."

"Something's come up at work that stands between us," she replied. "I'm ever hopeful it will pass, but we're under tightened security right now. July's going to be absolutely abysmal if these sanctions don't get lifted soon. Now, I see why freedom is so all-fired important."

Effie walked into the kitchen from the utility room. "Oh, Reggie. I didn't hear you come in. Will wonders never cease? I was just thinking about you and now, here you stand."

"My, my, Effie. You're going to swell my ego talking like that. I drove up to spend the day with Uncle Art. I even took him out for lunch, so he didn't have to cook."

She laughed and straightened her hair. "You would not believe how my garden had taken off. Why, there must be twenty dinners worth of squash and zucchini out there with more blooming. The green beans have taken up that trellis you set up for me at least waist high. Do you have time to come take a look?"

"My dear, I thought you'd never ask," he replied with a chuckle. When Effie held out her arm, he accepted it like she was royalty.

Myla watched them without a word as they strolled down the deck toward the garden plot. Her mother had male company, yet she did not. This came as her penance for cheap involvement where she had no business. Disheartened, she came back into the dining room and examined her progress. She could get this panel knocked out tonight and be done with the first pair. That would give her something productive to do in her spinsterhood each evening as June disintegrated into July. Independence Day popped into mind, and she squelched it right then and there. Their separation had to be over by the holiday. It simply had to.

~

Weston stepped into the stuffy room where the historic records were kept. The head librarian led him through a tight passageway, until they arrived at the back wall. For the seven hundredth time, he told himself the time investment would be worth the afternoon away from work. If he had known what he was looking for, it would help at this point.

She bent and opened the slant-top oak cabinet which exposed stacks of newspapers folded in neat rows. "This cabinet contains the years forty-six and forty-seven. You go right from here until present. Over there we have a card file for topics and some individuals by name, if they were well-known, that is. We cannot make an endless list of key words or the card catalogue would run out of room."

"That's perfectly understandable. I'll take it one stack at a time then, from nineteen forty-six forward. Thank you for getting me situated." He removed a notebook from his briefcase as she glared at him and surrendered her tidy reference section. He turned to the cabinet and found the year clearly labeled. He only hoped that the seven-shaped cut in the jet cover would save him considerable time in the research arena. If it represented an anniversary, he'd be able to ferret out the significance. He skipped the first stack and soon located the June papers. He cradled them in his palm to preserve the order and placed them on the work table nearby.

He eyed the card catalogue before sitting down. There could be something under Amherst in there, which would serve as a shortcut. He stepped over and pulled out the first narrow drawer and filed back alphabetically. No listings had been made under that name. Of course, there would be no shortcuts. He'd have to read through this fading typeset and get eyestrain to find the slightest clue.

He returned to the table and checked his scribbled notes. Yes, prioritize aircraft news and also check obituaries, ever looking for the A-name. Easy as pie, as though pies were easy at all, which they weren't.

A mind-numbing two hours later, he glanced at his watch and let out a long exhale. On June twenty-eighth, a fatal construction accident had made the front page of the Wichita Beacon. A picture caption lamented the need for women in the hazardous workplace. He turned several pages to the local section and scanned the obituaries. Nothing turned up. He slid the next paper off the stack and continued his process. The paper for the twenty-ninth held the obituary for the mother of two grown children. Something about the picture seemed familiar. The woman's eye teeth crowded her front teeth, making both appear crooked in her wan smile.

Onto something, he glanced at the name, Barbara A. Rondale. His palms broke out in a sweat, and he yanked his tie loose. As he read down, he discovered that the cause of death seemed sudden, but hadn't been specified. He pulled the previous day's paper back and reread the front page article about the construction accident. It identified the victim as a forty-four-year old female laborer. Back to the obituary, he found the date of birth and calculated the deceased's age at forty-four years.

His breath grew short. This Barbara Rondale shared her last name with the snack room attendant as well as her flawed smile, but not Hague Amherst. Yet the middle initial was 'A,' and that lent a single letter of possible connection, like Bette's hyphenated name. No children were specifically mentioned in the brief obituary, which ended only with the mortuary's name.

Weston took his notebook out and copied the obituary, word for word. He planned to do the same with the construction accident report. He could check other records for this Barbara Rondale, possibly a marriage record that might lead to an interesting maiden name or similar connection. On fire for the advancement, he wrote as fast as he could while keeping it legible.

The moon pie-crushing snack room attendant soon tangled his focus, recalling her crooked smile after she'd pulverized the treat, so he could legitimately take it. Those two were most definitely mother-daughter. He really needed to know Bette's age, so he could better track down the mother's marriage license. That would take a little prying, but he could add a touch of flirtation and make a game of it. She'd be making her rounds tomorrow morning. He would copy a play right out of Myla's game plan and turn on the charm.

He reached for the previous paper and the sensation of being outside of his comfort zone filtered under his shirt collar. Duncan Reed needed to get back to his position as safety manager and stop playing wet-nurse to his new son. *How much work could a newborn be anyway?*

He stopped writing to count out the days left in Reed's leave of absence. With the company closed Monday for the holiday, he wouldn't report back to work until next Tuesday, a week and a day from now. Surely he could continue to pick up wayward tools to fend off an FOD, find a missing connection for his culprit, and save his girlfriend from jail time in eight days. It was as easy as pie, squashed moon pie.

Chapter 19

Weston eased down the balcony stairs as rehearsed lines cycled through his brain. He had not encountered any new tool bundles in the snack room during his early inspection rounds this morning. Perhaps that would portend that the jovial snack room attendant might be somewhat approachable today. He'd been praying for favor, as he truly needed it.

When he reached the bottom step, it occurred to him that he'd been employing a surface scan to solve the case, though it deserved an eddy current inspection for deeper content. He never ranked psychology among the real sciences, but he sure could have used a crash course for this case. The picture in the obituary came back to mind. He shook his head at the woman's hollow expression. Like a haunt, it seemed reluctant to let go.

Noise up ahead brought him back to the shop floor. A gantry swung into place off a Bird Dog fuselage, where he spotted the bulk of Alice Granger in position to start her installation work. He tried not to scan the area for fear that Myla might be close by. He had a job to do this morning, so he couldn't get sidetracked. If the attendant hadn't arrived in the snack room yet, he'd head on down to talk to Skip about the QC meeting tomorrow.

In a matter of steps, he discovered that his delay tactic would not be necessary. The snack room rang with lively humming while a dozen cinnamon rolls met the vending machine. He enlivened his step and made the plunge into the room. "Aha! Fancy meeting you here." He smiled and cocked his head to one side.

"Hey there, Weston. I'm already three-quarters done. I

wondered if you'd show up for our regular rendezvous." Bette tossed a snack cake into the air and banked it into place for dispensing. A smirk spread across her face, both framed by a red bandana tied around her hair.

"There's lots of work yet to be done down in my lab, but a man cannot ignore his more primal urges, can he?" He chuckled and rubbed his stomach.

"Oh, I like a man who is aware of his own needs, that's for sure." She waggled her brow and turned to stash another handful of rolls into the machine.

"You're quite the enigma, do you know that?"

She stopped in mid-step, her face blank.

"No, I mean it. You know this place like the back of your hand. I'm an expert at quality control, and efficiency is one of our paradigms. I'm an admirer of yours, for sure."

"Well, if that isn't one of the sweetest things anybody's ever said to me." She reached deep into the crate and brought up the last carton of snacks. When she popped it open, the moon pie wrappers shimmered in the light.

"Anyone twenty-one years old that can handle this material so adeptly and get the individual pieces stocked in place deserves being raved over, believe you me." He propped up a foot in the doorway and then crossed his arms to lock her in his gaze.

"I thought a man like you would handle numbers better, my friend." She turned her back to tend the machine, but a blush of red worked up her neck before she could hide it. "Twenty-one came and went a couple of years ago without much excitement, all things considered."

"No—you don't look twenty-three. Why, you're as lithe as a teenager. That's not to say twenty-three isn't special. There's Shakespeare's twenty-third sonnet that's famous, and Psalm twenty-three. Dare I mention that it's a prime number, too?"

"Prime for what? A sonnet or a song? I don't know either one. All I know is stocking snacks and counting coins." She hoisted another handful of moon pies into the vending slots.

Had Weston been centered over a fulcrum's point, he would have easily snapped in half at his predicament. Far off his original game plan, he now had two directions to turn the conversation, and Shakespeare's ode to love positively would not do for this situation. He opted for King David's words, a ready balm for the wounded no matter how deep the psychological scarring. "'The Lord is my Shepherd, I shall not want.'"

Bette glanced up from the crate slack-jawed, and then diverted her eyes back to her work.

"'He maketh me to lie down in green pastures: he leadeth me beside the still waters. He restoreth my soul: he leadeth me in the paths of righteousness for his name's sake. Yea, though I walk through the valley of the shadow of death, I will fear no evil: for thou art with me; thy rod and thy staff they comfort me. Thou preparest a table before me in the presence of mine enemies: thou annointest my head with oil; my cup runneth over. Surely goodness and mercy shall follow me all the days of my life: and I will dwell in the house of the Lord forever.'"

Bette sniffed and made quick work of getting the money bag into the crate. She shoved a foot under the wheeled dolly and made toward him at the door. Before she could exit, she backhanded a tear off her cheek and gave him a sad smile. "Thanks for the poetry recitation. It means a lot. We didn't get church training when we were young, so I didn't know what to expect. That was comforting, Weston. Thanks for sharing it with me." Her face blotched with pent-up emotion. She looked up at him and seemed hungry for something more.

"God is a caring Father, more than we'll ever know." He reached for her without analytical assessment and landed a platonic pat on her shoulder.

She bounded from the room as though running scared. Only the squeak from the dolly wheels followed her until another round of riveting began.

Weston dropped his foot from the door frame and turned to head for his lab. He rounded the shop walkway and there stood Myla, a horrified look pinching her radiant facial features. Unchecked and well off-script, he held out an open palm toward her in minimalistic explanation, causing her to bound up the nearest gantry with a gasp. He didn't miss the subsequent swipe of her hand across her cheek, though her back was toward him.

A genius need not expound that he'd just made two women cry with the same recitation. Heaven help him, wedged in a war zone of truth versus deceit. Even he couldn't decipher his allegiance, friend or foe. However, he did have what he'd come for. He had a count of twenty-three years, which he'd take all the way to the county magistrate's office.

~

Myla accepted Skip's arm and allowed him to lead her into the meeting room. Other members of the QC circle nodded as they took their seats. Her navy linen dress, worn as a tribute to the upcoming holiday, made it difficult to sit with its tailored fit. She crossed her ankles and hid her high heels under her chair. With a flip, the notebook opened. She jotted down the day's date, June twenty-seventh.

Her regular practice, she gazed around the room to account for the members present. She wrote in the members' names and kept her gaze fixed on the page as Weston shared a laugh with Rich Yost. Only Ernie Pike was missing. Maybe she could maintain her distance from Weston and survive the meeting without an emotional breakdown. The river she'd cried in bed last night might serve her well in the long run. Her eyes felt gritty and dry this morning.

A man's voice split the room carrying a Jackie Gleason taunt. "And away we go."

Rich Yost stood and elbowed the late member. "If you'd lay off the doughnuts, Ernie, maybe you could be on time."

"What's the fun in that?" the man replied as he took his seat. Three-quarters of a glazed doughnut hung from his index finger.

The scene struck Myla as a slapstick rendering of an Abbott and Costello skit, making a smile tug at her lips. Skip harrumphed beside her, and she glanced up in the other direction only to lock gazes with Weston. Though stoic, his face seemed to soften before he looked down at his agenda. She swallowed the lump in her throat and pledged to focus on business—not pleasure—for the remainder of the meeting.

"Let's get started then," Weston said. "Thank each of you for being here. These are especially hard times for me, as I'm doing double duty for my work, as well as for the safety manager, Duncan Reed. By way of an update, his wife delivered a baby boy last week, but little Timmy is experiencing what the doctor's call 'failure to thrive' and seems to be struggling to gain ground."

Myla gasped, unaware of any such postpartum complication.

Duncan Reed must be worried out of his mind, and Lorna Rae at a complete loss as to what to do. She hung her head while making a cryptic note in the margin.

"At any rate, I'm certain your thoughts and prayers would be appreciated." Weston cleared his throat to work through the personal message. "I hope it doesn't seem egregious to start out with some wry Midwest wisdom, but I'd like to quote humorist Will Rogers to open our meeting. He once said, 'Even if you are on the right track, you'll get run over if you just sit there.'" He paused as the quote earned a few chuckles.

"That sure felt like my progress yesterday, as I stumbled on an important quantification for my investigation, but affected someone adversely in its extraction. I wanted to put it out there to this team that such a result was far from my intention. I should stick to quality control, where I hold more confidence."

Skip laughed, which took the sharp edge off the apology. "So much for continuous improvement on your behalf."

Myla fought off the urge to laugh, but received the cloaked request with modest acceptance. She wrote out the quote and stilled her pen waiting for the next remark, but the speaker seemed at a temporary loss for words. When she glanced up during the lull, Weston nodded her way as though to finish the effort. She blinked and looked across the circle at no one in particular.

"Will Rogers also said, 'Common sense ain't common' which serves as our introduction to this first bit of Old Business. Rich, would you update the team on your progress with the paint room issues?"

Myla smiled at the second quote while she wrote it into the minutes. Rich's ensuing explanation proved equally as humorous as he exposed the half-knowledge of higher-ups that were making unfeasible decisions between facilities. She entered a condensed form of his account and waited for the outcome to cap the notation.

"So, I get a brand spanking new paint room here at this facility, not Pawnee, right where it should be. I'd like to thank Weston for walking me upstairs to a VP who actually cared enough to listen. I witnessed continuous improvement fledge from lip service to actual implementation, so now I'm a true believer. We start construction July fifth. They've even offered me a shovel at the ground-breaking ceremony set for June thirtieth." Rich shook his head, but the smile wouldn't leave his face.

Myla felt moved to speak. "That's amazing Rich, and so fitting, too. You probably saved the company thousands of dollars on logistics, and now you can design ventilation improvements right into the blueprints."

Skip started to clap, which soon broke the entire circle into applause.

Myla attempted to catch up with the conclusion in her notes as the tribute came to an end.

"Poka-yoke." Weston's soft-spoken challenge rippled across the room.

The skin on Myla's writing arm tightened in goose bumps. Though she knew it had been meant for all to hear and gain inspiration, the coded expression seemed to hold special meaning for her. How could she avoid error when it seemed to have taken up as her long lost friend?

Weston held up a newspaper clipping and waved it. "One more item of Old Business then, before we move on. This comes to us from one highly satisfied customer, a Mr. Bart Connors of Missoula, Montana, courtesy of our marketing department. This front page article extols the attributes of the custom-made aircraft he received by special delivery earlier this month. The review is most complimentary of the Western Durango interiors, which Marketing thinks may open the door to future sales."

Myla's head jerked up at the specific mention of her design. Instead of the sting of unwarranted praise, she sensed freedom to extend the privilege of pursuit of an idea. "What that article may not say is that any promising concept is worthy of consideration, if given half a chance. Our privilege is to have this group, and the place to allow for the birth of innovation. I believe in what we're trying to accomplish here."

"And so do I," Skip added. "I've asked for training in some of Weston's scan tests and am willing to forego some previously used rudimentary techniques in favor of more diagnostic measures."

"Thank goodness," Ted Hastings said in a teasing tone. "We've been trying our best to keep you looking good with our sheet metal work, but you assembly guys can take it and run."

"Speaking of measures for improvement," Skip added, "our FOD incidental tool count is so low, we're about in negative figures over in Hangar C."

"Duly noted," Myla exclaimed, happy to share the victory. She glanced up at Weston as he sat agenda-in-hand, a look of satisfaction painting his expression. His quest for improvement had become contagious, and the entire circle now carried the banner. Maybe she could put the personal hurt aside and help continue to promote such a gallant effort, even if the messenger occasionally displayed a flaw. There were more altruistic things to strive for than emotional attachment, after all, though they didn't make the nights any less lonesome.

Ernie Pike twitched sideways in his chair. "If we're moving on to New Business, can I go next?"

Weston held out his palm to give the Tools & Fixtures manager the floor.

"I think I might have a porosity issue with material coming in from a Tier One supplier." The big man stopped to take a breath and gave a look around the room.

"Porosity problem? I just love porosity problems," Weston quipped as he leaned forward to receive the details.

Myla fixed her gaze on the notebook entry, though she fought the urge to watch Weston in demure action. The man was a genius in his element, yet a wrecking ball outside of it. Admiration for the angular mix rose in her chest, and it took every bit of control she had to keep it out of the notation at hand. She wrote the word 'porosity' as her respect for him hit a higher plateau. Though it didn't rant and rave like love tended to, it did seem better suited to the workplace. If they couldn't maneuver their way back to love, at least they would have respect, by far and away a steadier platform for the launching of airworthy planes.

~

He walked in to find a woman with her head tied up in curlers seated at the kitchen table. Soon the stench of ammonia curled his nose hairs. The whole scene looked alien. "Why do you have to do that home permanent thing to your hair? It stinks to high heaven."

She glanced his way over her magazine. "What in the world is that on top of your head? I think the pot is calling the kettle black on this one." She chortled and reached for her soda.

"It's called a pompadour, for your information. The barber said it would highlight my swagger. It's popular with the rebel-for-a-cause crowd."

"So what's with you? I bet it's a new girlfriend."

"Working on one, as a matter of fact. I'm trying to get her to see me in a new light." He strolled to the sink and began to wash his hands. "I don't see anything cooking for supper."

"Nope. I have forty-five minutes under this treatment, and then I'll think about it."

"I'll grab some chips then. You didn't leave any old tools around today, did you?"

"Nope. You said we'd run dry for a spell, right before the big bang, so I let off. Plus, somebody was nice to me today out there. He recited a poem to me. It left me feeling almost human, like my life mattered."

He leered over the table at her. "Don't get soft now, Curly Jean." He laughed and snatched the chips from the counter.

"You're the one getting soft, Mr. Pompadour, which means I must have loved Mother more."

"Don't forget she was mine first." He flashed a gaudy smile and headed upwind of the stench of self-improvement.

~

Weston dropped the bar, and it thudded on the carpet of the second bedroom. He traced the walls with his gaze while still lying on the weight bench. Duncan Reed had called earlier and informed him the baby had taken several ounces of formula from a bottle. Heartened by the progress, the new father felt like the lad had passed a critical turning point.

Ever since the house closing procedure after work, Weston could say the same. Now, he owned a nugget of real estate that came with a whopping mortgage attached. The furnishings he'd purchased last month already bore an accumulation of dust on their veneers. Besides wiping his T-shirt over it, he had no idea how to counter it. That and about a hundred other domestic things rendered him inept or inadequately disposed to, like the proper operation of a washer and dryer.

A small advancement, he'd purchased two ice cube trays and filled them in hopes of producing ice by tomorrow. With July on his front doorstep, that would bring some much-wanted relief. June would end with a trip to the county magistrate's office to inquire about marriage records from two decades ago, in hopes of finding something to link their culprit with a motive. He wiped the sweat from his forehead and considered doing another set of reps with the bench presses. The exertion would empty his mind and help him sleep.

He sat up for the bar, gripped it with focus and snatched it up from the floor to get the last set underway. He lowered onto the bench and forced the bar above his chest. He extended his arms and held it until it began to burn, then lowered the bar to his chest. Myla leaked into his thoughts while he pushed the bar back up. His elbows wobbled, but he held the control. She'd written *respect* into the margins of her meeting notes, an inclusion he could hardly ignore.

It might be an admirable raft for gaining ground down river, but it made for solitary recompense in a cottage too big for one man, a man who had no clue how to make a house a home.

214

Chapter 20

Weston stood on the flank of the airfield near Rich Yost to lend support as the paint shop manager booted his shovel tip into the ground. The ceremony halted upon command of the photographer, who hunched behind his tripod and snapped a succession of pictures. Dignitaries held their smiles and posed for the camera. Not his shindig, he'd come out to show support for his QC circle member. A man harrumphed behind him, and he turned to see Ernie Pike join the gathering crowd.

"Have I missed anything but rhetoric?" Ernie leaned forward and buried his hands in his pants pockets.

"Nothing more than a little Kansas wind," he replied. "Glad you could come out, Ernie. We'll have to congratulate Rich after the ceremony. He battled for a better plan and won."

"Sure thing. It's like a seven gold-shovel salute out there. This will be a good move for the company, wait and see."

Weston couldn't resist the urge to tease the typically indifferent manager. "Sounds like you might be coming around a little there, Ernie. Has continuous improvement struck your fancy at last?"

He chuckled, which made his ample girth bounce. "I reckon so. Going forward sure beats heading backwards. That might help us keep a few more planes in the air."

"Hey, I'll be glad to go with you on that Tier One supplier visit, if you want support. We can bring along my portable radiography gage and conduct a scan or two right in their shop. There's nothing like cold, hard facts to make a believer out of a skeptic." He dusted his hands together to indicate the task would be a piece of cake.

"Let me set it up over the phone first, and then I'll get back to you." Ernie paused and took a look around the crowd. "On a more personal note, I appreciate how you've befriended the team members. It seemed our Miss Templeton was more demure than normal this past meeting. She barely looked your way, which tells me something's up between you two. Call me nosy, but I want the old Myla back, the one with the beaming blue eyes."

Weston felt the burning insinuation right down his sternum. He couldn't talk about the investigation and risk compromising it. On the surface, the situation looked like a lovers' quarrel. Ernie merely wanted him to patch things up. He drew a labored breath and dropped his shoulders. "I don't know what to do. My hands are tied at the moment doing my job and Duncan Reed's tasks on top of it. That's on one side and Myla is on the other, a distant side that falls beyond arm's length right now."

"When you have a breach between what you have and what you want, the situation calls for a bridge to span the gap. You're a smart man, Mr. Durand. I'm positive you'll figure it out."

Someone gave his shoulder a squeeze, and he glanced up to see Skip Sellers had joined them. "Figure out what? Am I missing something intriguing?"

"Women," Weston replied. "We're designing a bridge to span the gap between men and women. Do you have anything to contribute?"

"Nope. Leave me out," Skip replied. "I'm not consorting right now, but when the stalemate's over, I'll swim the gap if I have to. That means I won't need the bridge you gentlemen are designing."

The crowd began to applaud as the front dignitaries tossed their first shovel-full of dirt on the project's interior. Weston clapped as though on automatic. Skip's response had said it all. If the desire existed, so did a way to traverse the impasse. His desire might be due for its sixty thousand mile check-up.

~

Myla allowed the disappointment to run through her frame as she exited the cockpit for a breath of fresh air. The ground-breaking ceremony had to go on without her, as she had earned restricted duty which turned out to be a constant date with leather seat covers. She sighed and brushed the hair back off her face.

"Hey, it can't be as bad as all that." Hague shook his head and gave her an impish grin.

"Who let you out of the wolf pen? It's not even Friday." Weary of cramped quarters, she sat atop the gantry steps. The tool salesman seemed to have polished his appearance with a new hair style—one looked like a poodle had perched on his head. Not eager to get too personal, she'd withhold her critique for now.

"Ha-ha. You're so funny. I delivered the rented ceremonial shovels for the ground-breaking. Those things are really earning their keep. Wish it had been my idea at the outset."

"Better luck next time. Good ideas have a way of popping up again."

"Speaking of good ideas, I was thinking you and me ought to go out this weekend." He traced his fingers through his top curl, and his bicep bulged under his T-shirt sleeve.

"I'm a lot more wary going into something romantic this time around," she replied with a shake of her head. "Too bad you don't work around here where we could see each other more."

"No offense, but that will never happen. Our family was burned by this company once. Never again." He shot halfway up the gantry to get closer and leaned in toward her. "We'll have to figure something else out, babe. I'm standing ready at the door. Believe me, I'm interested."

"It's too soon for me, Hague." A tiny dread pinged inside her chest. She'd started this dialogue. Now, look where it had dropped her, on trouble's doorstep.

"You make me feel better about myself. Let me show you how much." He reached for her and held his palm out.

Touched by his sincerity in the moment, she put her hand out and let him take it. "I don't think—"

"Don't think. Let yourself feel." He wrapped his fingers around her hand in a velvet touch chock full of physical interest.

"Myla?" Miss Granger called from the next aircraft down the line. "I need you over here right now." Her curt tone sliced through the moment with an icy blade.

Myla shot up like her coveralls had caught fire. "I've got to go."

Hague squared on the gantry to block her path. "How about the date this weekend?"

"No means no." She lowered her shoulder and skimmed right

past him. When her feet hit solid concrete, she pivoted and headed for her boss. One glance over her right shoulder unveiled a new level of trouble. Weston stood by the balcony steps with Skip Sellers and Ernie Pike in tow. How much they'd seen was questionable, but it might have been enough.

"You're about to get us fired, little lady," Alice huffed. "And I, for one, am not ready to pack in my career. What do you have to say for yourself?"

"I have a dire message to send Weston. Got anything to write on?"

Statue-still, the battleship gave her a hard glance that said she meant business. Then she dug into the pocket of her coveralls and handed her a triangular scrap of leather.

Myla took it with a nod and headed up the stairs to the next installation job. Whether it appeared that she'd been consorting or not, she had gained a key bit of information. The Amherst family had been burned by Cessna in the past, which would be motive aplenty for retribution. Weston would know what to do with the lead. She'd have it ready for Skip when he came to escort them to lunch. She found the pen in her tool kit and began to word the message. Her credibility hung in the balance. Which side of justice would she land on in the end? Would it be the same side Weston stood on?

~

Another shot in the half-dark, Weston strode into the county magistrate's office where a gray-haired woman sat beneath the front counter.

"Hello, sir. I'll need both parties present to issue the marriage license. Is your intended on her way?" Her eyebrows arched as she dropped her pen.

His thoughts scattered at the inference. The image of Myla holding hands with the tool salesman jabbed his midsection. "Uh, no ma'am. I may not be in the right place. I've come to research marriage records dating back maybe twenty-three years or so. Where would I go for that?" His words seemed to rattle around the room.

Her expression softened. "You're two doors away from your destination. Tell them Millie sent you down. Take a left and look for one-o-four."

Weston smoothed his tie and gave her a nod. "Thank you, Miss Millie. I sure appreciate the help today. Things have been a bit rough, lately."

"Come back and see me when you're ready." She smiled and picked up her pen again.

Weston backtracked to the hall and soon found the right room marked "Records" on the door. He entered and approached the female clerk at a small cluttered desk.

"Yes, sir. How may I help you?"

"Millie sent me here. I need to research your marriage certificates from approximately twenty-three years ago."

"I see. In regards to what? Are you working with the police?" She pushed her glasses up on the bridge of her nose and waited for his reply.

He had not anticipated the need to substantiate his research. It threw him for a loop. "Uh, no ma'am. Not the police. I'm working for the safety manager of Cessna. It's an employee security matter, you might say." He forced a swallow, since his throat had gone bone dry. Without taking his eyes off her, he loosened the knot on his necktie.

"Oh, a corporate matter. Well, seeing how it involves one of our largest employers in the county, I think we can accommodate your request. If you'll sign on this clipboard, I'll take you back to the records. There's a desk you can use to review the files."

"Thank you for your cooperation in our investigation, ma'am." He scrawled his name on the next available line and waited for her to come around front.

"Right this way then." She strolled by several closed offices and headed to a large room at the end of the hallway. It could have been a vault for its size, large and looming. "Everything is filed by year in here. Each year has been alphabetized, not kept in chronological order. Can I get you anything more?"

"No, ma'am. I've brought paper to write on. I'm set."

"Please check back in with me upon exiting." She turned with a nod and left the vault.

Weston dropped his briefcase on the table and approached the metal cabinets with some trepidation. He could easily fall victim to an avalanche in this place, if he wasn't careful. He scanned the drawer labels and soon found 1930, the year Bette had been born.

He pulled the drawer open. It scraped along the metal runner below. He found the tab for 'R' and leafed through halfway searching for Rondale. He slowed when he got to Rollins, let out a breath and turned to the next document. It read Rory in plain block letters. He'd landed in the wrong place.

Weston started to close the file cabinet to open a new drawer when the 'A' tab stared back at him from the front. On second consideration, he fingered through the 'A' section and soon passed Allen only to land right on Amherst. He blinked, not believing his good fortune. He removed the document and took it to the table.

According to this record, on February 14, 1930, Barbara J. Amherst had married Leonard H. Rondale at the Sedgwick County courthouse. A sliver of accomplishment rushed through his mind as he began to write down all the pertinent dates and information. This was the missing link connecting the two siblings, likely creating a blended family. He pulled Reed's Instamatic out of his briefcase and took two snapshots of the evidence.

Satisfied, he picked up the marriage license and carried it back to its resting place. This case floated on multiple levels, and he'd just uncovered a critical one. Reed would have this investigation wrapped up within a week of his return. For his part, Weston would give him the file and let him resume the lead. This detective work held no thrill for him. He would divest himself of any responsibility and get back to searching out cracks and defects, the harmless illegitimates of his chosen line of work.

He drove on an elevated buzz of success all the way back to Cessna. When he walked into Hangar C, he swung his briefcase as though warding away any further complications. He owed the surface penetrant machine some attention this afternoon and looked forward to its bluish company. Predictable and inerrant, he knew he could depend on it.

With a flick of the light switch, the lab sprang to life. He stepped to his desk and settled the briefcase into his chair. The case notebook needed to be updated, but he'd complete the marriage license entry later. Right now, he had some solid quality control inspection work to conduct.

Out of the corner of his eye, he saw something limp and curled on the desktop. Tucked under his calendar blotter, he discovered a piece of butter-colored leather. When he lifted it, he was struck at how supple the material felt. The small triangle flopped over, and he spotted lettering penned on the rough underside. *Amherst family burned by Cessna. Check employment records.—My.*

A cascade of numbness started in his frontal lobe and leaked all the way through his core. Not only did he know *who* they were, but now he had a chance to take a glimpse as to *why.* A shiver shot down his spine. The penetrant would have to wait. He grabbed for the briefcase and headed toward the Administration wing for Employee Services. As he flicked the light off, he brought the leather note to his lips and kissed it. "Excellent work, Myla, honey. Top notch, as usual." He threw open the door and pursued a specter with bloodthirsty intent. He tightened his grip on the briefcase as though to throttle the saboteur with one hand. It was a choke-hold, most certainly.

~

On her knees, Myla leveraged the cover into place and negotiated for more room between the front and rear seats. She pressed on the adjustment lever, and the front seat ratcheted forward, lending her a spacious reprieve. This set would be her last for the day, a long Thursday with its share of trouble. She heard a man's voice down below. *Where had Alice gone?*

With the surplus selvage gathered in one hand, she reached for the stapler to fix the cover in place. She eased the fullness across the padding, her experience disallowing wrinkles along the way. Susie had a lot to learn in that department, but installation was not as cut-and-dried as outsiders might think. By acquired skill, she soon had the seat cover installed and brought out the piped trim to cover her seams. She used the last of her glue and pressed the piping into place.

Before starting the companion seat, she thought to ask Miss Granger for her adhesive. She ducked out and found the woman standing toe-to-toe with Skip Sellers, deep in debate. The battleship looked more like a dinghy adrift at sea. *Will wonders never cease?* She hated to interrupt, but she sorely needed that glue.

"Sure it's a holiday weekend," Alice argued, "but you know we're not supposed to be together."

"I say blast it all and come out with me anyway," Skip insisted. "Fall River is lovely this time of year. The water's so refreshing.

With shade, water, and a handsome companion in your boat, what's not to like?" He tweaked his mustache to sharpen the offer.

"Can we discuss this over a cinnamon roll? I'm starved this afternoon, for some reason."

"By all means. Come with me. I'm buying." He offered his arm, and she took it.

Myla hated to play the intruder, but she had to have that mastic. "Excuse me, Miss Granger. May I borrow your glue bottle while you're gone? I only have one seat left to do this afternoon, but I'm out."

"You bet, Myla." She stooped and took the bottle with a firm grip. "Can you catch it?"

"Go ahead and fire away." She made a basket with her hands and bent her knees. When the glue bottle flew high over the gantry, she ended up making a one-handed grab. She nodded and returned to the cockpit to finish up the job. It didn't matter that her boss had gone soft this last half-hour of work, not to mention her defection to consorting with the restricted personnel. She grabbed the leather cover and lofted it in place over the padding. Better to stay here on the job where she could remain safe from further scrutiny.

Her brow beaded with sweat from the lack of circulation in the rear of the cockpit. As she adjusted the fabric, a lonely thought needled into mind regarding the three-day weekend ahead. Hers would be full of garden weeds and gathered curtains, nothing special by any stretch of the imagination. Pinned at the interface of good and evil, she could only work her way through it and trust God for the rest. She was innocent of corporate sabotage. That much she knew.

With the last strip of piping set by the borrowed glue, she backed toward the door. Her gaze swept the floor for any tools left behind. A shadow fell over the new seat cover, and she turned to find Weston standing in the cockpit door, her note flapping in his hand. She sat on her heels and steeled herself for the dressing down of having remained involved in the case.

"You know, this little scrap of leather reminds me of that story about David in the Bible," he said. His expression was impossible to read. "In an awkward moment, David cowers in hiding from the back of a cave as King Saul steps into the alcove to relieve himself. Are you familiar?"

Myla swallowed hard. A Bible lesson had been the last thing she'd expected. "Yes, I recall the story. Saul is hunting David down, though he's innocent of threatening the king."

Weston stooped to match her level, his eyes honest but not searching. "David cuts off a piece of fabric from the rampaging king's robe, but won't bring any further harm to him."

"Because Saul bears God's anointing as king." She shifted onto her knees, the topic of conversation unthreatening.

Weston made the leather scrap flounce in his grip. "He calls the king out after he leaves the cave and shows him the piece of his robe. That little swatch of fabric attested to more than David's innocence, it represented being close, yet not exacting vengeance. I came up here to tell you that we're close, thanks to your scrap here, plus some other pieces that have fallen into place. I'll allow Duncan Reed to take legal action to apprehend the guilty parties after the holiday weekend upon his return to work."

"A lonely three-day holiday weekend?" Her voice squeaked and made her sound like an adolescent beggar.

Weston tucked the leather scrap into his breast pocket and ran a palm across it like a caress. "I'm in charge and have to play it out straight by the rules, Myla. Your innocence means more to me than risking something less honorable."

"Like David, you're the noble one, Weston."

"Knowing when to strike is part of our strategy. We have to coast through one more work day and anticipate the freedom next week will bring. I hope you're in agreement with me."

She planted her face in her hands and tried to wipe away the sweat and grime. "Hague Amherst comes to Cessna on Fridays, so tomorrow will stretch on like an eternity for me."

"How so?"

"He's badgering me to go out with him this weekend. Unfortunately, he doesn't seem to take 'no' for an answer." She shrugged and wiped her hands on her coveralls.

Weston stood, his expression rigid. "One more workday. And then justice arrives." He descended the stairway, an eyebrow raised as if chiseled in stone.

"God, help me. I'm in too deep." She tried to stand but her knees had turned to jelly, so she stayed on the floor and ran a visual inspection over the installation work. Her thoughts turned to

Weston and how stalwart he had adhered to his mission. She wanted to be more like David, a vagabond cave-dweller who longed to be king. *Lord, help me not be weak.* She rose to her feet to practice having strength and took the gantry one step at a time.

~

Weston rubbed his eyes as the page blurred in front of him. Determined to have the investigation log finished for Duncan Reed's use next week, he transcribed the employment record findings onto the lined paper.

On April 1, 1946 during the second round of post-war layoffs of female employees to accommodate returning war veterans with jobs at Cessna, Barbara A. Rondale had her employment terminated along with seventy-two other female laborers. Mrs. Rondale filed a protest claiming the mitigating circumstance of being a single mother. Her petition for retention was denied, with her last day of employment recorded as April 6, 1946.

This employee documentation substantiates the suspect's verbal claim that "their family had been burned by the company" which is why he professed no future interest in working for Cessna. It also provides probable cause as to his motive for acts of sabotage against the company, a vengeful motivation heightened by the unfortunate loss of the family's primary provider, Mrs. Rondale, in a construction accident less than three months later.

Though it stabbed him right in the sternum, Weston added a note about the snack food distributor's representative, and her role as accomplice by virtue of family relation. He added a mention of her ease of access to Hangar A and tied in the circumstantial evidence of the documented tool cache that later appeared in the vicinity of the turbojet.

He rested his hand and soon found his chin nearly touching his chest. Weary, he'd likely be the last employee to leave the plant tonight. He glanced over at the stack of untouched business in his in-box and tried to alleviate the weightiness of being behind in his quality control duties by shaking his head. The gesture failed to work.

When he spied the leather scrap on his desktop, Myla came to mind. If he intended to render justice in this investigation log, one additional entry remained to be written. He considered how to countermand the solid evidence against her, a four-inch spike of metal in the form of a leather punch that bore her initials. People had been nailed to a guilty verdict with less incrimination, he presumed.

Myla deserved more favorable representation than omission from the investigation log. With her continued questioning of the main suspect, she'd been David cutting off Saul's robe, daring the proximity while flirting with disaster. Such courage in the face of threat spoke of integrity under pressure. Despite his jumbled personal feelings, surely he could write that account. He picked up the pen and began the journal notation.

In regard to the Interiors Department personnel who have been caught in the middle of this investigation, no evidence of adverse motive or clandestine activity in the vicinity of Hangar A has been documented. On the contrary, installers have been called upon to facilitate the protection of the target in question, the Continental-Teledyne J69-T-25 turbojet engines, by fabricating covers and insuring their repair as requested, always conducted proficiently and under escort. Upholstery installer Myla Templeton has also ascertained leads to evidence incriminating the main suspect and his accomplice, duly demonstrating her willingness to aid the investigation and ultimately clear her name. She should no longer be held as a suspect in this case.

What more could be written, he felt deficient to document. Instead of a well-ordered, sugar-coated affection, a gradual etching of trust and stabs of jealous encounters had marred their relationship. He didn't need a penetrant and special lighting to highlight that damage. Under closer inspection, love didn't have an unflawed surface, but came porous and pitted with human imperfection. *Why must I always look for cracks and defects?* Fed up with his position and the investigation's life-sucking drain, he slammed the notebook closed and stood up to go home.

Chapter 21

The first day of July broke over Hangar C like a Molotov cocktail. Myla blew down the neck of her coveralls while fingering the tab of its zipper making sure it stayed fully closed. She had her guard up today, her stiff-arm protector in place, and a prayer on her breath at every turn. Alice Granger seemed woebegone and had scarcely uttered five words while they set up the first installation. Susie scurried up and down the gantry of the adjoining fuselage, hitting her first assignment of the day full force.

A supply cart squeaked into position as the sulking battleship delivered the day's seat coverings for their use. Her hands flopped on top of the pile as though imparting a blessing.

Myla stepped up next to her. "You know, you can work along with Susie today, if it makes the day go any smoother."

"Best to stick with routine, I reckon. Got a lot weighing on my mind today, that's all." She tried to smile, but it fell as flat as a tail rudder.

Myla sensed the nudge to extend some empathy. "Remember that day the test plane's propeller chewed the tin off the door, and I got hurt?"

"Oh, yeah. That was the day Mr. Reed lost his safety-in-the-workplace record for most consecutive days. We've been on the skid ever since." She winced and straightened several covers sliding from the pile.

"I wanted to express how much it meant to me that you took me home and told my mother about the accident. I never got to express my gratitude, so I want to today. Thank you, Miss Granger. You take sewing girls and turn them into productive installers, all the while trying not to show how much you care. I'm not fooled anymore."

"Your welcome, Myla. Just don't go blabbing it around. I have a crusty reputation to uphold, you know." Alice winked and a few worries seemed to drop off her shoulders.

Myla stepped a bit closer. "Please don't let my situation in this investigation affect your personal life. Skip is a great guy."

"Yeah, my loyalties are torn. It's a lot to hold up sometimes. Managers have more on their load than most." She slid her arm under the top leather covers and lifted them from the pile.

Myla took the top two for her use. "I respect that. Plus, I expect you to do what's best in the long run for you. I'm a big girl now. I'm innocent of wrongdoing and plan to put in an honest day's work despite the investigation. I want you to know, I'm committed to the company."

"Listen, Myla. You're the best thing we've got going for us. You wouldn't even be in this predicament if Susie could get a handle on her tool placement. Or should I say misplacement? Criminy."

"Well, honest endeavor should speak for itself."

"You're a hundred percent correct, but right now your soapbox is in the back of this cockpit. You go up first and dress the two rear seats. I'll set the pilot's seat, and see if I can bring him the slightest bit of comfort by getting the seams in straight."

"Great attitude, Miss Granger. You should be the one sitting in on the Quality Control circle, not me."

"Oh, let's not do that to our fine Mr. Durand. Besides, he'd never look at me the same way he looks at you."

Myla climbed halfway up the gantry considering her personal comment. When the stairs quaked underfoot, she knew the boss was on her way up. She turned and regarded her mentor. "The way he used to look at me—before Newton's Third Law got thrown out of kilter."

She harrumphed and pressed the seat covers against her back to prod her along. "I don't think the laws of physics can change like that on any given whim. At least I hope not, or this world could get mighty wobbly.”

Myla took another step up and thought to challenge her on that. “Maybe you should go on that boat ride on Fall River after all. You know, to prove out the stability of the world.”

“I’m inclined to do just that.” She paused and huffed out a breath three steps short of the complete rise. Once she had tossed the covers in, she surveyed the shop floor from her elevated post. “All’s clear on the western front.”

“Good. Let’s get busy before Susie needs our help.” Myla snickered and knelt to get a better perspective on her next client. She tossed the cover and with a quick tug, it fell right into alignment. With that success, she lost herself in her morning’s work.

~

Pleased that the double-sized wing flap sample for the A195 had breezed through his preliminary inspections, Weston relaxed his pace. Two more test pieces waited on the table. Once those scans were run, he’d be caught up. Maybe the day wouldn’t turn out to be the train wreck he’d imagined. He pulled the wing flap from the machine and wiped over its surface to dislodge some of the residual Magnaflux.

He circled its length and had barely set it down when the phone rang. He cleaned his hands on the rag and grabbed the receiver. “Quality Control. Durand here.”

“Hey Weston. It’s Duncan. Thought I’d better touch base with you before the work week is over. Hope everything is under control out there.”

“Yes, I’m happy to report it is. The investigation log is in your mailbox and awaits your authority for total resolution.”

“Wow, I am glad to hear that.”

He pivoted and sat on the edge of the desk. “How’s your little Timmy getting along?”

“We can’t call him little anymore—he’s gained five ounces this week alone. The doctor thinks it’s a miracle, but he’s somehow gotten the hang of this nursing thing. Lorna Rae has taken to calling him her precious piglet. Those two have really been through it—all of us really.”

“That’s astounding, a real answer to all our prayers. Funny how the littlest things can throw a wrench in something you thought would be smooth sailing."

"Hmm. Sounds like we're not talking about the vagaries of lactation anymore. I'm looking forward to our debriefing when I get back in Tuesday. Try to block out some time to meet with me early, and we'll move forward from there."

"That's a solid plan. Good to hear you'll be back on schedule. This safety stuff is not for the fainthearted. Give me a good old shrink cavity on a shabby casting any day. That's what grinds my wheel." When he heard the safety manager chuckle over the phone line, he laughed with him.

"You are by far the best hire I've accomplished for the company, Weston. Thanks for joining us and making my life easier."

"Where else would a man want to spend Uncle Sam's birthday, but in the Air Capital of the World? I'm grateful to be here."

"Well, I'd better go. The baby is napping now, so Lorna Rae has a whole list of jobs for me to get done—every one of them to be conducted as quiet as a mouse."

"Okay, Duncan. Don't squeak too much then. Please give Lorna Rae my best. Goodbye." He hung up the receiver in a much-improved mood. How odd that a tiny baby's willingness to nurse would solicit that kind of mental adjustment. Perhaps failure to thrive could be considered a snapshot in time, a hiccup of momentary trouble that leads to tic-marks of height on a growth chart in the long run.

Somehow, the tender spot generated by the baby suddenly became filled with thoughts of Myla. Soft, sentimental discourses seeped into his chest and leveled his heart rate. Maybe they were having a momentary hiccup of their own. Soon, a more level plane could be resumed. He would have meditated on it a few seconds more, but his stomach growled. "Come on then, let's go get some lunch and try to thrive." He spun toward the door, lighter than air.

~

No question, Myla attributed her headache to the heat. Flat-footed, she stepped off the gantry and headed to the snack room. A Sun Drop soda would jolt her out of the temple-throbbing clamp and restore her ability to think. Maybe they could go ahead and break for lunch, once Alice had Susie's latest wrinkle ironed out.

She soon halted at the door. A "Closed for Service" sign was not what she'd expected. Through the glass window, she could see the snack lady inside cleaning off the vending machine with a blue rag. She knocked on the window and shrugged her shoulders. When the woman beckoned her inside, Myla pushed the door open and set the chock wedge at the bottom.

"Sorry to tie the room up. I'm pretty much done now anyway."

"It's Bette, isn't it? I apologize for crashing in on you, but the heat is unbearable today. I've got to have a drink."

"I'm running late over here as I dropped by Hangar A first. Guess it's good to go counterclockwise now and again." She chuckled and stashed the rag on her crate dolly.

"Hey, I like what you've done with your hair." She slid the coin into the drink box and reached for the green bottle.

"Aw, it's just a home perm. Guess I about gagged my brother putting it in." She snickered and brought a double handful of square crackers out of her crate. She turned and loaded them into the vending machine.

"Guys don't give us enough respect, right?" She chuckled and lowered the bottle neck under the opener. With a jerk of her wrist, the cap came tumbling off. A tiny mist of carbonation rose from the bottle rim, and she trapped it with her lips. In seconds, her favorite refreshment trickled down her throat.

"I'm really trying to catch the attention of that guy from quality central something-or-other." She looked sheepish as she grabbed another handful of snacks. "He quoted me a nice poem earlier in the week. Maybe he'd feel like a date over the weekend."

Myla froze, her drink halfway to her lips. She'd accidentally walked up and caught the tail end of that encounter. Bette was talking about Weston, and from the sound of it, seemed to have a red hot crush going for him. An invisible canyon opened up under her feet, and she had the sensation of falling into it, right where all the old flamed-out crushes landed. She felt nauseous and considered fibbing her way through it. Instead, she found her fortitude, lowered the soda, and locked gazes with the snack lady. "He's a nice guy. I bet if you'd ask, he might take you out somewhere."

"Well, that would be better than my plans." She halted, her expression freezing to chiseled granite. She dropped her gaze to the snack crate and busied her hands with more stock.

"Hey there, beautiful," Hague called as he leaned into the room. "Got a minute to talk before lunch? I'm on a short rope today, so what do you say?" He quirked his brow at Myla and locked in his keen interest.

She wiped off the sweat from her soda bottle. "I need to go back to the shop floor where the other installers are, but Susie's having a problem. Guess I have a few minutes, until they get it resolved." Her stiff-arm resistance locked into place, and she felt adequately guarded.

"I'm all yours then. Lead the way." Hague gestured toward the aircraft. As she passed through the doorway, he gave a pronounced wink.

A strange sensation prickled her skin. His misaimed wink didn't seem meant for her. Myla glanced back through the snack room window as she passed. The snack lady appeared to be swallowing a wry grin. For an instant, she wondered if Hague had previously tried out his wolf-charm on the rough-edged woman, but soon dismissed the errant thought. She wasn't flashy enough to be wolf bait. Still, her reaction bordered on oddball.

"Killer hot today, isn't it?" Hague stepped up even with her and fanned his face. "Wish I had a convertible on days like this."

"Maybe that wouldn't be suitable for a work car." She took a sip of her drink and glanced around for Alice Granger. She might need her battleship in the wings after she declined Hague's invitation to go out again. She spotted the cart that the covers had arrived on and headed for it.

"Well, here it is Friday," Hague said. "Both you and I knew it was coming down to this. How about we mark the beginning of something incredible on this first day of July? What do you say? Light my firecrackers early and go out with me, Myla. I'm hooked on you, babe, so don't put me off anymore." He polished off the rehearsed lines with a guileless look as he stroked an enticing finger around his jawline.

"Don't think—" Myla saw Skip Sellers headed straight for her between two rows of Bird Dogs. She clamped her mouth shut and watched him approach. He shook his head once, his mustache bent in a slight twitch. As she stalled, she arranged her hair back behind her headband.

Hague sized up the floor inspector for a few seconds and returned his attention to her. "What was that you were saying, doll?" He reached for bare skin and caressed the top of her hand with his thumb.

"Don't think—"

A piercing siren sounded the lunch hour across the tops of the hangars. Twelve o'clock noon landed on the airstrip outside where visible waves of heat bounced back off the tarmac and made the air contort. Too short-lived to help her out, the lunch siren completed its here-and-gone announcement before she knew it. She took a sip of her drink.

"I do believe you were saying something about thinking," he said, his tone curt.

"Yes, thank you. Don't think that I don't appreciate the notice. I mean a James Dean guy like you noticing a wallflower girl like me." She tipped the bottle mouth toward him in a salute.

"Really? You think we're different, but we're not. Together, we could be something special." He leaned closer, his eyes keen. "You might even make me respectable."

"You possess the wherewithal to make your own self respectable." She looked directly at him and could almost see the flawed ego that kept him going in perpetual motion like an animal. Hungry until sated, that was his type.

"How about we skip the lecture? You're afraid you might enjoy yourself if you went out with me, aren't you? Tell the truth?" He pressed his full lips into a little pout to mock her.

"I'm not going out with you, Hague. That's final. Therefore, we'll never find out the answer to your question." Her voice started to quiver. Vulnerable, she shot a glance up the next gantry to find reinforcements. No one came into sight.

"They say an ounce of fear can turn volatile and set off a blinding blast of passion. Should we add a touch of fear, Myla?" He snatched her hand before she could react and balled her fingers into his for a fist. He leered at her and, in one deft move, twisted her arm behind her back. "I want you to stand up now, lovely. We're going to take a walk to my car and try out the volatility of passion for ourselves. I'll prove to you we're a good match, Myla, and you're going to have no choice but to let me."

When he tightened his hold on her trapped arm, pain exploded across her shoulder. Determined to resist his forced advances, she resolved to find a way out of this coerced situation. She remembered the cart was on casters, but her feet were too far off the floor to push off.

"Let's get going. They'll all think we're having lunch together. This will be better than lunch. A real oasis of touch amid the heat, like that first kiss revisited."

"I'm not going with you, Hague. Let me go and leave the plant." She pulled against his hold, but made no progress.

"Give me one good reason to let you off easy." His breath fell hot on her neck as he shifted behind her.

She dropped her head, begging God to give her something to counter with. When the truth came to mind, she had to use it. "I'm still in love with my old boyfriend. I can't get beyond him, because we're not finished."

"Tough break. That makes me even more of a trespasser, but once I get a woman in my sights, I zero in on her. Besides, I can make you forget about old starched shirt in about five seconds." He threw his free arm around her waist and lifted her off the cart.

Tucked into his side, Myla had to think beyond the panic. The soda bottle almost slipped from her hand. She tightened her grip on the sly. Her only weapon, she waited for the right moment to leverage it.

With a series of pushed steps, he maneuvered them through the hangar toward the tarmac. His grip locked tight, a fuselage's length remained to freedom outside. He paused and peeked around the huge tin doors as if to make certain the immediate coast was clear.

Unwilling to take one more step, Myla stiffened her spine and planted both feet. Her every breath spoke a wordless prayer for divine intervention. Unable to overpower Hague, she only had the element of surprise in her favor. When she felt his next push make contact, she ducked. Off-balance, they collided with the door. She swung the bottle in a broad sweep. When it struck a crowning blow, she twisted from his grip and gained a degree of freedom.

Hague growled his displeasure and tried to force control, but she'd moved out of reach. Lemon-lime drink dripped down his face. In seconds, red intermingled with the flow. When he spotted the first drops of blood dripping from his jaw, he went ballistic. After grabbing her hair, he leveled a back-handed a blow right toward her face.

A split second after ducking, she heard the air rush out of his lungs as someone's fist collided with Hague's midsection, doubling him over. Determined to escape, she fell to the floor and rolled under the closest fuselage. The world swirled and reality blurred while the sound of blows landing buzzed the distant horizon like a high-flying plane. Her heart pounded like a rivet gun. Fear nailed her to the concrete floor, daring her to move.

Chapter 22

Weston thanked the Good Lord for every lonely night he'd spent on the weight bench. With double-handed force, he sank a chopped blow across Hague's left shoulder and heard something snap. Wiry and quick, the tool salesman maneuvered out of range and tried to clear his effeminate bangs off his forehead. Blood streaked from the cad's hairline, bolstering his efforts to deliver justice. *Myla always does top-notch work.*

Hague gestured palms-up for peace. "How about we call this a little misunderstanding?"

"Too late, troublemaker. Reap what you sowed." He lowered his shoulder and bowled the infiltrator over against the hangar door, which echoed in a tinny crash.

Skip stepped into the fray and tugged him back. "Myla's all right, Weston. The security officer is on his way to escort the abductor out."

Weston glanced around and saw that Alice Granger had Myla locked in her protective arms. She stared back at him, resolute in her retaliation. Out of the corner of his eye, he caught motion as Hague attempted to bolt away. He landed a palm against the man's boney chest and pinned him back against the door. He slid a hand up to the man's throat and locked it in place.

"She said she's still in love with you," Hague croaked. He spat some blood off his lips and gave a mocking look. "Kind of hard for me to believe that, starched shirt."

"You should have listened to the lady," he replied, short of breath from the exertion. He savored his advantage and wanted to drive his point home before security got there. "We don't like your type preying on the women in our labor force. You might just have to find a new route for your pitiful sales ploy." He felt a laugh trickle through his clamped fingers.

"She was about to go on a date with *me*." Hague spat more blood and tossed his hair.

"No, I wasn't," Myla replied. She stepped closer. "Everything I told you was the truth, Hague. You just can't take 'no' for an answer. I'll testify to that, when and if I have to."

A growing pride in Myla's exemplary behavior began to swell Weston's chest. She had confirmed everything she'd told the tool salesman to be true, including the part where she still loved him. That glimmered like a diamond of hope in this whole dark mess, a gemstone he'd return to as soon as possible. He glanced out onto the tarmac and saw that the XT-37 had been shoved out for an afternoon test flight. Wariness leaked into his consciousness.

"No need to testify, babe. This is only a he-said she-said lover's quarrel," Hague insisted. "Even if you dare to press charges, I'll be back home before you working dogs will be tonight."

"Save your pleading for the judge," Weston warned. "You might have gotten yourself in too deep, this time. We know more than you think we do." He squinted and tightened his grip.

Susie shrieked. "Myla—watch out for her!"

A guttural grunt came from nowhere. "Run, Hague. Go!"

Weston turned in time to see Bette launch the broad side of a tool box at his face in a desperate Herculean heave. The red projectile headed toward him with considerable mass.

"Weston, no!" Myla screamed.

The vengeful scene played out in slow motion as he braced. His field of vision filled with tousled black hair and red metal, but the crushing impact he anticipated never landed. Instead, Myla intercepted the blow, knocked sideways by the full force of contact. While distracted by the turn of events, Hague managed to slip out of his grip and fled for open ground.

A she-cat grappled him next, tying him up in clawing scratches and a hulking body lunge. Bette knocked him to the ground in the attack. He fought to overpower her while remaining a gentleman combatant at the same time—a tenuous tumble through a minefield of contact.

"This one's on me," Skip said. With a heavy-handed tug, he pulled the stocky woman away and pinned her to the floor with his knee. Alice appeared at his side and put a choke hold on the accomplice.

Freed, Weston crawled over to Myla who lay crooked but still, her cheeks wet with tears. His next breath struggled. "Tell me where it hurts. We'll get you some help right away."

"Don't," she replied, her tone air-filled. "Don't let them move my head—not even a jiggle. It hurts too much." When they locked gazes, he saw her pupils were huge.

"Alice, get over here," he ordered. "Myla's going into shock." As he stood, he caught a glimpse of the tarmac. The female pilot ascended to the cockpit just as Hague arrived. The scene landed like an unmitigated threat. Once Alice moved into place next to Myla, he shifted his attention. "Whatever you do, no one moves her until the medics arrive. Got it?"

"Yes, boss. We'll have to brace her head to lift her onto the gurney."

"Kid glove treatment, promise me." He hadn't meant to beg, but he somehow felt her helplessness. It should have been him knocked senseless.

"Don't let Hague in that jet," Bette cried. "He doesn't remember. I set the big bang."

The skin down Weston's neck tightened. The last unthinkable puzzle piece clanged into place with deafening authenticity. Though precious little time remained to thwart tragedy, he rose and began to sprint out onto the tarmac. Details of the case rolled through his mind while his lungs clamored for air.

Hague climbed the gantry and followed the pilot into the plane's cockpit. In seconds, the twin jet engines roared, a blood-curdling shriek.

Anticipating its forward momentum, Weston angled ahead on the tarmac. Bette's words returned to him like a pulse threatening his ears. *Why would Hague head right for the aircraft knowing the FOD had been planted?* It didn't make any sense. The turbojet accelerated with a noisy jolt and soon outpaced him, headed for the taxiway.

He tried to make out the pilot and caught a glimpse of streaming blonde hair beneath the cap. Hague had saved his best flirting pass for his most desperate emergency move and had duly hoodwinked the unsuspecting female pilot. The realization drove the last ounce of air right out of Weston's lungs, forcing him to stop running.

Torn by two allegiances, he bent and heaved in place under the scorching July sun. He should go back and help get Myla to the hospital, but he somehow could not let go of the investigation while his number one suspect rode off scot-free into the wild blue yonder. *What about the jet?*

In seconds, he looked up to find Skip Sellers standing with him. He straightened and tried to read the face of the veteran employee who'd proven his allegiance by requesting apprenticeship. He drew a long breath, trying to extinguish the fire in his chest.

"The woman accomplice admits she set the FOD inside the left engine first thing this morning. That's why she's so beside herself to warn him." He smoothed over his mustache and glanced up at the sky.

"Hague's unaware, but he's poised to be caught in his own trap. That's the big bang they'd planned to occur over the holiday weekend, only now it could happen at any moment."

"She says she taped it to the inside chamber. Whenever that tape gives way—"

"There goes the XT-37. Lord, have mercy. We need to call the air traffic control tower and get them to bring the pilot back in pronto. You go alert the fire crew for stand-by."

"Roger that. Security now has the snack room gal in custody. The ambulance for Myla remains inbound." A worried look followed as his gaze drifted toward the main gate. "She's in and out, chief. I don't know how she'll hold up under all that transport movement."

Weston broke off in a run, refusing to believe it could end like this—the enemy flying a tenuous arc to heroism while courageous Myla faded into an unconscious nothingness. That lackluster fate should have been his. He held out his hands as he ran faster. Life seemed to slip through his fingers like airborne sand. He choked back his protest, which made his lungs burn as tortuous as his thighs.

He arrived at Hangar C as a medic team lifted Myla and loaded her into the ambulance's gaping back door. A padded brace blocked all her features except for a tuft of black hair matted with blood. "God in heaven, help her, I pray." It was all he could manage as mounting anguish blocked every other thought.

He needed the phone. Like a manic man, he ran around inside the hangar to locate one.

Out of the gathering crowd, Rich Yost stepped forward and took him by the shoulders. "Tell me what you need."

"Call the tower and have them stop the XT-37. Bring the test flight straight back in. One of its jet engines has been sabotaged with an FOD. It could break loose at any moment." He bent and tried to suck a lung-full of air, but it came to him as inhospitable matter.

"Heaven above. Let me get the tower on the line then." Rich made quick work of the call and soon held the phone on his shoulder. "They want to know on whose authorization they should proceed."

"Tell them Duncan Reed's name, the safety manager. Give my name as his proxy."

Rich turned his back and provided the authorization information. Seconds passed. Restless, Rich turned and shook his head. His brow knit with the wait.

Weston took stock of where they stood. He'd wait at the tarmac's edge and take Hague Amherst by the scruff of the neck all the way to the police department, if that's what the situation required. Fed up with the investigation, he'd had it to the hilt. As far as he was concerned, it was over. The deeper gut stab remained. *I must get to Myla.* Out of nowhere, a burning sensation began to scold his left bicep. He turned to find Alice Granger dabbing a cotton swab down his arm that reeked of rubbing alcohol.

"You didn't give that hangar door a chance," she said, straight-faced. A crooked smile slid into place. She looked at him with newfound admiration. "I must admit, I enjoyed your little one-on-one scuffle. You landed a pretty nice upper-cut."

"Thank you, Miss Granger. I've sent Skip ahead for the emergency fire crew. Once we bring this cad into custody, we can all move on with lives, starting with our weekend plans."

She sniffed and looked at him with sympathetic eyes. "Looks

like yours might be spent at the hospital, my friend."

"I should be so lucky," he replied. A tap on the opposite shoulder caused him to redirect his attention.

Rich still had the receiver clamped to his ear. He covered the mouthpiece with his palm. "They've successfully engaged radio contact with the aircraft."

"Great job, Weston." Alice slapped him on the back. "Now, let's reel them back in."

He winced at the blow, already feeling black and blue. His left arm throbbed while his head held a fire of unknown origin. Maybe that was his empathetic connection to Myla. "Hold on, baby," he whispered to the aircraft. "Everything's going to be all right. Let's get that precious landing gear back on the tarmac."

Rich flapped his elbow to gain his attention. "The pilot has reversed the test flight pattern and is now returning to Cessna. The tower estimates five minutes, max."

Weston touched a hand to his head in an attempt to stop the strengthening drumbeat inside. A commiserating hand patted his shoulder blade. Sirens blared from the tarmac, and an array of emergency vehicles arced around the connection to the airport's main runway.

"That's my man out there," Alice said. "Who wouldn't want to spend the live-long day out on a boat with him?" She elbowed him for a response.

He snickered, though the levity about broke his face. "Go ahead, you two lovebirds. Float away and don't look back upstream, because there won't be a soul coming to bother you."

Rich covered the mouthpiece. "Four minutes till touchdown. They have a sheriff's escort patrolling down MacArthur Drive eastbound, keeping a visual on the aircraft."

Alice pumped her clinched fist in celebration.

"You know, once this part is well in hand, I need to head for the hospital. Could you call Duncan Reed for me?"

"You bet," she replied. "It might not be a bad idea for you to clean up a little, or they may not let you in over there."

"Good point. I'll stop by the house first and grab a fresh shirt."

"Remember to comb your hair to cover that goose egg popping up under your cowlick there." She took his fingers and guided them back to the right spot.

No wonder his head pounded. He had a lump larger than a quail egg back there.

Rich sucked in a sharp breath. He covered the mouthpiece again. "The tower reports losing contact with the XT-37, right at three minutes. They're holding for the sheriff's ground verification that the jet is no longer airborne."

"Lord, please, not now when we had them so close." Alice pressed the back of her hand over her lips to stop them from quivering.

His brain numb from the threshing, Weston held his face in his hands and waited for the unfathomable outcome to receive verification. The seconds stretched in a torment of eternity.

Rich cleared his throat. "Impact has been marked by a ball of fire east of Lake Afton, as confirmed by the sheriff's department. They'll have a man on the scene in half a minute."

The air sucked out of his lungs. Weston stood on wobbly legs and headed to the Pontiac. "Alice, call Duncan with the outcome. Rich, get word to Skip and the fire brigade. There's nothing more I can do here."

He walked away from the investigation, an hour past high noon on the last day he had to hold down the fort. How it all disintegrated into hell-in-a-hand-basket, he would never understand. Only one thing remained certain. If he couldn't get to Myla, he was the casualty, at least on the inside. When he broke into a trot for the parking lot, his legs immediately protested.

~

Painfully awake, Myla estimated her field of vision to comprise the width of a seat cushion and a half, forty-five degrees at the most. A straight-laced nurse of sour disposition paced in and out of that field which comprised her entire world. Unable to turn her head, they had screwed her cranium into the framework hovering above the bed for a safety net they referred to "traction." She cared little for the stern treatment.

Effie had been in to visit, her eyes puffy from crying all the way over to the hospital. Myla had dictated a list of personal items to be brought from home. Not knowing how long they might keep her made the list mostly guesswork, but she wanted something to wear under the hospital gown at a minimum. The nurse ushered Effie out after a few scant minutes, so as not to tire her. That left her feeling even more alone.

She tried to remember the sequence of events that had brought her here, but large chunks of information had gone missing. Hague intended to force himself on her, no matter how much she objected. Then Weston appeared out of nowhere and fought him off with unbridled gallantry. The snack lady had come at him with the tool box but, for the life of her, she couldn't understand why. She tried to stop her from striking the most brilliant man she'd ever met though, and she had succeeded. Now, she bore a halo of screwed-on traction and time, lots of empty time.

Surely someone would come in and provide some details in a follow-up. Had the sabotage investigation concluded? Did she even have a job anymore after being seen with Hague again? She moaned to swallow. From nowhere, the busy nurse leveled a straw into her mouth to let her drink. She closed her eyes and gave thanks for being alive.

~

The Catalina slipped into a parking spot and Weston switched off the engine. With a clean exterior and a heavy heart, he made his way to the hospital's front entrance. After a barrage of questions, plus some cajoling of an elderly volunteer, he garnered directions for Myla's whereabouts and headed up an elevator to the third floor. Why she had to end up in a pre-surgery ward he failed to understand, though that aspect made him uncomfortable.

When the elevator opened, he diverted to the right only to find a small gathering of familiar faces. Reggie and Effie met him partway up the hall. He reached for them both, and they shared a brief commiserating embrace.

Effie dabbed at the corners of her eyes. "They don't know much yet, only that the next twenty-four hours will be critical."

Reggie pointed his cane toward the sitting area. "The doctor would like her to stay awake as much as possible. Swelling is the greatest risk."

Weston placed a hand on Effie's elbow and walked her a few steps closer. "Swelling? Do you mean her brain?"

"Yes," she replied. "Evidently, she received quite a blow."

"A blow that was meant for me," he clarified. Guilt tightened his throat. "Would I be able to see her?"

Reggie made a sideways nod. "That depends on the door

guard."

Back to them, a large-framed man rose to his feet. He turned around and regarded their group, grim-faced. "I'm afraid admittance won't be possible, since you two are responsible for shattering my string of consecutive days of on-the-job-safety *again*."

Weston couldn't hide his astonishment. "Duncan? How did you beat me to the hospital?"

"Lactation visit. The call from Alice Granger caught us as we headed out. I'm playing door guard for the floor nurse while little Timmy is downstairs learning how to perfect his latching-on move."

Weston extended his right hand, and Duncan shook it. "Congratulations on the new family member, by the way. Nice to see the wind is back in your sails after a week floating through the doldrums."

"Yeah, it's mighty unusual for Kansas not to have any wind, right?" He chuckled and squared around to block the door to the closest room. "I'm not kidding about refusing you entrance, though. It's shift change for the nurses, and I pledged to guard Myla's door."

Weston shuffled his feet. He'd have to better state his case and win admission. "Duncan, I have to go in. Things are not settled between us. She took a hit for me, an act of utmost bravery. I can't let that go without the proper sort of follow-up."

Reed crossed his arms, looking more like a body guard than safety manager. "Well, I'm certainly not going to let you in there, if you don't have any better plan in mind how the encounter could end up. Like I told you before, there's no wasting precious time, Durand." He opened his stance, a formidable obstacle.

Rethinking his whole approach, Weston blew out a labored breath. For an instant, it seemed like Reed had everything, and he had nothing. Notwithstanding, he'd spared the safety manager the complication of closing out the case. That should offer enough leverage to pry the door open. He moved so close their shoes almost touched toe-to-toe. "You have some audacious nerve, you know that?"

The man's eyebrows shot up to his hairline, but he didn't move.

"You bow out on personal leave and hand the whole volatile case over to me. Now, the guilty parties are apprehended, and the whole thing gets handed back in a tidy package for you to take to legal. Plus every night, you go home to a loving wife and two beautiful children. By comparison, look at what I have—the cold metal of my weight press and empty cupboards in the kitchen. How about a little empathy for a Christian man trying to do the right thing? Won't you consider that and allow me passage? Or are you just one more obstacle standing between us?"

Duncan's face winced at the wife and children part. He narrowed his gaze as if to burn a hole through his half-thought out intentions. "Do not make me regret this, Durand. You come out of there with something resolved—or else."

"Thank you, sir." Weston ducked by the man's elbow and depressed the latch. The heavy wooden door swung open. He entered the spacious room already hot under the collar and fresh out of words. When he closed the door, Myla made no notice. Maybe she'd already fallen asleep. With a finger tugging at his shirt collar, he examined the array of wiring that held her captive to the bed frame, a considerable rig. Undetected, he decided to unbutton his shirt and cool down from his face-off with Duncan. He yanked off the starched shirt and tossed it on the guest chair. A fan-generated breeze swept across the exposed skin around his undershirt, a saving grace.

"Weston? Is that you?" Myla asked in a frail tone.

A dagger pierced his heart. He stepped closer, taking care not to touch the bed. "Yes, Myla, I'm here now. Sorry it took so long. Are you okay? Tell me where it hurts."

"They're giving me something for the pain. I think it's jumbling up my thoughts. Guess I won't be the sharpest mind around the QC circle for awhile."

"Skip and Rich send their best, by the way. Your bravery will be legendary by the time those two finish retelling the showdown." He smiled when her eyes gleamed at the compliment. "Then there's Alice. She cannot seem to do enough to help us wrap up the case and get life back to normal."

"Tell me. Did she give in about their holiday weekend plans?"

"Skip may have mentioned winning that war. Since the investigation is over now, there's no need for the separation anyway." He smiled and stroked a single finger over the top of her strapped-down hand.

"Weston, I don't remember parts of what happened. Some portions are there and some are missing. I'm struggling with that, quite honestly."

"I'm not supposed to give you cause for alarm in here, so some of the details will have to wait. Still, I'd be honored to answer a few specific questions, if it would help settle your mind. Remember, we need to get you healthy, so you can break out of here." He stepped back and dragged the chair up closer. He sat on its arm to remain at the height of her bed.

"The cut down your arm there, was that from the fight?"

"So, you're in traction, but not blind. Good show on that surface analysis, Myla. Yes, I must have met up with the metal hangar door, but it matches the goose egg Alice found on the back of my head. By the way, she lacks the tender touch of a proper nurse. Take my word for it."

She snickered and followed it with a moan. "They're going to make you leave, if you inflict more pain on me like that."

"Okay, definitely no more funny stuff, because I don't intend to leave. Any other questions I can help you resolve?"

"What about the snack lady? Truly, I could not have been more surprised. I thought she was getting sweet on you."

Shame burned his cheeks. "I used a script right out of your play book, Myla, the flirt-to-learn-more act. Bette is the sister you told me to find."

"Hague and Bette?"

"Yes. And your clue about the family being burned by Cessna led to me finding their mother's name on the list of women relieved of their jobs post-war to allow the returning veterans opportunities for employment. Call it an unfortunate circumstance. The mother must have been forced into a high-risk job and was killed several months later during a construction accident. You could guess how long ago by your stitch repair work on the jet engine cover."

"Seven years? Oh, that's so tragic for the family."

For a few seconds, Weston allowed her sympathy to soften his consideration of the siblings, but their deliberate acts of sabotage held a hefty price tag in both equipment and loss of lives. The tender emotion came chased by something more heated as he remembered Hague's scandalous intent with Myla. Heaven help him, he still bore jealousy over that attempted taint of purity, although the man had long since been pronounced dead at the crash scene. He'd withhold that for now, as it even riled him to think about it.

"Did Hague get away, Weston?"

He pressed his lips together and dropped his gaze to her hand. There, life-connecting blue veins stood out, winding around her knuckles to feed her fingers. He stretched his pinky finger out and covered hers. "He did. That's all I can tell you for now, except for one thing." His throat tightened. In seconds, he had to blink back extra moisture in his eyes. "You're a brave woman, Myla. I told you that the day we met. Once again, I haven't proven trustworthy enough to keep you from getting hurt. For that, I came to ask for your forgiveness."

She blinked and fixed her gaze on him. "I'm not sure you need forgiveness."

A lump formed in his throat, taken by her readiness to let his inadequacy go. At a loss, a less weighty topic came to him. "I closed on the cottage this week. It seemed a hollow affair, with lots of signing and a handy book of bank notes to pay in monthly installments. I'm up with the sun every morning, because I don't have any of the windows covered yet. You'd think the neighbors would have complained by now."

She snickered and moaned again. Her fingers lifted to touch against his.

He had to figure this demure reaction thing out for the time being. "Okay, no more laughing, young lady. I'll put my hand in yours, so you can squeeze it or thump it, whatever the reaction might lend." With care, he slid his hand under hers. The connection heightened the affinity of their closeness. If he ignored the traction, the scene even struck him as intimate. That rattled through his chest and stirred a deeper response, as though his love had reawakened. The surge came with too much magnetism to hide.

The door squeaked open and Duncan Reed's face appeared. "Shift change is complete. Rogue nurse headed our way in fifteen seconds. I'll stall as long as I can." He pulled the door closed with a click.

"Myla I…well, I've missed you like crazy. It's not the same without you, not by a long shot. I think you had my heart the day we met under the belly of that plane."

"Weston—"

"No, Myla. Really. I have to say something important, as Reed warned me not to come out of here without settling this."

"You could—"

"My-la. I want you to be mine. You have to get better, so I can take you home. So we can be together."

A knuckle knocked against the door. Voices began to filter in. It all fell as a threat.

Her eyes twinkled with the brightest blue, though the raven-black of her pupils held perfectly still. "Kiss me, Weston, so I can feel your heart's genuine intentions."

He rose from the chair, his mind battling warnings not to touch her or make her move. To his knowledge, no one had ever died from the presence of love. Maybe death came from the absence, a fate which he had feared for his future. He locked gazes and angled his head to avoid the wiring that held her in place. With a hairsbreadth of distance between them, he examined the rich field of her face and detected only beauty, not imperfections. "I love you for waiting this out, Myla, not with merely words or ticks off the clock, but with your actions as well." He bent and brushed his lips across hers, an infinite pleasure.

"That's what I love about you, Weston, continuous improvement." She winked as the dam holding the door closed broke and a commotion of movement spilled into the room.

A squatty nurse came over and checked the monitors. "Hmm. That's her best blood pressure reading all evening. I don't know who you are, mister, but you just might be a keeper."

His heart racing, Weston slumped back into the chair. With a thought for modesty, he shirked an arm through his shirt sleeve.

The new nurse trapped him by the wrist. "Better let me get some iodine on that bicep first, young man." She shuffled off to a wall-mounted cabinet.

Weston caught the smile on Myla's lips and paid her back with a sheepish grin. He slid his right hand under hers, and the tender caress from her fingertips launched him to the moon. Not to minimize the role of the medic, but he could hardly wait for her to leave them alone again. The cold pad of a cotton ball reacquainted him with pain as the iodine seared into his cut.

"Was this wound made by metal, by any chance?" the nurse asked.

"Yes, ma'am, a tin door to be more specific," he replied.

"That's going to mean a tetanus shot for you. I'll have to go get it prepped. Sit tight."

"Oh, good." He locked gazes with Myla, whose parted lips already invited him back for more continuous improvement. Now the recorder for a different kind of QC circle, he'd be sure to write a note in the margin about being good medicine for her blood pressure, as soon as he could find a pen.

Epilogue

Weston reached up and steadied her hips as Myla clipped the dining room curtain panel to the rod. She'd insisted on removing her shoes. Now, her painted toenails added to the many distractions keeping him entertained. He could not be happier. Labor Day weekend had arrived without additional labor, which was fine with him.

"Next ring, please." She lowered her hand for the next fancy pleat clamp.

He dug into the package and freed up the next candidate. "Do you think we could take a break soon?" He needed a little time to pull off his magical moment, but didn't want to tip her off.

"Come on. Stick with it until the job is done. Shouldn't perseverance be another tenet for your continuous improvement program? If it's not, I'll propose it at our next QC circle meeting. Besides, your parents will be here by four o-clock, and I'm not about to show them a half-finished project." She snapped her fingers for the clip.

He tapped her palm and the curtain ring dropped off his index finger to meet her demands. "I like this fabric pattern a lot. Not too feminine, but kind of classic along the lines of Roman architecture. It complements the dark furniture, too. I can't believe you worked on this the whole time we were apart. Once again, I've underestimated you."

She tugged at the pleat, set the clip in place, and slid it along the round curtain rod. "Thank you very much, Mr. Durand, for your generous admiration. Little touches like the right fabric tucked in tend to make a house a home. Only two more clips to go. Another ring, if you please." She stepped further back onto the seat of the dining room chair and held out her hand.

Again, he dug into the cello bag and freed up another circular clamp. He deposited it with vigor, and watched it disappear into the higher tier. "Did you happen to buy any extra fabric? We might need a few more touches of color around all this walnut furniture, don't you think?"

"I'm way ahead of you, as usual. Plus, I bought a contrasting pattern that has a bit more gold. I'll make the toss pillows for the living room out of that solid for a punch of color rather than pattern." She made a little throat-clearing noise to adjust her tone. "You may want to keep a closer eye on me, Weston. You might learn a thing or two."

He hid the smile that wanted to meet and match her challenge. So happy to have her in his arms, his heart might have burst right then and there. It had been a rough few weeks after her release from the hospital, but Effie had welcomed him as he'd stopped by daily after work. They'd come a long way to regain what God had lent them previously, and he knew to cherish it for all the promise it held.

Her demanding palm dropped down level with his chin. "Last ring, please."

He bent and pressed a kiss into her palm as a diabolical alternative plan came to mind. He dug into his pocket and produced a special gold clip, one that held a three-quarter carat diamond instead of curtain prongs. He popped it into her hand and waited for the equal-and-opposite reaction Sir Isaac Newton had promised.

Her knees trembled first, giving her away. "What is this?" Her words floated down full of airy wonder.

Weston wrapped his arms around her legs and lifted her off the chair. He held her close, not allowing much space between them. "Just testing out Newton's Third Law of Motion." He searched her face as her expression ramped through several stages of astonishment, each one more beautiful than the last.

"Oh goodness me, oh my. Does this shiny thing come with any sweet words attached?" She looked up at him, her mouth open in a perfect circle.

He let the wonder of holding her affect his pulse for a second. By the time he wanted to say something formal and important, the tightness in his throat almost prevented him. He found her free hand and wove his fingers through hers. "Myla Templeton, will you consent to be my wife, stand by me each day through thick and thin, and help me build a family under the nurture and admonition of the Lord? Say you'll be mine, Myla. Let's start an incredible life together as man and wife."

Her eyes rimmed with unshed tears as she centered the engagement ring between them. "Yes, I will, Weston, consent to be your wife. You bring me joy beyond measure. There's no place on earth I'd rather be."

"Well, there is for me," he replied with haste. He scooped her into his arms and made for the back door while her nuzzled giggles tickled his neck. He let the door fly open and soon passed the little shed. "Might you get the gate for me, my dear? It seems I have my hands full of wife-to-be material."

"By all means," she replied. In seconds, she had the latch tripped. The gate fell open.

The river ebbed by with a steady flow, the late-morning sun glinting from its surface. Weston placed her on the approximate spot where they'd enjoyed that first kiss many moons ago. The spot hadn't changed a bit, as though it had been waiting for their return.

Myla held the ring up. "Put it on me?"

He took possession of the trifle and slid it onto the ring finger of her left hand, the permanent location for such a symbol of devotion. He bent toward her and held her shoulders with tenderness. "I love you so much, Myla. Thank you for saying yes." The ensuing kiss proved to be all the response he needed. The water kept flowing, but all else stood still while they became one-of-heart there on the river bank.

She brought another kiss and leaned onto his chest in the process of delivering it.

He dropped his hands around her waist and held his fiancé as if she was the most precious thing on earth. Pleasure and promise wrapped the moment while a bluebird dropped to the river's edge nearby to take a sustaining drink of water.

"Yoo-hoo, Weston." A woman's voice called up by the driveway.

He passed his cheek over hers and whispered into her ear. "My parents are here."

"Our parents," she corrected with a grin. "That is, if they'll claim me."

"They're already claiming you. Ask my dad." He grabbed her hand and led her back into the yard past the little shed that he might have to convert to a playhouse sometime in the next five years. He'd hold that in the offing, since it might be nice to keep a few surprises in his pocket yet. He waved when his father appeared by the garden, tucking Myla to his side for a lifetime of safekeeping in his little cottage by the river.

The End

AUTHOR BIO

Cindy M. Amos has enjoyed being a resident of Wichita, Kansas since 1999, when her husband came to work as a materials engineer for Cessna Aircraft. Familiar with his role as a "crack and defect guy," the author couldn't resist fashioning a hero from her husband's job description for Book 2 of her "America's Fabulous Fifties" series. With her oldest son a recent college graduate in aerospace engineering and her youngest reaching the midway point in biological systems engineering, the Amos household continues to remain all about science, math, and predictable outcomes. With career experience in natural resource management and endangered species conservation, the author enjoys weaving realistic natural settings so her characters can live close to the land. Sometimes that appreciation comes from a bird's-eye view, especially when one lives in the Air Capital of the World.

Find her complete booklist on her website at:
http://cindymamos.wixsite.com/natureink

Also check her Amazon author page at:
https://www.amazon.com/Cindy-M.-Amos/e/B01JTDIPOQ/ref=ntt_dp_epwbk_0

On Facebook at: https://www.facebook.com/natureinkbooks

OTHER BOOKS BY CINDY M. AMOS

Landscapes of Mercy Series
Redeeming River Rancher
Saving Bicycle Man
Justifying Sound Strider
Sanctifying Ace Aerialist
Lifting Lock Runner
Salvaging Doctor Junk

National Parks 100th Anniversary Romance Collection
Everglades Entanglement
Mesa Verde Meltdown

Christmas 3-in-1 Collection
Running Out of Christmastime

Taming the Cowboy's Heart Collection
Warming Stone Cold Lodge

50 States Collection
Secondhand Flower Stand (Kansas)

Red Cloud Retreat (Nebraska)
Tidewater Lowlands (North Carolina)
Canyon Country Courtship (Utah)

John Denver 20th Anniversary Collection
Calypso Reimagined

Loving the Town Hero Collection
Cascading Waterworks

America's Fabulous Fifties Series
Oil Field Maven

257

Cowboy Brides Collection
Renegade Restoration